CONVOY EAST

BY THE SAME AUTHOR:

CONVOY EAST

Philip McCutchan

St. Martin's Press
New York

CONVOY EAST. Copyright © 1989 by Philip McCutchan. All rights reserved. Printed in the United States of America. No part of this book may be used or reproduced in any manner whatsoever without written permission except in the case of brief quotations embodied in critical articles or reviews. For information, address St. Martin's Press, 175 Fifth Avenue, New York, N.Y. 10010.

Library of Congress Cataloging-in-Publication Data

McCutchan, Philip.
     Convoy east / Philip McCutchan.
         p.   cm.
     ISBN 0-312-03310-9
     I. Title.
PR6063.A167C64   1989
823'.914—dc20
                                       89-34843
                                         CIP

First published in Great Britain by George Weidenfeld & Nicolson Limited.

First U.S. Edition
10 9 8 7 6 5 4 3 2 1

ONE

John Mason Kemp, hunched into his bridge coat, shivered in an icy wind coming off the dark waters of the Tail o' the Bank: no snow, it was a little late in the year for that, but a nasty heavy drizzle blown along the wind. Smoke from the funnels of the drifters lying in the comparative shelter of Albert Harbour joined the drizzle. Some of the drifters were moving out, their wet decks crammed with libertymen returning to the ships at anchor or at the buoys; more seamen waited on the dock wall, or moved for the remaining drifters as the shouts of the petty officers directed them aboard. A typical Greenock scene, far from new to Kemp, for the war had been going on now for more years than he cared to remember: so many sinkings, so many shattering deaths among the crews of the merchant ships in convoy, among the ships' companies of the naval escorts.

'There she is,' a voice said at Kemp's side.

'What?'

'The picquet-boat, Commodore.'

'Ah, yes.' A dark shape was moving in through the entrance, edging past an outward-moving drifter. In the shaded lights of the port Kemp saw the bowman and sternsheetsman, clad in oilskins, lift their boathooks high above their heads then bring them down to a horizontal position across their chests as the picquet-boat closed the gap towards the waiting Convoy Commodore.

Kemp turned to the officer at his side, a lieutenant-commander of the Naval Control Service staff, wearing, as Kemp himself did, the gold stripes of the Royal Naval Reserve, the professional

5

reserve of merchant service officers in naval service for the war's duration. 'My thanks again to FOIC for the use of his boat.'

'The least we could do, sir. Goodbye – and good luck.'

They shook hands. The NCS officer saluted as the Commodore went down the steps, greasy with rain and oil and seaweed, to be saluted again by the midshipman of the picquet-boat as he stepped aboard.

'Permission to carry on, sir?' This was the midshipman.

Kemp nodded, thinking of his own sons in naval uniform, little older than this youth. 'Carry on, please,' he said. No time was lost now; there was more smart work with the boathooks fore and aft as the picquet-boat was borne off the wall and headed for the harbour entrance and the windswept waters beyond, out to where the convoy and its escort lay waiting. The sailing orders were for midnight; the destination was Alexandria through the war-torn Mediterranean, and then Trincomalee in Ceylon. A troop and armaments convoy, under very heavy escort that as far as Alex would include the battleship *Nelson* currently lying at the flagship buoy and wearing the flag of a vice-admiral.

ii

Kemp had reached Upper Greenock station early that afternoon, after a long train journey from his home at Meopham in Kent, via Charing Cross, Euston and Glasgow Central. He'd had a month's leave following an exceptionally arduous convoy, the longest leave he'd had since the start of the war when, as Master of the Mediterranean-Australia Line's *Ardara*, he had arrived in Tilbury from Sydney to be greeted by the chairman of the Line with the news that he was required for Admiralty service as a commodore of ocean convoys; and from that moment his life had changed irrevocably even though within a couple of years of convoy duty in various ships chance had found him aboard the old *Ardara* again, for she too had been mobilized into the fleet and was acting as Commodore's ship leading a convoy of former liners to pick up Canadian troops on draft for service in Britain. Gone for as long as the war might last were the days of glamour, of soft light and the music of the liner's orchestra, of a whole spectrum of passengers, rich and important or not so rich and seeking a new life in

6

Australia or New Zealand. Old and young, crusty and convivial, all of them more or less interesting when, as Master, Kemp met them at his table in the first-class saloon or at the cocktail parties that were his lot to give and which on the whole he didn't much enjoy: what he called social tittery was not in his line and he was always thankful when bad weather or other navigational matters gave him the excuse to hand over to his Staff Captain, who, together with the purser, was more directly involved in formal entertainment than the Master himself.

With the transition to war, all was grey paint and austerity, the expensive furnishings gone, the cabins and staterooms largely ripped out for conversion to troop accommodation and the decks strengthened to take gun-mountings. And the casualties had begun right at the start when on the first day of the war the liner *Athenia*, filled with women and children, had been torpedoed in the North Atlantic.

Leave, as for everyone else in the services, was a welcome oasis and a necessary one if sanity was to be preserved. But this last leave had been a disturbing one. Mary his wife was overtired, not to say overwrought; a husband and two sons at sea, and all the worries of wartime housekeeping – the shortages, the queues, the ration books, the blackout, the air raids, the transport difficulties. Not only all of that, but granny too. Kemp believed he must be the only master mariner in his early fifties with a grandmother still alive – not only alive, but resident in his home. It was hard on his wife to have a grandmother-in-law who was bedbound and cantankerous and getting more and more trying, but both of them were fond of her and Kemp, of course, especially: Granny Marsden was not only his grandmother but a lifelong friend, a mother to him after his mother had died young, and she was now not far short of her century.

Loyally Mary had tried not to add to her husband's worries but, knowing it was better for her to unburden, and guessing easily enough at the trouble, he had come right to the point after the first week's leave.

'It's granny – right?'

'Well – '

'Yes, it is. And I understand, of course.'

'That stick,' she said. 'That *bloody* stick!'

Granny Marsden was in the habit of banging her walking stick

7

on the floor, which to those below meant the ceiling, for attention. Bedpan, false teeth dropped, open the window, shut it
again, a glass of water, draw the curtains, bedpan again.

Kemp asked, knowing the answer, 'Can't we get help? A
nurse? Even a daily woman.' He said it without hope; they'd
been into all that before. Everyone was on war work, factories,
buses, trains, the women's services, forces' canteens and clubs.
There wasn't even a nursing home available, and she wouldn't
have gone if there was, and Kemp wouldn't have had the heart to
throw her out in her last remaining years. But they did go into it
all again and Kemp ended a fruitless discussion by saying, 'Well,
she can't go on for ever, Mary.'

Mary sighed. 'She's got a better chance than Hitler,' she said. A
banging of the stick summoned her, and she went up the stairs,
came down again to say John was wanted in the sick room, and,
like a little boy, the Commodore obeyed. He guessed what it was:
granny had a chocolate for him, or a biscuit. She always had; and
fifty-odd years couldn't be easily set aside.

It was another worry for the Commodore to carry with him to
sea; Mary was only human, could take so much and no more.

iii

In Glasgow another worry had awaited Kemp: he had break-
fasted in the station hotel after the night train from the south –
there were no longer any restaurant cars on the trains. At his table
he was approached by a lean woman, spinsterish and hungry-
looking, in the uniform of a first officer WRNS, two-and-a-half
blue stripes on her cuffs.

'Commodore Kemp?' she asked brightly.

'Yes.' His heart sank as he got to his feet, napkin in one hand.
So soon! He knew who she must be: the niece of old Sir Edward,
chairman of Mediterranean-Australia Lines, who had told him
she would be aboard the Commodore's ship – there had obviously been an unwelcome breach of security somewhere – and
would he keep a friendly eye on her. 'You're – er – Miss Forrest?'

'Jean Forrest, yes.'

He indicated a chair. 'Do sit down, please. Er – you've break-
fasted, Miss Forrest?'

'Yes, I have, thank you, Commodore Kemp. But I'll join you if I may.' She sat down facing him across the coffee pot with the ersatz-like coffee, the toast, the tiny pat of butter, the dried egg powder masquerading as scrambled egg. He summed her up: fortyish, nervy, potentially bossy but currently anxious to please and, above all he feared, for he had a long experience of women at sea, anxious for a man. Not unattractive in a bony, rather arid way. She shouldn't have found it all that hard to get a man, at any rate in wartime when the old inhibitions were slipping away fast.

She fiddled with a spare fork. 'The convoy – '

'We'll not discuss that in a hotel dining-room, Miss Forrest.'

'No, I'm sorry.'

He gave a cough, feeling embarrassed: she had looked what she probably thought of as prettily contrite. He said, 'Your uncle – '

'Yes, he'll have spoken to you, I know.'

'He asked me to – '

'You mustn't bother *too* specially about me, Commodore Kemp.'

'I'll do what – '

'It's my girls, you see. The Wren draft.'

'Again, that should not be – '

'Discussed. No. I'm awfully sorry. I wasn't going to say anything important.'

Kemp frowned. He had a strong dislike of being interrupted when speaking, an even stronger dislike of having his sentences finished for him. He said, 'Well, I'm relieved to hear that, Miss Forrest. It's unwise to say anything at all that might be picked up. Tell me, is Sir Edward better?' When he'd called upon the chairman half-way through his recent leave, being caught up in one of the London air raids for his pains and spending a fraught two hours with his shoulders holding up a beam so that the rescue squads could bring out the injured people from inside a building, Sir Edward had complained of a vicious attack of lumbago. He was indeed better, Jean Forrest said, and went on to talk of London and the blitz. Safer conversation: Kemp kept her at it for a polite ten minutes, then excused himself. There was something about her that suggested she found the war boring as well as dangerous, an interruption of her peacetime routine of coffee at Harrods, meeting friends for lunch, then afternoon tea followed

9

later by a dinner party or perhaps a theatre. In Kemp's view, there were more important things in life.

Reaching Greenock, he attended the convoy conference where the shipmasters and naval escort commanders were given their route instructions by the staff officers of the Naval Control Service. There was an overall appraisal of the situation in the Mediterranean and in the waters beyond the port of Suez at the southern end of the canal: the Italian fleet and the German dive-bombers continued to be active in the Mediterranean, and as ever the period of most danger would come between Gibraltar and Malta. The escort, however, was strong and would remain so until arrival off Alexandria where the troops would be disembarked in support of the armies fighting west from Egypt where a big push was expected soon. When the convoy sailed from Alex, *Nelson* and the covering aircraft-carriers, *Indomitable* and *Victorious*, would be withdrawn and the merchant ships would sail on with four heavy cruisers and six destroyers. As far as Alexandria at least it was a big escort for a comparatively small number of merchant ships: a vessel to detach to Malta with supplies of food and medical equipment, three troopships for Alex, eight large cargo vessels fully laden with armaments – guns, ammunition, tanks, armoured vehicles – for Trincomalee. And aboard the Commodore's ship, the freighter *Wolf Rock* of 15,000 tons, a draft of twenty WRNS ratings together with First Officer Jean Forrest and two Third Officers, one-stripers, taking passage to Trincomalee to join the base staff of the Admiral commanding the British East Indies Fleet.

The conference was a long one, extending into the afternoon. It was followed by an informal meeting with the Flag Officer in Charge and his Chief of Staff. There was a farewell drink before Commodore Kemp left Naval HQ in the early dark for Albert Harbour and the *Wolf Rock*.

iv

The Commodore's staff, those who went with Kemp from one convoy to another, had joined the ship the previous day. Now, Petty Officer Lambert, yeoman of signals, having checked his flag locker for the umpteenth time, had gone below to the petty

10

officers' mess to write a last letter to his wife in Pompey. Last before leaving he meant – no call to be too pessimistic; the *Wolf Rock's* Chief Officer, Mr Harrison, had announced a final mail that would leave the ship aboard the last drifter to come alongside, ready to go inshore with some base maintenance men at 2200.

Lambert wrote slowly: fast as you like at reading a lamp in any weather, fast to interpret a flag hoist, mostly without need to refer to the signal books, he was a poor composer of letters home. There never seemed to be anything worth writing, not unless you wanted to have the letter mutilated by the censoring officer before it left the ship. You even had to be careful in writing of the weather, in case Hitler got a buckshee weather report, and you could never mention where you'd been or where you were now or where you were going next, of course. That stood to reason. But what else was there? Assure the wife of your undying love, but she knew that already. Repetition could become stale, though there were different ways of expressing it, some of them carnal, but he'd gone through all of them too over the years, pre-war and since it all started. Testimonials of love and desire from Hong Kong, Singapore, Sydney, Colombo, Port Said, Malta, Gibraltar, the West Indies, South Africa and other places. In his ditty box he kept a number of nude photographs, snaps really, of Doris to keep the fires fuelled. She had a good figure still and it was useful to look at it before going ashore: by proxy, she kept him away from the world's brothels and likely disease. When you had a body like that to go back to, you kept yourself clean, not like the single men and the ones married to old bags. As Yeoman of Signals Lambert laboured pencil-wise with expressions of basic love, he was interrupted by heavy footfalls and a loud voice.

'Finished, Yeo?'

Lambert looked up, met the sardonic eye of Petty Officer Ramm, gunner's mate and in immediate charge of the *Wolf Rock's* armament of one 6-inch gun, obsolete for years, and assorted ack-ack and close-range weapons mounted fore and aft and in the bridge wings.

'Nearly, GI. What's the rush?'

'Subby.'

'Subby, eh.' The reference was to Sub-Lieutenant Finnegan, RCNVR like the Commodore's previous assistant who had been killed in action. Finnegan had the chore of censoring the outward

11

mail. Finnegan, again like the dead Cutler, was an American who had pre-empted his own country's call to arms by joining up in Canada early in the war. Lambert knew the story behind Finnegan's appointment to Kemp's staff: Commodore Kemp had had a lot of time for that previous assistant, Cutler, had been so impressed with American keenness and efficiency that he'd asked for, and got, a replacement from precisely the same stable. There were not so many of them; Kemp had been lucky, but he was highly thought of at the Admiralty and all the strings had been pulled. Now, Lambert knew the new Commodore's assistant was dead keen, anxious to prove himself worthy of his predecessor, to prove that any American was as good as if not better than any limey officer. So he took even his censorship duties seriously, as those on the Commodore's permanent staff were well aware. Lambert said, 'Wetting 'is pants to get the job done, eh?'

'Before the drifter leaves, yes.' Petty Officer Ramm gave a large yawn. He'd been ashore, sampling the fleshpots of Greenock and, as he would have put it, was shagged out. Pre-war, he'd been known in every ship he'd served in as Ramm by Name and Ramm by Nature. He changed the subject. 'Any buzzes, Yeo? About this run.'

Lambert shrugged. 'Routine convoy, that's all.'

'Routine my arse! Not known convoys before, run through Alex to Trinco. Not that you'd say, I s'pose.'

'That I wouldn't.' Lambert looked surprised. 'Where d'you hear about Trinco, then?'

Ramm winked. 'A little bird told me. Jenny Wren to be precise. Know we were embarking Wrens, did you?'

'Not officially, GI. And you – '

Ramm jeered. 'Come off it. Accommodation's all ready, as near the officers as possible, lucky sods. Met one of 'em ashore and got her talking. Ever hear the one about the Wren that went for a swim on a cold day, did you?'

'No.'

'Two blue tits came out.' Ramm gave a loud laugh. 'Better get that letter done, Yeo, or subby'll close the mail.' He left the mess; Lambert stared after him with a jaundiced eye. Thick as a plank, was Ramm, like all gunnery rates in Lambert's view. The signal staff were the brains of the outfit, the ones without whom all

12

would be lost. Even Lord Nelson had depended on his signal lieutenant, among other things to get that last message hoisted for the eyes of the fleet. Ramm was all gas and gaiters, loud voice, left-right-left along the deck and swing those arms, cap square on his head and boots banging like Ramm himself on a night's liberty. Lambert sighed, finished his letter, put it in the envelope, left the flap open for subby to get his thrill, and wrote S.W.A.L.K. on the back flap. He could only hope Doris was OK and would remain so, what with the perishing air raids and all. What he would do without that figure he knew not. Doris was his mainstay in a wicked and now dangerous world, always there to come back to. As Lambert got off the mess stool he reflected, not for the first time, that the sealing, loving kiss would in fact be the tip of the censoring officer's tongue . . . and as he was thinking this the tannoy from the bridge came alive.

'Commodore coming alongside starboard.'

Lambert left the mess, depositing his letter in the mail box on the way to the starboard accommodation ladder. The Commodore would expect his yeoman of signals to attend upon him: there were often last-minute signals for the shore. As he reached the upper platform of the accommodation ladder and stood at the salute for Kemp's embarkation, he saw the last drifter, the one that would take the mail and the dockyard mateys, lying off to come alongside after the Commodore. A lot of young faces looking up from beneath floppy-brimmed hats of navy blue: Wrens. Some were looking seasick already, for there was a chop on the waters of the Tail o' the Bank.

TWO

Captain William Champney, Master of the *Wolf Rock*, was also at the accommodation ladder to welcome the Convoy Commodore. He was not without a degree of wariness: this was to be his first experience of having a commodore aboard, the first time his command would wear the Convoy Commodore's pennant, and he suspected there might be friction. Captain Champney was not a man to share his own command and he had heard yarns of commodores who tried to take control of the ship. Not many, but a few. The facts of seafaring life and of maritime law were that the Master and no-one else was in full command. The Convoy Commodore was no more than a passenger as regards the conduct of the ship in which he found himself. His responsibilities were to the convoy as a whole, to act as co-ordinator and as leader – not dissimilar from the role of an admiral commanding a fleet of warships, who commanded the fleet itself but did not interfere with the duties of the captain of the flagship. Some convoy commodores, notably those who had themselves been admirals and were now on the retired list and recalled to serve in a very different role, seemed – so Captain Champney had heard – to think that when not aboard a King's ship they could do just as they wished.

But probably not Kemp: Kemp, as Champney knew, was RNR and as a basic merchant service officer he would be easier to get along with. They had met at the afternoon's conference, had had words before Kemp had been taken off by the Flag Officer in Charge. Champney had liked Kemp's very direct eyes and his easy manner, assured but far from pompous.

14

Now, he watched as Kemp climbed the ladder, reached the top platform and gave a friendly grin. Kemp said, 'A dirty-ish night, Captain, but not unusual for the Tail o' the Bank, of course.'

'Not unusual, no. Welcome aboard, Commodore.'

'Thank you.' Kemp looked shrewdly at Champney, appreciating what he had already seen that afternoon, an alert face, weather-beaten like his own. Obviously very tired: keeping the seas in wartime was a tough and demanding job, and the one man who had always to be on the bridge in danger or difficulty, in altering formation, when entering and leaving port and a hundred other times, was the Master. It was often enough a case of 'watch on, stop on' as the saying went. 'You're all ready for the off, I take it?'

Champney nodded. He introduced Harrison, his chief officer. The chief engineer, he said, was busy in the engine-room and sent his apologies.

'That's all right,' Kemp said, and caught the eye of Yeoman of Signals Lambert. 'All well at home, Yeoman?'

'Yessir, thank you, sir.'

'How was Portsmouth?'

'Bit knocked about like, sir. Barracks and all . . . and a lot o' civvies killed in the last raid, sir.'

'It's turned into a filthy war,' Kemp said, and added, 'All right, Yeoman, no signals, you can go and get some sleep until the convoy weighs – but have a signalman standing by on the bridge please.'

'Aye, aye, sir.' Lambert saluted and turned away, his signal clip-board in his hand. It was just like Kemp to take the trouble to ask personal questions, not nosey ones, and take an interest. They'd not met for a month, not since Kemp had brought the last convoy home and they'd both had leave; it was good, Lambert thought, to be back with him again even though he'd have preferred to stay on permanent leave and bugger the convoys – but if you had to go to sea, then Commodore Kemp was the right bloke to go with.

Coming fast past Lambert and making for the starboard ladder was Sub-Lieutenant Finnegan, looking harassed.

'Commodore aboard?' he asked.

'Yessir. Reckon you've missed the boat, you 'ave, sir.' Finnegan moved on fast and Lambert grinned to himself. Subby had

15

had his head down, most likely. He'd come aboard earlier, off one of the drifters, having attended upon the Commodore at the conference but not having been asked to remain behind when Kemp had gone off with FOIC and the Chief of Staff. Kemp would probably give him a bollocking now, for not being with the others at the ladder. Kemp, however friendly he might be, was a stickler for things being done properly and never let slackness pass.

ii

The three WRNS officers were to be accommodated in the mid-ship superstructure, using the deck officers' spare cabins. First Officer Forrest was in a single cabin, the two Third Officers, Susan Pawle and Anne Bowes-Gourley, shared a cabin in which an extra bunk had been fitted at the start of the war. The Wrens, nineteen of them under the immediate charge of Petty Officer Wren Rose Hardisty, were accommodated in the engineer offi-cers' accommodation aft, in five four-berth cabins, spaces also fitted-out for possible passenger use in wartime. A little before sailing Jean Forrest encountered Kemp outside the door of the Master's spare cabin, now allocated for the Commodore's use.

She gave him one of her bright smiles. 'Oh, Commodore, I do hope you didn't mind my speaking to you this morning?'

'That's all right, Miss Forrest.' Kemp's tone was gruff: he had an idea the encounter was not entirely fortuitous; but he had no wish to be impolite. He asked, 'Has your party settled in all right?'

'Yes, thank you, Commodore.' She paused: Kemp's hand was on his cabin doorknob. She went on with a rush, 'It's such a new experience for all of us, you know. Aboard a ship – well, there can be problems as I'm sure you'll realize.'

Kemp smiled briefly. 'Yes. Men. They can cause problems, but I'm sure you'll cope, Miss Forrest. However, if you're in any difficulty, you can call upon me. You're part of my responsibility, of course, as a Naval draft.'

'Yes, thank you, Commodore. I'm – '

'Goodnight, Miss Forrest.'

Kemp turned away abruptly. There was something potentially

16

effusive about First Officer Forrest and that was not to be encouraged. He wondered if she would find a man aboard, but reflected that she was probably a snob. WRNS officers had a reputation, perhaps not wholly deserved; they were all, or nearly all, young ladies of impeccable upbringing who were said to bed only with officers of commander's rank or above. Jean Forrest just might settle for the ship's chief officer and what Kemp had seen of Harrison, albeit briefly, had suggested that he might well be co-operative. But time would tell. Just one thing was cast-iron certain: if she had her eye on himself, she was barking up quite the wrong tree. Not only was Kemp faithful to his wife, but convoy commodores on sea duty didn't dirty their own nautical doorsteps or risk ships and mens' lives by having their minds on dalliance of that sort. But Kemp found part of his mind on the general subject of the WRNS when, at a few minutes before midnight, stations for leaving harbour were taken up and he joined Captain Champney on the bridge. He asked Champney if he'd sailed with women before.

Champney hadn't. Not, that was, other than his wife on the occasions when his company's regulations had permitted the Master's wife to accompany him. 'You'll have had experience of them in the liners, of course.'

'Yes. But there are differences.'

Champney laughed. 'Sure thing! Lavatory and washing facilities, as an instance. I've had to mark off the washrooms and – '

He was interrupted by the yeoman of signals. 'Message from the Flag, sir, addressed Commodore. Report when ready to proceed, sir.'

Kemp lifted an eye towards Champney. 'All ready, Captain?'

'All ready.'

Kemp said, 'Make to the Flag, ready in all respects.'

'Aye, aye, sir.'

Kemp and Champney paced the bridge. In the wheelhouse, the helmsman stood ready at the wheel. Chief Officer Harrison was seen in the eyes of the ship, ready to supervise the operation of weighing the anchor when the order came from the bridge. The lookouts were in position. The wind was still cold and seemed to be increasing. A few lights flickered from Albert Harbour but otherwise the area was darkened. Greenock lay to port, Helensburgh and the Gareloch to starboard. Quickly on the heels

17

of Kemp's response to the Flag, another signal came, this time addressed generally to all ships in company. Lambert reported again: 'From the Flag, sir, shorten in cable.'

Champney took that up. He called down to the fo'c'sle-head. 'Shorten in, Mr Harrison, two shackles on deck.'

'Aye, aye, sir.' Harrison passed the order to the winchman. When the steam winch had been put into gear the slips and bottle-screws were knocked away and the weight of the cable came on to the drums of the winch. As the drums revolved and the cable came home, with seamen on the fo'c'sle directing the wash-deck hoses on to the links to clear away the Clyde mud before they dropped down into the cable locker, there was a metallic rattle and a cloud of steam from the fore well-deck, steam that was blown across by the buffeting wind.

When the second joining shackle appeared at the lip of the hawse-pipe, Harrison stopped the winch and reported to the bridge: 'Shortened in, sir!'

Champney lifted an arm in acknowledgement. The next signal from the *Nelson* was as brief as the others and was final. The yeoman of signals reported, 'Weigh and proceed in sequence as previously ordered, sir.'

Kemp caught Champney's eye. 'We go ahead of the main body of the convoy, Captain. Immediately after the destroyer escort.'

'Yes. I was at the conference too, Commodore.'

Kemp grinned. 'Of course you were – I'm sorry! No offence?'

Champney grinned back. 'Of course not.' All the same, Champney reckoned a point had been made. As Master, he didn't propose to be treated as a mere watchkeeping officer. He kept a careful lookout as the destroyers of the escort began moving ahead past Rosneath Patch, sliding past the sides of the *Wolf Rock* and the other ships of the convoy, slim shadows in the night, moving as to war, moving to take up their positions ahead of the merchantmen for the long passage out through the anti-submarine boom laid across from Cloch Point to Dunoon and on beyond the Cumbraes to the open waters off Ailsa Craig where they would take up station on the flanks of the convoy to act as an anti-U-boat screen. As the last of the destroyers came up on his port quarter Champney called the order to weigh and rang down Stand By Main Engines on the telegraph. A matter of minutes later the Commodore's ship was moving out in the wakes of the

18

destroyers, to be followed in their due time by the rest of the convoy. Behind them would come the cruiser squadron, and finally the great battleship *Nelson*. Once into the open sea off the Northern Irish coast, a rendezvous would be made with the two fleet aircraft-carriers, *Indomitable* and *Victorious*, on passage north about from the Firth of Forth and currently coming down past the Outer Hebrides, through the Minches with their own destroyer escort.

Aft of the bridge as the *Wolf Rock* passed the boom, moving cautiously through the darkness and following the shaded blue stern-light of the destroyer immediately ahead, Third Officer Susan Pawle stood in the lee of one of the ship's lifeboats, between it and the funnel casing. Heat and fumes were blown down upon her from the funnel as the wind eddied around the open decks; it made her cough, made her eyes run. There was a flap of canvas where one of the boats' covers had been improperly secured, and it had an eerie sound like the tappings of a supposed corpse inside a coffin . . . horrid simile, she thought, and shuddered. The deck was lifting slightly to rough water, and she clutched at a davit for support. She didn't like the motion and she didn't like the fumes but she stayed where she was and would remain there until the ship had passed Toward Point and the entry to Rothesay Bay where not so long ago she had been happy. Only twenty-three and for a little over a year married to an RNR lieutenant serving as First Lieutenant of a boat of the Seventh Submarine Flotilla based on Rothesay. That submarine had failed to return from a patrol and she had been left shattered, to see in her recurring nightmares a body trapped in a broken, depth-charged steel hull, floating sightlessly, bumping against the torpedo-tubes and the useless periscope housing and the spider's-web of pipes that threaded through the close confines of the boats.

Susan had been working at the Greenock naval base, handy for Rothesay, and it had been no problem for her to get night leave when Johnny's submarine had been in Rothesay, lying alongside the old depot-ship *Cyclops*. Nights spent in the Victoria Hotel just behind the pier where the Greenock ferries came in . . . parties aboard the *Cyclops* where the submariners relaxed after their patrols . . . all happy days, so suddenly and cruelly brought to an end. Afterwards she had wanted desperately to get away, and had asked to be reappointed. Passage aboard the *Wolf Rock* to the base at Trincomalee had been the Admiralty's sympathetic response, in fact somewhat unexpectedly since requests were often enough met with a dusty answer and an appointment very different from what one wanted.

As the ship came abeam of Toward Point the past came back once more. The point where the ferries, the paddle-steamers from Greenock, had turned to starboard for the entry.... The ship moved on, coming off Kilchattan Bay. They had often done the long walk across the high ground from Rothesay to Kilchattan to have a drink in a friendly pub and look across the water to the Cumbraes lighthouse, and the other way to Inchmarnock Water and the great peaks of Arran, Goat Fell rearing to blue skies over Lamlash Bay and the summer-sparkling waters of the Firth of Clyde.

Oh, Johnny, Oh, Johnny, heavens above.... They had courted to that song. Once past the island of Bute, Susan, stiff-faced, went below to her shared cabin.

Her cabin mate, Third Officer Anne Bowes-Gourley, stared at her face and asked if she'd seen a ghost or what.

'I – I – ' she couldn't go on: of course, Anne didn't know. She didn't want to talk about it.

iii

Peter Harrison, chief officer, had once been a junior second officer in the liners but had fallen foul of authority because he didn't mix well with passengers, whom he had regarded as perishing nuisances very largely. Not entirely: there were the women, and that had been where his final downfall had come. Peter Harrison had a simple and direct way with women, an approach not unlike that of a stallion or a bull. Select the most likely-looking prospect, usually but not always a married woman travelling without her husband, get her into his cabin, shove a whisky in her hand, put a suitable record on his gramophone, move closer on the settee, then make a grab.

It worked nine times out of ten because he had taken trouble over the selection in the first place, but there was the tenth that cropped up now and again and that woman didn't usually complain to the Master because she knew she had herself at least partly to blame. But it could happen, and finally it did, that you could pull a complete boner and go too much on appearances. One of those tenths had been both virginal and scandalized and had gone straight along to the purser's office to lodge the worst kind of complaint, short of professional negligence, that could be made against a ship's officer.

Sacked, Peter Harrison, tall, blue-eyed and handsome and well-preserved in his middle thirties, had found a coasting berth for a while and then had started the climb back by joining a foreign-going freighter company when war had broken out and there was a shortage of officers due to so many being called into the Royal Naval Reserve. By now the climb back was well under way: one more step in promotion and he would be a master. Which was why he didn't entirely welcome the fact of women being aboard the *Wolf Rock*: the temptation would be great, and he had to keep his nose clean. Champney, who knew his record, would be keeping a weather eye lifting, and there was also the Commodore to be stood clear of. In peacetime, the then Captain Kemp had been a well-known shipmaster on the Australia run, and although Harrison's company had not been Kemp's, he knew of Kemp by repute. Kemp ran a happy ship always, it was said, but a very taut one.

Even though he wasn't running the *Wolf Rock*, he could make his weight felt.

Harrison sighed: continence was not easy. When the ship had passed down the Firth of Clyde under a heavy sky and was bringing up the Pladda Light and the great rock of Ailsa Craig on her starboard bow, the order came from the bridge to secure the anchors for sea. When the ready-use anchor had been lifted from the waterline and hoisted to the hawse-pipe, when the slips had been secured and the bottle-screws drawn tight, Harrison left the fo'c'sle and reported to Captain Champney.

'Fo'c'sle secured for sea, sir.'

'Thank you, Harrison. I'm remaining on the bridge at least until we've rendezvoused with the carriers.'

That was as expected. Harrison asked, 'Boat drill, sir?'

'Yes, please. I was about to give the order. Exercise abandon ship stations – and see to it that those Wrens are fully instructed.'

'Aye, aye, sir.' Harrison turned away and clattered down the

21

ladder. As he reached the boat deck Champney gestured to Logan, Second Officer, whose bridge watch it was, and a button was pressed in the wheelhouse. The alarm rattlers, sounding boat stations, blared throughout the ship and men began turning out from below carrying cork lifejackets. Most of them, expectant of the routine exercise, had already dressed in a variety of warm clothing. With them came the WRNS contingent, warned in advance by First Officer Jean Forrest. They assembled at their allotted stations and Harrison, moving from group to group with the ship's third officer and the bosun, carried out the Master's instructions carefully. The set of lifejackets round the chest was of paramount importance.

By dawn the rendezvous with the carriers had been made, the huge dark shapes coming down on the convoy from the north and taking up their positions astern of the merchant ships and ahead of the Flag moving along in rear. The concourse of ships, not yet taking up the zigzag pattern that would help to protect them against enemy submarines when farther out, proceeded on course to leave Malin Head in County Donegal behind them. It would be from Malin Head that the convoy would take its final departure from the British Isles.

iv

The routeing orders had followed the usual procedure for ships bound in wartime for the Strait of Gibraltar: first of all they would steam well out into the North Atlantic until they were beyond the range of the German bombers based in Occupied France; then they would turn south, and finally, when well down towards the South Atlantic, east for Cape St Vincent and the entry to the Mediterranean – or *mare nostrum* as Signor Mussolini presumptuously called it. Kemp was taking a look at the chart when a message came from the ship's radio room, manned now by naval telegraphists on the Commodore's staff as well as by the *Wolf Rock*'s own Marconi operators. The message was brought to Kemp by his assistant, Sub-Lieutenant Finnegan.

Finnegan said, 'Starting early, sir.' He handed over a naval message form, the brief Admiralty cypher broken down into plain language. Kemp read it, frowning. The signal was ad-

22

dressed to the Flag, repeated Commodore; and it indicated that a U-boat group was believed to have left the occupied port of Brest and was heading into the North Atlantic. The pack's course could cross that of the convoy.

That was all. Kemp said, 'Too much to expect that the Admiralty could give a more precise indication of their damn course and speed, I suppose!'

'Crystal balls, sir – '

'All right, Finnegan. Frankly, it doesn't add much, does it? The U-boats are always out, it's nothing new.'

'Any action, sir?'

'Not from me! The Admiral may decide to alter course, I suppose. We'll just have to wait for him to react.' Kemp left the chart room and walked out to the port wing of the bridge where, in an increasing wind, Captain Champney was standing looking back towards the last of the land and the waves battering against the great mass of the Bloody Foreland and, closer, the heaving hulls and flight decks of the aircraft-carriers with the massive 16-inch turrets of the *Nelson* astern. Kemp passed the message form over and Champney grunted. His response was much the same as Kemp's had been. In wartime, you got used to such signals. Intelligence was often wrong; you made a mental note and carried on until such time as the intelligence grew more precise or the Asdics of the naval escort came up with an echo from beneath the sea.

Within the next five minutes a signalling projector began winking from the *Nelson*'s flag deck. Aboard the Commodore's ship the signalman of the watch read it off and reported to Kemp.

'From the Flag to Commodore repeated escort commanders, sir, convoy will maintain course and speed. Follow zigzag commencing on the executive.'

'Acknowledge,' Kemp said. 'Then make to all merchant ships, zig-zag pattern as indicated in NCS orders will be followed on the executive signal from the Flag.'

The executive came quickly, the hoisting close-up of a pennant flying at the dip from the starboard upper yard of the *Nelson*. Kemp watched with interest and some trepidation as the merchant ships, each with its own handling characteristics, began the turn to starboard on the first leg of the zigzag. At such moments collisions could occur, although by this stage of the war the merchant shipmasters had become more accustomed to sailing in convoy. This time there were the usual hair-raising moments but on the whole the initial manoeuvre was expeditiously carried out. For some fifteen minutes the convoy would maintain the course and then alter to another leg; and so it would go on throughout most of the voyage.

Below in her cabin First Officer Forrest felt the list of the ship as course was altered, heard the chatter of the telemotor steering gear as the helm was put over for what seemed like a long time. Fear struck, imagination taking hold: the ship was moving away from a U-boat attack . . . but if that had been the case, then surely there would have been a warning from the bridge? Of course there would: she remained in her bunk but sat up and stretched out towards the cork lifejacket hanging on a hook behind her door. As she did so there was a knock; she went back beneath the bedclothes.

'Who is it?' she called.

'Botley, ma'am. Tea up, as they say.'

'Oh . . . come in.' Botley was the Captain's steward; he had presented himself when she had embarked, telling her that he was to be looking after her as well as Captain Champney and the Commodore. Botley entered, a tray balanced on the palm of his hand.

'Good morning, ma'am.'

'Good morning, Botley.'

'Comfortable night, ma'am?'

'Yes, thank you. Are we . . . is everything all right?'

'All right, ma'am?' Botley looked surprised. 'Course it is, ma'am. Was you worried, like?'

'We seemed to alter course just now.'

'The zigzag, ma'am. And something of a near miss. Possible collision, but nothing to fret about, we're still afloat.'

'I see. Thank you, Botley.'

The steward placed the tea tray on a shelf by Jean Forrest's bunk. 'Anything else you want, any time, just ring, ma'am.'

'Thank you,' she said again. Botley took a quick look around the cabin as though establishing likely female requirements in his mind, then left. Jean Forrest drank the tea and shuddered: it was very strong and made with condensed milk – filthy! She was forced to leave it. Botley would need instruction in making tea. In the meantime Botley was reporting on WRNS officers to the ship's chief steward, Jock Campbell.

'The boss one . . . proper bleedin' virginal. Sheet right up to 'er chin, hiding the scrag I reckon. Toffee-nosed with it. The other two, they're not so bad. *Smiled*, would you believe it?' Botley paused. 'Got any tips, have you, Chief?'

'What sort o' tips?'

'How to tidy up a lady's boodwar.' Botley had come to sea with the war, had never attended upon the Master's wife. Campbell on the other hand had been a bedroom steward in the liners, years before.

He said, 'Main thing's tact. Things you don't notice, women's things. Knickers and that. Not that you're likely to see any. When they do leave knickers around, it's an invitation and *you* don't look the romantic sort.' He added with a wink, 'No offence, eh?'

'Oh, bollocks,' Botley said. Short and fat, too much gut, no hair and a squint. Each look in the mirror was torture. No, he wouldn't expect to find any knickers if Campbell was right. Botley went on his way, humming a tune. Never mind what he looked like, he had a wife at home and he was basically a cheery soul and if you couldn't get the odd popsie there was always booze when you got to port somewhere. It was a hymn tune that he hummed but the words were not those of any verses in the hymn book. There was a fantasy in his mind: if the Jerries made an attack at night there would be some interesting sights, twenty-odd wrens in nighties. Sometimes, the sea life held its compensations.

Botley went out on deck to take a look at the heaving sea. Glancing aft, he saw the ship's surgeon, old Dr O'Dwyer, puking his guts up over the side. Botley tut-tutted: the quack wasn't doing his first voyage to sea, far from it; the puke was due to the night before. Botley had become accustomed to ship's surgeons, anyway to Dr O'Dwyer, since the *Wolf Rock* had been fitted out with passenger cabins – Board of Trade, or rather, now, Ministry of War Transport regulations required a ship carrying more than twelve passengers to have a doctor on Articles. Dr O'Dwyer had been dredged up from some scrapheap or other to fulfill the requirements and had been glad enough to have the chance once again of imbibing duty free whisky. Rumour had it that the doc had been given the bum's rush from a liner company in pre-war

25

days after throwing up over the feet of the chairman of the line at a sailing-night cocktail party in Tilbury.

Botley studied the sea again. It was grey and nasty and heaving; not rough enough to send the U-boats deep and give the convoy a degree of safety. It was, in fact, good U-boat weather; just rough enough to hide the feather of spray that would show up the presence of a periscope. Botley gave a sudden shiver: they had a long way to go and most of it bloody dangerous, especially until they got to Port Said and the Suez Canal.

Even after that: the Jerries were everywhere, and if not the Jerries then the Japs, coming out across the Bay of Bengal from Burma to be a nasty threat to the waters around the naval base of Trincomalee. And all those troops in the liners: prime targets which, come to think of it, was probably why the girls hadn't been aboard the liners. Too risky. Same with the escort: more prime targets. The *Wolf Rock* was perhaps regarded as the safest bet even though she carried the Convoy Commodore. In that thought lay a little hope, and Botley cheered up, pulled his yellow duster from a pocket of his blue serge trousers, and went through the watertight door into the officers' quarters just as Jean Forrest began emerging from her cabin. She nipped back in and banged the door shut.

Botley grinned to himself: he'd seen a dressing-gown and fancied he'd frustrated a visit to the lavatory. He had just reached the Captain's pantry when there was a racket from the telemotor steering gear and the *Wolf Rock* heeled over sharply, much more sharply than would have been the case with a mere shift as per zigzag.

THREE

It had been Yeoman of Signals Lambert who had spotted it – the trained eye of a long-serving signalman beating the lookouts to it. He could be wrong but he reported immediately.

'Periscope on the starboard beam, sir!'

All the officers on the bridge trained their binoculars on the bearing. They saw nothing. Kemp said, 'So soon?' They were scarcely away from the land. Then he picked it up: drawing a little aft now, slap in the middle of the convoy and nothing reported from the escort: that tell-tale feather of water, almost impossible to be sure in the breaking seas, could have been anything really.

Then Champney saw something else. 'Torpedo trail, or I'm damn sure it is!'

It was impossible to be sure in fact, but Kemp didn't hesitate. 'Hard-a-port, Captain!' They had to turn away, present the smaller target of their stern to the oncoming torpedo if that was what it was. 'Yeoman, make the warning to all ships, masthead light.' Over the harsh noise of the action alarm Kemp heard Champney passing the order to close all watertight doors and Finnegan shouting down to the guns' crews as they manned their weapons. Then at last the reports came, a little late, from the Naval escort: the Asdics had picked up the echo, just the one. The U-boat, Kemp thought, must have been right down deep and had come up fast in a lucky spot. He awaited the outcome helplessly: the turn away was all that could have been done. He let out a long sigh of relief as the track of the tin fish was seen – just – passing close down his port side, passing harmlessly towards the land, away now from the convoy. By this time the destroyers of the

27

escort were reacting, signals flying from Captain (D) in the flotilla leader and the ships moving in at high speed, water gushing back along their decks, towards where the periscope trail had been seen. By now there was nothing: the U-boat would presumably have gone deep again after loosing off her fish, but how many had she fired?

Kemp got some of the answer within the next few seconds. There was a sudden mighty explosion from farther down the Commodore's column, and a great sheet of flame, blue, orange, white, crimson, a terrible firework display in the makings of the North Atlantic storm. Kemp looked astern in horror as the *Wolf Rock* under Champney's direction resumed her place in the column. Debris was rising into the sky, whirling bodies, pieces of wood that fell, slowly as it seemed, back towards where the water swirled over a vanished ship.

At Kemp's side Finnegan said, 'S.s. *Luton Town*, sir. Armaments.'

'Poor sods!'

'They won't have known much, sir.' Finnegan paused. 'Survivors, sir?'

'Don't be bloody naive, Finnegan.'

Sub-Lieutenant Finnegan didn't respond. Was it naive, to have a thought for someone who might, just might, have lived? He didn't reckon so. However, he did see Kemp's point. Kemp was no mean, cold bastard who would willingly leave any man to die if there was anything he could do about it. You didn't delay the convoy for the picking up of hypothetical handfuls of survivors, you didn't hazard other valuable ships or the lives of thousands of troops and seamen. You took the larger view; you had to. The winning of the war, and more pointedly at this moment the winning of the long-running battle of the North Atlantic, was paramount.

There were more explosions, but not this time of ships – the destroyers were mounting their depth-charge attacks. The repercussions of the deep explosions could be felt throughout the plates of the *Wolf Rock*, the great spouts of water were seen to rise again and again and fall back in crescendoes of foam. But the attack was abortive; the destroyers dropped behind the convoy, which with their so much greater speed they would easily overtake, to carry on searching and depth charging but when they

28

came back to rejoin the report was a dejected one: the lone Jerry, a brave man admittedly, had got away with it.

'Murderers,' Kemp said, his face grim.

'Not the first time, sir.'

'Don't·state the obvious, Finnegan.'

'Sorry, sir. I guess I just thought – '

'Can it, laddie. Or in English, shut up.'

Finnegan looked sideways at the Commodore's weather-beaten face. Square, solid, dependable, tough. But often toughness was only skin deep. Kemp didn't like death, didn't like seeing seamen blasted into shreds of bloody flesh. None of them did, of course; but Old Man Kemp, as Finnegan thought of him, always seemed to take it personally, blame himself for some dereliction of duty, some lack of alertness, though God alone knew what else any commodore could do. A commodore's broad gold band of rank didn't make its wearer superhuman although often enough it seemed expected of him.

Kemp put a hand on his assistant's shoulder, a kindly gesture to take the sting out of the rebuke. 'Send down for Petty Officer Ramm. Those guns' crews were too damn slow to close up.'

ii

Petty Officer Ramm came down from the bridge after getting an ear-bashing from the Commodore in person. Ramm didn't like being told off; it wasn't consistent with his dignity as a gunner's mate. Gunners' mates were something special. Kemp hadn't held back, though he had walked into the bridge wing and spoken quietly so that the reprimand wasn't obvious to the guns' crews. Well, it wouldn't happen again. Ramm moved aft from the bridge ladder, arms swinging, shoulders back and a nasty glint in his eye.

'You, Leading Seaman Nelson.'

'Yes, GI?'

Ramm looked his number two up and down. Stripey Nelson, so called on account of his three good-conduct badges. 'Next time the alarm goes, move yourself, right? Just because your bloody namesake's in company, doesn't mean you can sit back and bask in glory.' Ramm rose and fell on the balls of his feet. 'Slow to close up, Commodore says. Gets the 'ands fell in and we'll have some gunnery practice, put some dynamite under their lousy fat backsides, all right?'

29

'All right, GI.' Leading Seaman Nelson, fat himself and never very fast, lumbered away to pass the order. It was probably true that they'd been a bit slow, but that often happened at the start of a convoy; the fleshpots of the shore had to be overcome and the gunnery ratings aboard the *Wolf Rock* were no great shakes. None of them were active service, by which Stripey Nelson meant they weren't on long-service RN engagements; nor were they pensioners of the Royal Fleet Reserve, which both he and Ramm were, nor was this lot composed of the normal hostilities-only ratings of the fleet: they were DEMS, which stood for Defensively Equipped Merchant Ship ratings with little more than a smattering of gunnery knowledge, a ham-fisted bunch – at any rate, the *Wolf Rock*'s lot were. Moaners, too, but the moaning stopped when Petty Officer Ramm marched along to where Stripey Nelson had assembled them.

'Right, you lot, any more sotto voce remarks about my ancestry and you'll wish you'd never been bloody born. And any more slackness and you'll be on the bridge and in the Commodore's Report.' Ramm paused, his eye travelling along the guns' crews. 'Now. We shall exercise closing up on the action alarm, and we shall bloody exercise it until I'm satisfied you've all moved your arses as fast as is yumanly possible and more so.' He nodded at Stripey Nelson. 'Right, Leading Seaman Nelson. Dismiss. And stand by for a blast on me whistle.That constitutes the alarm, all right? In the meantime, get below as if you was sitting in the messdeck dreaming of 'ome.'

Ramm gave it five minutes, then blew his whistle down the hatch leading to the naval messdeck. He held a pocket-watch in his hand. The men tumbled out, were sent down again. And again and again until Ramm believed he had shaved off the last second. After that, he exercised gun drill, imaginary firing at an imaginary target. That, too, went on and on.

iii

First Officer Jean Forrest sat in an easy chair in her cabin, face tight, her hands shaking. She had now come face to face with war, with the sheer horror of an armaments carrier blowing up as the result of a touch on the firing lever aboard a submerged

U-boat. An almost casual act once the sights were on. And then the terrible deaths, the shattered bodies, the burned flesh, none the easier to take for being at a distance, and the convoy steaming on regardless, steaming almost certanly to more such explosions.

Jean Forrest had seen little of the real war so far. It had been back in the phoney war period that she had joined the WRNS, back in the days of leaflet-dropping over Germany, of Hang Out the Washing on the Siegfried Line, and Run Rabbit Run. The days when, after the initial reaction that had closed the theatres and cinemas was over, life had been little different from peacetime except for the constant digging of air raid shelters and the new self-importance of little Hitlers metamorphosed into air-raid wardens with their hectoring shouts of 'Put that light out, don't you know there's a war on?'

Days when the socialite thing to do had been to apply for a commission in the WRNS. Miss Forrest had had to do a more or less token period as an ordinary Wren rating, but that had been no great hardship and a combination of her greater age than the rest of the girls and the help of highly placed relatives had quickly got her a commission; subsequently some string-pulling and again her age got her promotion to First Officer. Her service to date had kept her out of the areas subject to the bombings by the *Luftwaffe*: latterly she had found herself doing naval liaison duties in that section of the War Office that had been evacuated to Woodstock in Oxfordshire and she had spent her days in the splendour, a little muted by the exigencies of the war, of Blenheim Palace, home of the Dukes of Marlborough, and her nights in Keble College, Oxford, being bussed in daily.

She wished fervently that she was there still. She had applied for a posting after an abortive affair with a brigadier whose wife had turned up unexpectedly, whereupon the brigadier had lost interest in her. She had been used and she knew it; a move had been a matter of urgency, or anyway of hurt pride, and she hadn't thought too much about consequences. Now she was stuck with them: out at sea in a convoy subject to heavy attack.

No way out now.

Her nerves were playing her up: she almost reached screaming point as the repeated, hectoring tones of Petty Officer Ramm ripped into the cabin despite the closed glass of the port and its protective deadlight of heavy metal. Shouts, ship noises, the increasing turbulence of the sea, the heavy swell as the *Wolf Rock* moved out from home waters into the North Atlantic.

A knock came at her door.

'Come in,' she said. Third Officer Pawle appeared. 'Yes, what is it?'

'PO Wren Hardisty, ma'am.'

'What about her?'

'She'd like a word with you. A complaint, about the seamen.'

'Oh, God! Molestation already?'

'Language rather than molestation,' Susan Pawle said. 'Shall I send her in, ma'am?'

'Yes, all right.' First Officer Forrest remained seated as the petty officer wren entered. Dorothy Hardisty was squat, virtually square, with a big bosom and firm jaw and once inside the cabin she stood at attention like a sergeant-major, very formal, eyes gazing over Jean Forrest's head in the regulation manner, ready to state her complaint.

Bidden to do so, she stated it unequivocally. 'My girls, ma'am, have heard such things they *never* ought to. Filthy words, such as I couldn't repeat – '

'The ship's crew, or the naval ratings?'

'*Both*, ma'am. And it goes on and on –'

'But the girls aren't . . . they've not been cotton-wool wrapped, have they?'

'That's different, ma'am. Quite different. The odd swear word heard in barracks. Not continual filth, muck. On deck, outside the wrens' mess . . .'

Jean Forrest sighed. 'We all know what sailors are like. Is it really that bad?'

'Yes, ma'am, it is. Words like – well, I dessay you'll not have heard them, ever. So I –'

'I probably have,' Jean Forrest said.

'Well, ma'am that's as maybe.' PO Wren Hardisty's bosom heaved upwards. 'I think the men need to be reminded that there are young ladies on board, with ears. The ship's Captain and the Commodore –'

'Very well, PO, you've made your point. I'll see what I can do. I agree with you really, I don't like coarse language, but men are men, you know.'

'Yes, ma'am, I do know. More's the pity.'

'Yes.' Jean Forrest sighed again. Miss Hardisty was standing her ground still. 'Is there anything else?'

'Yes, ma'am, there is. Wren Smith.'

Ena Smith, the tarty one, more suited in Jean Forrest's view to the WAAF. What language had *she* overheard that she hadn't heard before? 'What's it about?'

'Wren Smith reports having missed her second period, ma'am.'

'Oh God, no! *Second*? Why in heaven's name didn't she report having missed her first?'

PO Wren Hardisty shrugged: her face was doomful and in a way accusing, as though First Officer Forrest was responsible. Miss Forrest asked, 'How on earth did the MO at the embarkation inspection miss *that*?'

Again the PO shrugged. 'Naval doctors, ma'am, are not used to pregnancies. Not the RN ones. The RNVR, they may be. What should we do about it now, ma'am?'

'In the middle of an outward bound convoy?'

'We're not that far out, ma'am –'

'That won't wash.' Jean Forrest had no intention of suggesting to Commodore Kemp that the convoy might turn back on account of a possibly pregnant Wren: missed periods didn't always mean a pregnancy. She said, 'If necessary she could be landed at Gibraltar, or Malta I suppose. But it's early days . . . there's no real reason why she shouldn't have her next period before we get to Trincomalee . . . is there?'

PO Wren Hardisty looked ominous. 'Regulations, ma'am. Wrens that *are* pregnant –'

'Yes, yes, I know.' Pregnant Wrens were normally discharged back to civilian life; it had not been unknown for disillusioned Wrens to get themselves in the family way as a means of getting out, but usualy these had been the married ones. Ena Smith was not married.

'If I might make a suggestion, ma'am?

'Yes, of course, do.'

'Thank you, ma'am. The ship's doctor.'

'An examination? Well, yes, I suppose that's the obvious answer. But before making any decisions, I'll see the girl myself and then I'll put it to the Commodore.' Miss Forrest, PO Wren Hardisty thought, was looking very agitated and no wonder: it

33

was not nice to be faced with a likely pregnant, unmarried Wren. The world had become like a cesspit, thanks to Hitler, not at all what it had been when Miss Hardisty had been young. She stood in the cabin like an affronted fortress and was about to speak again when the First Officer said, 'The girl herself. What's her attitude?'

'Cocky, ma'am. Defiant, you might say.'

Jean Forrest said, 'What I can't understand is why she didn't come out with this before embarking – the missed first period would have been a reasonable excuse. No chances would have been taken – she'd have been off the draft immediately. I take it she wants her discharge?'

'No, ma'am, she doesn't.'

'Doesn't? Then why, for God's sake, make an issue of her condition now?'

PO Wren Hardisty said, 'It came out by accident, ma'am. Wren Smith was boasting to her friends on the messdeck. I happened to overhear and I instituted questioning.'

'Boasting?'

'*Boasting*, ma'am, yes. That she'd been – er. That she thought she might . . . have a bun in the oven, ma'am, those were the words used.'

Jean Forrest kept her face straight: Miss Hardisty's tone, like her expression, had been outraged. Miss Hardisty, asked about her questioning of the girl, reported further. Wren Smith had committed the act behind a bush in Victoria Park not far from the Naval barracks in Queen Street, Portsmouth. The man involved had been a sailor: Ena Smith had refused to reveal his identity.

'Thoroughly sordid, ma'am. I don't like having to speak to you about it, that I don't.'

When PO Wren Hardisty had left the cabin, Jean Forrest wondered about sordidness. It hadn't got to be. Her own experiences with the Blenheim brigadier had been a little sordid, perhaps; but often there could be love. And such persons as Wren Smith and her sailor, probably from the barracks, hadn't the advantages open to brigadiers. Behind a bush in Victoria Park had very likely been the only available place. She had to keep an open mind, at any rate until she herself had spoken to the girl.

It was all a bloody nuisance; but at least it took one's mind off the dangers of submarine-infested waters for a while.

34

Yeoman of Signals Lambert, an oilskin covering his number three uniform with the red badges of his rank and his non-substantive status of Visual Signalman First Class, checked round his little kingdom in rear of the chart room, fluffing at the flags of the International Code in the flag locker, checking his signal halyards and glancing now and again down at the boat deck where some of the WRNS ratings were draped over the lee guardrail and looking a nasty shade of green. Lambert sucked at his teeth and thought; poor little lasses, far from home and getting farther with each turn of the screw, feeling as if they'd rather die than carry on being seasick. He wondered what their daily shipboard routine would be: so far, they didn't appear to have anything to do other than keep their quarters cleaned and swept, maybe washing their smalls as his own wife and daughters called their knickers and bras and so on. No doubt, before long their officers would organize something. Maybe they'd be put on to darning the matlows' socks or something useful like that. Or, when the better weather came, PT on the boat deck, a sight for the sore eyes of seamen, tits lifting and falling while they cavorted and jumped in the air. A year or so back, Lambert had been in an aircraft-carrier that had brought a bunch of Wrens back to the Clyde from Gibraltar. A deck hockey match on the flight deck had been organized, WRNS against the ship's company. The seamen had behaved as proper gents but the girls had been murder, real savages once they had hockey sticks in their hands, and the seamen hadn't had a chance.

Checking and wren-watching done, Lambert lifted his binoculars and looked around at the ships now once again altering to their set zigzag pattern, coming round on the port leg. He looked at the immensity of the battleship *Nelson*, her great camouflage-painted sides heaving to the increasing ocean swell, seas coming over her bows to wash aft past the three massive 16-inch turrets, each carrying three guns with their tampions in position to keep the seas out of the barrels.

Those guns were a welcome sight, solid and heavy, with a nice long range. Something to make any Jerry surface raiders think twice before attacking the convoy as it made its westing towards the position where the ships would alter to the south.

Lambert rolled a fag from a tin of Ticklers', using a Rizla

cigarette machine. Shielding his face behind his flag locker, he lit the fag. Some captains didn't allow smoking on the bridge, but so long as the ship's master had no objection Commodore Kemp permitted it in daylight hours – not at night because even just the glow of a fag-end, let alone the striking of a match or lighter, could be seen by the perishing Jerries who might be lurking beneath their periscopes – and so long as you didn't approach him with a fag dangling from your lips . . .

Lambert's thoughts drifted homewards.

Pompey. Pompey at war, Pompey under the spasmodic hammer of Goering's *Luftwaffe*. Palmerston Road in Southsea, and King's Road, all flat. Likewise parts of the barracks and the dockyard, and a good deal of Commercial Road going north from the Guildhall, and more south and east of the Guildhall, little streets that had never expected to be blown sky-high by German bombs, helpless civilians dying by the dozen despite the heroic efforts of the rescue squads and firemen. Lambert's home was off Arundel Street, which itself led off Commercial Road, and he worried about it continually, right there in the firing line as he saw it. He worried the more now because he and Doris had had words the night before he'd left to rejoin Kemp and report aboard for the new convoy.

There had still been a cloud next morning, and all over what Lambert saw as nothing. Or anyway, not much. Women were funny. When he'd pulled his pen out from the top pocket of his jacket, a french letter had come out with it. He'd forgotten it was there; he'd had it a long time. Doris had pounced.

'Well I never!'

'It's nothing to worry about, dear.'

'Nothing to worry about! What you been up to, eh?'

'Nothing. Else it wouldn't have been there, would it?'

She'd sneered. 'I'm not green. That's a daft answer.'

'Well, I'm sorry, love. It – it's just precautions, like. Just in case. I'd forgotten all about it. Sort of thing any man has on him,' he'd added lamely.

'A particular sort of man, yes, maybe.'

'I swear I haven't done anything,' he said, and it was the truth. He had those snapshots, and they sufficed. He'd been loyal to them, if sometimes tempted. Women in the world's ports went for sailors, men with saved-up cash to spend on a good time, men

36

who had been deprived at sea, sometimes for long periods. Some of those women were bags, others were hard to resist. But he had resisted them nobly. He said this, and repeated his assurances, and she'd cried but in the end had calmed down about it and he'd taken her out for a drink in the Golden Fleece and then a bit of supper, and when they'd got back both their daughters turned up with their husbands to say goodbye to dad. Then bed, which hadn't been very successful what with one thing and another, and come the morning Doris had nagged again. Cried again too. Not the best send-off back to war. Lambert was feeling remorseful now but could only hope and pray that Hitler wouldn't get Doris before they'd patched up the bad feeling. When he'd written that letter before sailing from the Clyde, he'd wondered whether or not to mention it but had decided not to on the principle of least said, soonest mended.

A little later, when Lambert went below to the petty officers' mess, he listened to the BBC news: there had been another raid on Pompey and two of the Jerries had been shot down in Spithead. There was no mention of damage or casualties but Lambert's anxieties became that much sharper.

v

The majority of those aboard the *Wolf Rock* and in all the other ships of the convoy had their home worries. That was part of war. The exceptions were those who had homes in the safe areas of Britain, the remoter country districts away from the ports and the factories and the armament depots and the airfields. The *Wolf Rock*'s chief engineer, Edgar Turnberry, came from Kirkby Stephen in Westmorland, high up and on the northern fringe of the Yorkshire Dales. The Pennines were pretty safe in his view, Hitler wouldn't be wasting his armadas on sheep and mountains, farm buildings and waterfalls. Edgar Turnberry was a widower; when his wife had died some years before the war he had sold up the little home in Liverpool and gone back to spend his leaves with his ageing parents and the elder brother who ran the farm for them.

So remote from the sea and the dockyard hustle, Kirkby Stephen was a good place to relax. Turnberry liked horse riding, an odd hobby perhaps for a ship's engineer, and he'd covered the area from Kendal east to Richmond by way of the steep road leading down by the Birkdale Beck to Muker and on through Swaledale; or the right turn to Thwaite, past the Buttertubs along the track to Hawes; and the narrow road from Reeth through Arkengarthdale and back again to Thwaite. Long days in the good fresh air, so far removed from the clamour and oily smell of an engine-room.

Currently Mr Turnberry was making an inspection with his second engineer, Bob Guthrie, checking round, feeling bearings, probing now and again with a long-necked oilcan, wiping his hands on a ball of cotton-waste. When that armaments carrier had gone up, the reverberations of the huge explosion and of the depth charges from the destroyers of the escort had hit the *Wolf Rock*'s engine-room, making everything shudder and clang. It was doubtful if any actual damage had been done but prudence dictated a looksee.

'Bloody buggers,' Turnberry said with feeling. 'All those blokes trapped below.'

'They won't have known much about it, Chief.'

'No? I wouldn't bet on it. Not unless the bottom was blown right out of her. Which I grant it probably was.' Edgar Turnberry had himself been a survivor from a dry-cargo ship that had been torpedoed in the North Atlantic. No bottoms had been blown out on that occasion, but the ship had settled pretty fast and Turnberry, along with all the engine-room complement, had been trapped and helpless when the entry hatch had jammed, trapped at the top of the maze of steel ladders that criss-crossed the engine-room from the top of the double bottoms to the deckhead above. The deck gang had been working on it and those below had scrambled through with just a couple of minutes to spare before the ship had gone down. By the time he reached a lifeboat, Turnberry's hair had taken the first step towards going grey. Thereafter he had lost a lot of his enthusiasm for the sea life, but he'd had to see the war through in the only way he knew how – as a ship's engineer.

His tour of inspection completed, Turnberry went back to the starting-platform and used the voice-pipe to the wheelhouse. Captain Champney answered.

Turnberry said, 'Chief here, sir. All correct.'

'Thank you, Chief.'

'What's it like up top?'

'Fair weight of wind, sea increasing, otherwise all quiet. But we're still in the area where we can expect the *Luftwaffe*, remember.'

Turnberry grunted. 'I'll try not to forget. Meantime, there's paperwork to see to. I'm going to my cabin if that's all right, Captain?'

'All right with me, Chief.'

Turnberry replaced the voice-pipe cover, nodded to his second engineer, and climbed the ladders to the air-lock and the hatch to the engineers' alleyway. Emerging, he heard girlish laughter coming from the converted spare cabins: the wrens. As he passed an open doorway he saw a male figure, one of his off-watch junior engineers, sitting on a bunk with a girl on his knee. He halted, looming in the doorway. 'Out of there, lad, pronto.'

The young engineer got to his feet, face scarlet. Turnberry said, 'Wrens quarters are out of bounds. You know that. If it happens again, you'll be up before the Captain. Maybe the Commodore too. There's a touch of the RN aboard now and don't you forget it.'

Turnberry went on his way, duty done but leaving him with a feeling of age and curmudgeonliness. What was more natural than to seek female company? Turnberry cursed the presence of the Wrens and the threats of dalliance they had brought with them in the middle of a convoy. In a sense, they were worse than Hitler: they were closer, and they would be there all the way to Trinco.

In his cabin, Turnberry started on the paperwork, returns of engine-room stores and bunkers for the company and for the Ministry of War Transport. The official work done, he turned to personal matters. He examined what had become, since his wife had died, his whole interest: his three passbooks. His bank account, and his savings accounts with the Leeds Permanent and the Halifax Building Societies. He was getting quite well lined: his expenses were few, so were his desires. Money mounted when left alone at two percent.

Turnberry was thus engrossed when the strident call of the action alarm burst into his reverie.

FOUR

'Relax,' Kemp said.

All binoculars were turned on the aircraft, circling distantly, out of range of the ack-ack. Kemp's first instinct had been to sound the action alarm when the German was sighted, but now he ordered the stand down, the falling-out of the guns' crews. The intruder had been identified by the yeoman of signals as a Focke-Wulf Kondor, the four-engined long-range reconnaissance aircraft of the *Luftwaffe*. It could be left to the Seafires, the fighter planes of the Fleet Air Arm now moving along the flight decks of the carriers. It was probably, Finnegan said, from Merignac in Occupied France.

'Or Norway', Kemp said. 'Stavanger . . . they're working from there as well now.'

He studied the aircraft. It was very unlikely it would attack; the FW 200s had been known often enough to attack single ships, or stragglers from convoys, but currently the escort would be far too much for a lone reconnaissance aircraft. The bugbear was that she would already have reported by now to the German command; the convoy's position, course and speed would have been radio-ed, also its composition – the heavy, laden merchant ships and troop transports, the size of the naval escort – the presence of the *Nelson* and two fleet carriers alone indicating the importance of the convoy. Sooner or later the big attack would come. The U-boat would have made the first report; now the FW had come for a proper bird's-eye view, and it was likely that the convoy would be shadowed distantly. In the meantime the FW had turned away, beating it for home. It was unlikely, Kemp thought, that it would get away from the Seafires but it wasn't all that important now: it had done its work.

Now the day was darkening, sinking towards the bleakness of a stormy, windswept night. The rain had come, was slicing across the open bridge-wings of the *Wolf Rock*, and the ship was labouring somewhat to the swell and the breaking seas that crossed it, giving an uncomfortable motion. Below in her cabin Third Officer Susan Pawle lay sleepless, feeling not so bad so long as she remained flat in her bunk but desperately seasick if she stood up. Her mind was in a turmoil: the ripping apart of the armament ship earlier in the day had brought back her miseries. Something like that could have happened to Johnny for all she knew. The Admiralty didn't go into details. Johnny could have been blown into fragments, not trapped at all. If so, that was of course a kinder way but it didn't assuage widowhood.

The recce had left its sinister shadow over all: everyone in the convoy knew the score. It was just a matter of waiting now, and probably the wait wouldn't be very long. The attack would come before the convoy had moved too far out for the fuel capacities of the German dive-bombers and their fighter escort. Aboard the flagship the Admiral conferred with his staff officers and with the Flag Captain, together with the fleet gunnery officer: all would be on the top line, extra vigilance throughout the convoy and escort, ready-use ammunition lockers rechecked, the parties in the shell-handling rooms deep below the armoured belts set to move fast in getting the shells into the hoists to the guns, damage control parties rehearsing what could happen when the bombs came down so that they would be ready with an instant response.

ii

The knock came at Kemp's cabin door when he'd been about to turn in, fully dressed except for his seaboots and monkey-jacket, to snatch as much sleep as possible before things hotted up. He was not needed on the bridge when things were quiet: Champney and his deck officers had no need of a nanny and Kemp had no desire to appear to be such. Hearing the knock, he gave a sigh: no peace for a commodore.

'Come in,' he said testily.

The door opened: it was Jean Forrest.

'Well, Miss Forrest.' Kemp's tone wasn't welcoming.

'I'm so sorry to disturb you, Commodore.'

'Get it off your chest, Miss Forrrest, and be sharp about it if you don't mind. I assume it's important?'

'Yes, it is.'

Kemp indicated a chair; Jean Forest sat, crossing her legs, hands clasped around a knee, the two-and-a-half blue stripes on each cuff catching the electric light from the deckhead. She said, 'We have a pregnancy –'

'*What*?'

'A possible pregnancy, I should say. That's being optimistic though. The girl's pretty sure.'

'That's all we need,' Kemp said heavily. 'A damn Wren up the spout! Well, what's the story?' He glanced at the brass-bound clock on his bulkhead. 'In as few words as possible, please, Miss Forrest.'

She told him. When she'd done he asked, 'What do you expect me to do about it?'

'Well, I have to keep the regulations in mind.'

'Bugger the regulations . . . I'm sorry, Miss Forrest –'

'That's all right,' she said quickly. PO Wren Hardisty would have had a fit, probably. 'But really she ought to be put ashore –'

'Put ashore?' Kemp stared, eyes exaggeratedly wide. He gestured towards the deadlighted ports of the cabin. 'On a Carley float, or something? With Finnegan to navigate?'

'Not exactly, Commodore. What I meant was, she should be landed in Gibraltar.'

'The convoy's not entering Gibraltar, Miss Forrest.'

'Or Malta.'

'The convoy as a whole is not entering Malta either. A transfer at sea would be out of the –'

'I thought perhaps a boat –'-

'Think again, Miss Forrest. The Admiral's not going to delay the convoy for a pregnant Wren. Nor would I! She'll have to go through to Alexandria and await passage back to UK. Have you contacted the doctor?'

'Not yet, no.'

'Going to?'

'I think I should. But –'

Kemp gave a harsh laugh, a sound of no humour. 'I wouldn't like any daughter of mine to be examined by Dr O'Dwyer – breath like an anaesthetic! However, I suppose it's the form. Your Wren high command'll expect it – won't they?'

She nodded. 'It's all very unfortunate.'

'That's an understatement. Tell me one thing: does the girl love this man? Did you find that out?'

'I believe she does, Commodore. I really do. I asked her why, that being the case, she hadn't got herself off the Trincomalee draft. The answer was quite interesting. The man concerned was also on draft to Ceylon, to Trinco. Seamen replacements for casualties in the Eastern Fleet.'

'You're saying she wants to go on with the convoy?'

'Yes, Commodore.'

Kemp gave a hard laugh. 'Some hope, once your Wren bigwigs get their teeth into the girl!'

'Well, the regulations do –'

'Yes, yes. But I've a suspicion it could be a damn sight easier all round if we played Cupid, Miss Forrest. It's very early days, isn't it, pregnancy-wise? I mean . . . she won't – show is the expression I believe, all that quickly?'

'That's true, Commodore, but I gather she's talked more than she should, which is why PO Hardisty –'

'Yes, so you said. Let's sleep on it, Miss Forrest – and you'll have to see Dr O'Dwyer in the morning. We have to have a care for her health, come what may. That's the first consideration. Good night, Miss Forrest.'

Kemp got to his feet. So did Jean Forrest. She said, 'You look terribly tired, Commodore.' There was what he took to be womanly sympathy in her eyes. He agreed abruptly that he was indeed very tired, and held the door open for her exit. Then he slumped on to his bunk and was dead asleep within the minute.

iii

By next morning the weather had worsened. The wind was up to Force Ten on the Beaufort Scale and the wave crests rolled in apparently unending numbers ahead of the convoy, still steaming due west. Spume flew from those crests like a white carpet;

43

the wind howled like a company of evil spirits through the standing rigging. Both the Commodore and the ship's Master were on the bridge with Chief Officer Harrison, whose watch it was until his relief came up at 0800. Kemp was clearly anxious: the ships of the convoy were scattered all over the show, some of them visible only when they rose between the crests, coming briefly up from the valleys of the deep ocean. The weather had played hell with the station-keeping. Kemp said, 'It's the worst lash-up I've seen since the early days.'

Champney shrugged. 'It's the times we live in. I mean, the sea service is getting thinned out. So many dead, so many yanked off into the RNR. There's a lack of experience that's starting to show now.'

'I don't envy the destroyers their job this morning,' Kemp said, scanning the convoy through his binoculars. The destroyers, the shepherds, were everywhere, circling the spread-out convoy, weaving dangerously in and out of the disordered columns, the signal lamps busy as the commanding officers strove to get the merchant ships back into some sort of station. The aircraft-carriers had dropped farther astern, prudently: there was danger of collision while the convoy sorted itself out. Through the spume-carpet the *Nelson* was no more than semi-visible as the water rose over her fo'c'sle and streamed back along her flush decks, turning her superstructure into an island moving through the sea. The great turrets were submerged for most of the time, appearing now and again like three more islands on the move. As Kemp watched, there was a shout from the yeoman of signals.

'Flag calling up, sir.'

Kemp waved an arm in acknowledgement. Lambert read off the flagship's lamp, his words being taken down on a signal pad by the signalman on watch. The message received, Lambert reported to the Commodore, handing over the torn-off message form. Kemp read: *Commodore from Flag, s.s. Langstone Harbour dropping astern with engine trouble. Am detaching two destroyers to stand by. Remainder of convoy to maintain formation, course and speed.*

'Formation,' Kemp said sardonically. 'All right, thank you, Yeoman.' He looked around the plunging ships again. Some two hours earlier, when the weather had started its deterioration, the order had gone to all ships to cease the zig zag and steer the mean course of the convoy: there was no likely danger from U-boats in such conditions. 'Finnegan?'

44

'Yes, sir.' Kemp's assistant came across, sliding downhill along the wing as the *Wolf Rock* rolled heavily to port.

'*Langstone Harbour*, Finnegan.'

'Dry-cargo, sir. 10,000 tonner. Foodstuffs, for detachment to Malta.'

'I know that.' The Malta garrison and civilians had been under long siege, were said to be down to eating rats. The *Langstone Harbour* was very badly needed but the real chances of her entering the Grand Harbour at Valletta were pretty slim: the Italians were determined that Malta should be starved into submission and they would throw in all they'd got as the convoy came within striking distance of Malta. And now the *Langstone Harbour* looked like being a sitting duck, at least for a while. Kemp asked, 'You've got the list of convoy? What's her Master's name?'

Finnegan brought out a typewritten sheet. He scanned it. 'Captain Horncape, sir. Weird sort of name –'

'*Horncape*? Christian name, Finnegan?'

'Jake, sir. Captain Jake Horncape.'

Kemp smacked a fist into his palm. 'Jake Horncape! Well, I'll be damned! *Can't* be anyone else of that name . . . I don't recall seeing him at the convoy conference, but of course he'll have changed. So've I, come to that.'

'You know him, sir?'

Kemp laughed. '*Knew* him, yes. I certainly did! He and I were apprentices together in sail . . . oh, more than thirty years ago. Our paths never crossed since. We had plenty of fun with that name of his, rounding Cape Horn in the old days!'

'I'll bet you had, sir.' Finnegan had his binoculars to his eyes. 'Destroyers detaching now, sir. *Hindu* and *Pindari*, 34th Flotilla.'

Kemp picked them up, battling through the heavy seas, making for the rear of the convoy. He dictated a short signal to the yeoman, a message of good luck. He asked if Lambert could raise the *Langstone Harbour*.

'Yessir –'

'Then make by light, best wishes and all luck from John Kemp. Thirty-odd years is a long time.'

'Not from Commodore, sir?'

Kemp said, 'Not from Commodore, Yeoman.' As he braced himself against the corkscrew, roll-and-pitch motion of the *Wolf Rock*, his mind went back over the many years, the long years of

45

sea service from apprentice in sail to Master of a great liner. The days of sail were little more now than a memory, but one that would never fade from the minds of those few mariners left at sea who had served their time under the great spreads of canvas, bowling along before a fresh wind, or tacking into a blustery storm, or lying becalmed in the Doldrums as they dropped down through the South Pacific to come past the Falklands for the terrible east-west passage of Cape Horn, battling into the teeth of the westerlies that stormed around the world's bottom virtually without cease, to come into the kinder waters of the South Pacific. Then the long run to New Zealand and Australia, or up the coast of South America to Chilean or Peruvian ports to load for home. Largely the cargoes from Peru had been guano, the acrid, stinking droppings of sea birds for use as fertilizer. But it was not the cargoes that Kemp was recalling: it was Jake Horncape, a frivolous youth in those days and one inclined to be slow at times to obey the orders of the Master or mates. On one voyage he had been sent aloft as a punishment, sent to sit on the fore upper tops'l yard minus his trousers whilst the ship had been on passage of the Horn. When ordered down again, he was frozen to the ice-covered yard. Young Kemp had been sent up with one of the fo'c'sle crowd to bring him down. He'd only just about lived, that time. On another occasion he had been confined for three days to the hen coop carried below the break of the fo'c'sle . . . less lethal, but more smelly. Jake Horncape had survived all that with a rather impish grin on his face, shrugging it off as one of the penalties of going to sea in a world of hard men engaged in what was perhaps the hardest way ever known of making a living.

Would Jake Horncape survive this lot, with his broken-down engines?

Kemp spoke again. 'Finnegan, get a signal made to the Flag. I'd like the details of what's happening aboard the *Langstone Harbour*.' Kemp leaned across the guardrail, chin resting on his hands. His mind was still half back in sail, remembering and wishing . . . sail might have been hard, might have had its almost insuperable difficulties, but at least pregnancy was not one of them.

When the answer came from the *Nelson*'s signal bridge it didn't sound too good: the *Langstone Harbour*'s main shaft was in trouble from a hairline crack in the metal.

Captain Champney, making his own forecast of disaster, rang

down to his chief engineer for confirmation. Mr Turnberry's answer was swift. 'Curtains, I'd say. She *might* be able to go ahead dead slow but I wouldn't be sure.'

Kemp's face was grim: without power on her main shaft, the *Langstone Harbour* really was a potential dead duck, sitting prey for the Germans when they came in.

Champney said, 'She'll need a tow, Commodore.'

'Yes. But that's up to the Admiral.'

'Or you, surely? It's your convoy. The Admiral . . . he's just the escort.'

Kemp laughed, an edgy sound. 'It's not quite as clear-cut as all that, Captain. But if – I say *if* – it should come to that . . . do I take it you could pass a tow?'

Champney nodded. 'Yes, I could, But it'd be better done by those two destroyers. You know the limitations of single-screw ships, and the strain put on any towing ship by constant yawing in a seaway.'

iv

'Looks like we've got ourselves an arse-end Charlie,' Petty Officer Ramm said. Word had spread fast about the plight of the *Langstone Harbour*. 'Poor sods! Sooner them than me, just waiting for 'Itler. Wonder when the buggers'll turn up. The *Luftwaffe*, I mean. Would 'ave expected 'em before now . . . funny, really.'

He was speaking to Leading Seaman Nelson, the nearest in age to himself among the Naval draft except for the yeoman of signals, and the age proximity permitted Ramm, in his own view, some relaxation of the normal distancing of a gunner's mate. Besides, you had to talk to someone or you'd go barmy: what Ramm didn't admit was that he liked the sound of his own voice.

Stripey Nelson drew on his fag, shielding it from the wind with a horny palm. 'Something else expected an' all, GI.'

'What?'

'Patter o' tiny feet, that's what.'

'Now what are you on about?' Ramm stared in bewilderment.

Stripey said, 'Seems you 'aven't 'eard it. One of them Wrens. Got a nipper up the spout.'

'Never!'

47

'It's been known. Childbirth –'

'All right, all right, Leading Seaman Nelson, no need to be funny.' Ramm paused, all agog now. 'How do *you* happen to know, eh?'

Stripey closed an eye in a wink. 'Got ears, GI. So's the Captain's steward. You know what captains' stewards are. All lug and key'ole eyes. 'E 'eard a thing or two outside the Commodore's cabin, see. It's Wren Smith, the one with the goo-goo eyes and sharp tits, kind of pointed like, very sexy, more'n the sort like barrage balloons '

'All right, all right,' Ramm said once again, testily. 'When's the happy event, know that, do you?'

'Long time off yet, GI –'

'Who did it?'

''Ow should I know? Wasn't me any road. Some matlow in Pompey.'

Ramm sucked at his teeth, ruminating, seeing Wren Smith in his mind's eye, Wren Smith doing what she shouldn't have done. Maybe she'd be easy if the opportunity ever showed itself, maybe she'd be a little overawed by a gunner's mate's rank and dignity: you never knew your luck. Keeping his feet against the motion of the ship by holding on to the guardrail round the after gun-mounting, Ramm saw an unwelcome sight: coming aft, a hefty figure wrapped in an oilskin, a barrel-like arm raised aloft to retain a WRNS uniform hat against the wind. He said to Stripey Nelson's ear, 'I'm off below. That old bag's coming up fast. Ma Hardisty.'

Stripey chuckled. 'Bloody coward,' he said, but he said it to himself. Ramm had no sense of humour at all. As the gunner's mate vanished down a hatch, the PO Wren came on aft and passed harmlessly below the gun-mounting, eyes darting to left and right. She went right aft, peered for a moment over the stern into the curfuffle made by the screw, then started back for'ard again. Stripey fancied she was seeking something that she hadn't yet found. Maybe more Wrens in danger of becoming pregnant, though it would take a tough Wren and come to that a tough matlow to do it in this icy wind, and the spray and all.

On her return swoop Miss Hardisty halted below the gun platform and looked up. Her voice boomed. 'Morning, killick.'

Some Wrens, Nelson thought sardonically, were more RN

48

than the Navy: Miss Hardisty's reference had been to his leading seaman's badge of rank, the fouled anchor known as a killick that stood above his three good conduct stripes. Formally he said, 'Morning, PO. What can I do for you?'

'Nothing that I know of, thank you.' She marched off again; Stripey thought: and sod you too, mate! Viewed from astern, Miss Hardisty resembled a tank. She might as well be landed in Alex as reinforcement for the armoured divisions waiting in Egypt for when the big push came against Rommel. Stripey was thinking this when he became aware of the lamp flashing from the signal bridge of the *Nelson*, and more signalling from the cruisers as well. And a matter of seconds later he heard the threatening sound of aircraft engines coming in from the east.

v

Aboard the *Langstone Harbour* Captain Horncape had been intrigued to get the personal signal from the Commodore's ship. John Kemp . . . John Mason Kemp in full, as Horncape had recalled – he'd seen the Commodore, naturally, at the conference, and had recognized him through the mist of years. He would have liked a word then, but there hadn't been the chance: the Convoy Commodore was a busy man and the proceedings had been official, all very RN. He was glad now that John Kemp had remembered him; as the signal said, it was all a long time ago.

Jake Horncape's mind, like that of Kemp himself, drifted back into the past, a long reverie that was interrupted by the sound of the aircraft engines that had also reached the Commodore's ship.

FIVE

'Petty Officer Ramm!' Finnegan was yelling down from the bridge: Ramm had reappeared by the after gun-mounting. 'Target astern!'

'Seen for meself, sir,' Ramm shouted back.

'Right. Fire when ready.'

'Aye, aye, sir.' Ramm started chivvying the guns' crews as they turned out from below. He sent Nelson for'ard to take charge of the close-range weapons' crews on the bridge and on monkey's island above the wheelhouse. Stripey lumbered along as fast as he could, overtaking the PO Wren who went down a ladder towards the girls' quarters. The WRNS contingent was under orders from the Commodore to keep out of the way when the ship was in action.

Kemp was watching the approaching air armada, suffering the customary feeling of helplessness that visited everyone other than the guns' crews when air attack came. It was the gunners who counted: all the bridge could do was wait for the fall of bombs and dodge as best as possible. Kemp looked across at the carriers: the Fleet Air Arm squadrons were already mostly in the air, just a few Seafires still waiting their turn to take off behind the leaders. Kemp had already ordered the merchant ships to scatter and move independently as required; and the Naval escort was moving widely out on the convoy's flanks, two cruisers, *Derbyshire* and *Glamorgan*, heading to starboard and *Belize* and *Guiana* to port, with the destroyers constantly altering course in an attempt to confuse the enemy bomb aimers.

Just the *Nelson* was ploughing along stolidly, her heavy guns

50

useless against air attack but her ack-ack blasting away into the sky as the Germans came in. Kemp had been informed by lamp that the flagship was increasing speed to her maximum of around twenty-two knots: speed was the best protection after the anti-aircraft batteries – speed and manoeuvrability, but the *Nelson* had little of either.

Lambert was reporting. 'Ten bombers, sir, FWs. Escort o' twenty fighters.'

'Thank you, Yeoman. Any word of the *Langstone Harbour*?'

'Not a thing, sir.'

Kemp searched the seas to the east, binoculars clamped to his eyes. In the big waves his search was useless: ships appeared and disappeared again, and now the attack was starting. As the German four-engined bombers roared across the convoy, the sea became peppered with spouts of water, some wide, some very close to the ships. Captain Champney was handling the *Wolf Rock* expertly: this was by no means his first experience of avoiding bombs. Nevertheless, there was a close shave when a heavy bomb took the ship on the port side aft, slap on the deckhouse over the engineers' accommodation, and went through without exploding.

There was a shout from Petty Officer Ramm.

'UXB, sir, gone into the Wrens' quarters.'

Kemp roared out, 'Evacuate pronto. Report casualties – and get the doctor along.'

'Aye, aye, sir.' Ramm vanished down the hatch, taking two men from the after guns. By now the sky was puffy with shrapnel as the ack-ack shells burst, and a rain of fragments was coming down on the decks as the ships twisted and turned. Below in the *Wolf Rock*'s engine-room Mr Turnberry had heard the crump from above and felt the shudder as the heavy bomb broke through the poop. Even before the bridge passed the warning, he had diag-nosed what had happened: not very nice. If that bomb went up, there wouldn't be much left of the engine spaces. Or of himself. His impulse was to clear the engine-room, get to hell out, get for'ard as far away as possible. But you couldn't do that: Turn-berry grimaced across the shining steel of the ladders and across the sweaty vests of the oilers and greasers. There was after all, a war on. . . .

The *Langstone Harbour*'s chief engineer reported to the bridge: the crack was getting worse under the battering of the sea on the screw. He was forced to shut right down.

'All right, Chief.' Captain Horncape banged back the cover of the voice-pipe as he faced the gale and the German activity overhead. You had to be philosophical: this was no-one's fault except maybe the shipyard's, or the owners' for exercising too much economy during the last years of the peace. If they couldn't move, well, they couldn't and that was that. If only he was back in sail again ... there was more than enough weight of wind around to carry a square-rigged ship on at around fifteen knots, maybe more. Not so much slower in fact than the great bulk of the *Nelson*, known to the Navy as Queen Anne's Mansions on account of her immense central superstructure housing the senior officers' sea cabins, compass platform, admiral's bridge, flag deck, conning tower, gunnery control and what have you.

Horncape spoke to his chief officer. 'We'll let the sea take her. No damn choice – have we?'

'How about a tow, sir? Those two destroyers – '

'Not yet, anyway. They have their hands full.' Horncape ducked as a spout of water came over the bridge from a near miss, adding to the general drench of rough weather. More helpless now, with way right off the ship, he watched the fall of bombs as the Focke-Wulfs came over, watched the Seafires from the carriers get in amongst the Germans, saw two of the Seafires spin down trailing smoke. Then one of the bombers sprouted a thin line of red along its fuselage and a moment later was a ball of fire dropping from the overcast skies to come down in the water some ten cables'-lengths to starboard of the *Langstone Harbour*.

Soon after this, one of the destroyers, the *Pindari*, was hit for'ard. Her fo'c'sle erupted in flame and smoke and when the smoke began to clear a little in the strong wind Horncape saw the deck plating ripped up almost to the conning tower, the two fore gun-shields vanished with their guns and, presumably, their crews. Then he saw the damage control parties moving for'ard with hoses and axes as the destroyer continued firing with her remaining HA guns. She began turning to starboard through one hundred and eighty degrees to proceed stern first in an obvious endeavour to keep the weight of the sea off her for'ard collision bulkhead, which seemed as though it must be holding yet.

In the meantime, the *Langstone Harbour* remained somewhat miraculously unhit. If they came through, Horncape would proceed under tow so long as the Navy could spare one of its escort, which would henceforward be hamstrung when further attacks came, as come they would for certain before the convoy passed out of range of the air bases.

If it was humanly possible, Captain Hornpipe was going to get his cargo into Malta. In his time he'd come through plenty, getting his cargoes around Cape Horn and then serving as third officer in steam through the last lot, the 1914–18 War.

Two minutes later the cruiser *Derbyshire* took what looked like a direct hit, a bomb coming in at an angle to explode just below the waterline on her starboard side, a little for'ard of the after turrets on her quarterdeck. There was an upsurge of water, of boiling foam, and a raw red flash followed by clouds of thick black smoke.

'Engine-room,' Horncape said. 'Slap in the engine-room.'

The cruiser was seen to slew violently off course for a while until she steadied under helm. She continued making way through the water, obviously with her port engine-room intact still, two of her four shafts turning. Distantly from the bridge of the *Wolf Rock*, Kemp had her in his binoculars. The sense of helplessness increased, and he clenched his fists impotently. He looked down aft, where Ramm was keeping the ack-ack gun firing constantly but with little apparent effect. Kemp took stock. One cruiser and one destroyer crippled, one armament carrier sunk in the submarine attack earlier, and the *Langstone Harbour* drifting at the mercy of the sea and the Germans.

So early in the convoy, with thousands of sea miles yet to be covered to Trincomalee.

He turned as an unshaven face appeared at the head of the starboard ladder from the Master's deck: Dr O'Dwyer, looking haggard and shaken, skin white behind the stubble. The man was trembling like a leaf in a gale, Kemp noted.

Captain Champney went across. 'Well, Doctor?'

O'Dwyer licked at his lips. 'It's bad down aft, Captain. A number of injuries . . . and one dead.' He turned to Kemp. 'One of the young girls, Commodore, I'm sorry to say. I – '

'Let's have the details.' Kemp saw blood, quite a lot of it, on the doctor's uniform jacket and shirt.

'A girder . . . it carried away, and came down across the girl's head and neck. The neck was broken. The head . . . ' The doctor's voice trailed away; there was a look of horror in his eyes, which were badly bloodshot. 'There was nothing I could do, you understand.'

'Yes, I understand. The others, the injuries?'

'Various. Mostly not serious. But there's a young girl with her leg trapped. I think the leg is broken – '

'Trapped, in what way, Doctor?'

O'Dwyer said, 'Another girder that fell and became wedged. The bosun has men trying to lift it, but I believe it may be necessary to amputate. Of course, the girl's under sedation, a morphine injection. She's not conscious.'

'Do you propose to amputate at once?'

'I . . . I don't know. Really, I'd like a second opinion as to how long it can safely be left. One of the Naval doctors from the escort – '

'In action, Doctor? That's not possible – you must realize that. I think you must use your own judgment.'

'Yes. But don't you see, Commodore . . . it's a very final verdict, and it's possible the girder may be shifted eventually. For a young girl to lose a leg . . . if it should not be necessary, you see – '

'Yes, I do see. And I appreciate your honesty if I may say so.'

Dr O'Dwyer looked down at the deck, away from Kemp's eye. He had read behind Kemp's words: the Commodore had seen that there was a strong desire not to amputate on the part of a doctor whose surgery, such as it had ever been, was years behind him. The skill, the touch, had gone over long years of disuse and too much drink. But O'Dwyer also knew that without amputation the girl could die. Not just because she lay trapped when at any moment the ship could be blown sky-high but because of the possibility of infection; the leg was badly lacerated. And he believed that Kemp, too, knew the risk.

Kemp did: gangrene, perhaps, was one of the risks. Just one of them; there were so many. Blood poisoning . . . but gangrene might be the worst threat. Kemp, during his days in the sailing ships as apprentice and then as second mate, had become more or less familiar with shipboard injuries such as broken legs and arms, men falling from aloft, men with clumsy fingers caught in the sheaves of blocks, flayed hands resulting from rope friction

54

when the wind-filled sails took charge of halliards or downhauls or sheets or braces in the days before steam winches had been fitted for the handling of the sails. In a ship carrying no doctor the Master had been the medical authority, the physician and surgeon, with the printed assistance of *The Ship Captain's Medical Guide* and often with the assistance of his officers as well if only for holding down purposes when limbs had been amputated under the only available anaesthetic – an uncorked bottle of rum or whisky set between the patient's teeth.

Gangrene or the possibility of it had been the bugbear. Injuries – crushing, freezing, burning – could not be left. Limbs could become swollen, could go dead white and then blue-green or black, and there would be moist putrefaction, and the condition could extend.

Kemp put the question: 'Gangrene, Doctor?'

'Oh, it's early for that, of course, but . . . ' O'Dwyer shrugged.

'But,' Kemp said flatly. 'Quite! Anyway, the next thing is to try to release the girl. You'd better get back aft, Doctor.' He added, 'I'll be down myself as soon as I can leave the bridge. Where's Miss Forrest?'

O'Dwyer said, 'Aft, Commodore. She's very distressed.'

iii

There were further hits on the convoy but no more serious damage: their bombs dropped, the Germans withdrew towards the east, harried by the carrier-borne Seafires. Seven of the FWs had been shot down, together with eight fighters. When the attack pulled off, the signals flew from the flagship, the senior officers of the cruiser and destroyer escort, and from the Commodore. The convoy reformed into its steaming columns and the cost in terms of losses was counted. The *Derbyshire* was under control, but reported seventy-eight casualties including fourteen dead; *Pindari* had blown up, turned turtle, and sunk. There were fifty-three other crew casualties in the rest of the convoy and its escort, some serious, others not. The *Langstone Harbour* wallowed on astern, attended by the *Hindu* and the *Burgoyne*, the latter having taken over from the *Pindari*, and a tow was being passed. Kemp, who reckoned that his own ship was of less significance to the convoy than the guns and free manoeuvrability of the destroyers, would have wished to undertake the tow himself, but had recognized that this was not the proper function of the Convoy Commodore, who had other considerations than an arse-end Charlie to worry about.

When the convoy was back in its proper steaming order, Kemp went aft to the engineers' accommodation and was met at the port doorway from the after well-deck by Jean Forrest.

He asked, 'How is it now, Miss Forrest?'

'Bad,' she said. Her face was grey and her lips trembled as she spoke. 'Third Officer Bowles-Gourley – she's dead. It was – horrible.'

'And the one who's trapped? Any progress?'

She said, 'The bosun's done his best, Commodore Kemp. He and his men. No use so far. The girder's wedged down hard. They're trying to burn it away with – blow-lamps, I think. The chief engineer's there.'

'The doctor was unsure whether or not to amputate.'

'Yes.' Jean Forrest's tone was bitter. 'I don't believe he has any idea what he's talking about, Commodore Kemp.'

'But if the leg's trapped – '

'It is, and I don't mean that. I mean I don't think he's fit to operate. Which is a different kettle of fish.'

Kemp didn't comment. As he went through into the alleyway and came clear of the teeming rain and the wind's buffetting he asked, 'Who's the girl – her name?'

'Third Officer Pawle. Susan Pawle ... she and Anne Bowes-Gourley had gone aft to take charge of the girls.' She added, 'To reassure them, really. I hadn't told them to. I was there myself anyway. It's such filthy luck.'

Kemp nodded. He went on towards the shattered compartment where the bomb had gone through. The bomb was still there, wedged like the young Wren officer by the girder that had come down on top of it. Presumably it could go up at any moment; on the other hand it was very likely a dud: the British arsenals often produced duds, and the Germans were known to suffer the same. Kemp sent up an urgent prayer that this was one of the aborted efforts of Krupps or whoever. Petty Officer Ramm was bent in an attitude of listening, his ear against the bomb casing – a brave man Kemp thought, like all the others in the bomb's vicinity. But he doubted if the bomb had a timing mechanism and he said so.

'Just making sure, sir. But I reckon you're right, sir.'

'Get the hands round it, Ramm. Get it over the side.'

Ramm wiped a hand across his forehead, which was streaming sweat. 'Jammed solid, sir, bloody solid. It's the girder, sir ... same as the young lady.'

Kemp moved across to Susan Pawle. He didn't believe she was fully unconscious; her face was tear-streaked and deathly white, and she was moaning, a sound that went to Kemp's heart. He knelt by her side. Her eyes opened but she didn't appear to be aware of his presence. Kemp looked at the leg. He believed the knee was smashed. The flesh had been laid bare almost all the way along and there were tendons, as he believed them to be, showing. He got to his feet, bending away from the damage overhead. Deck beams hung, and the overcast sky was visible through the shattered poop decking, and the rain was coming through.

Kemp spoke to First Officer Forrest. 'I'm no doctor, but I think an amputation's essential. Look at that girder!' The heavy steel had cut into the thigh, right down to the bone. So far the deck gang, assisted by the Naval party, had been unable to shift it so much as a fraction of an inch. But on his way aft from the bridge Kemp had seen Harrison unsecuring the after derrick and preparing to swing a boom over the poop. With the whip of the derrick lowered through the gaping hole and hauled taut around the girder it should be possible to lift it clear enough to release the girl. Thus far it was a question of seamanship, but from the moment of release it would be purely medical. In Kemp's lay view the leg couldn't be saved anyway: the injuries were too horrific. He looked round for O'Dwyer: the doctor had disappeared. A few moments later he came through the door from the well-deck. Kemp's diagnosis was that he had gone to his whisky bottle for support.

O'Dwyer caught the Commodore's eye, then looked away. He said, 'Really there aren't the facilities aboard. No proper operating facilities, that is.'

'In emergencies, Doctor, you dispense with all that goes with operating theatres, don't you?'

'Yes.' O'Dwyer stared across at the girl, pulling at his chin with a shaking hand.

'If it's the after-care you're worried about,' Kemp said, though he knew that wasn't the doctor's chief concern, 'it may be possible to transfer her to one of the capital ships, but not until the weather moderates.' Kemp's voice was cold. 'I suggest you make up your mind, Doctor.'

'Yes,' O'Dwyer said again. There was a sound from overhead, and he and Kemp looked up. The whip of the derrick was over the hole made by the bomb, and Harrison was visible, giving hand signals to the seaman at the winch. As the whip came down it was grappled by the men waiting below and was lashed to the girder under the orders of the ship's second officer. As the slack was taken up there was a shouted warning from Petty Officer Ramm.

'Mind that bomb, sir! Best not let it shift, not suddenly.'

Kemp said, 'Get some hands round it, Ramm. Hold it steady.'

'Aye, aye, sir. Leading Seaman Nelson?'

Stripey Nelson approached the bomb, sweating in spite of the chill of the rain from overhead. Ramm said, 'Get your gut alongside it. Act as a fender!' Ramm gave a short laugh: no-one responded. Above on the deck, Harrison gave the order to start lifting, dead slow. The strain came on, the whip tautened and began trembling slightly, there was a sudden scraping sound as the lashing settled; but there was no movement of the girder. Kemp swore beneath his breath. The winch clattered again to the chief officer's order, just briefly, then was ordered to stop.

Harrison called down, 'It'll start stranding any minute if I put more strain on. I don't think that bugger's going to shift.'

Once again Kemp met O'Dwyer's eye and, very reluctantly, the doctor nodded. As he did so the action alarm sounded: it seemed another attack was about to develop. Kemp left the after compartment and went at the double to the bridge.

Petty Officer Ramm, before going up to take charge of the armament, took the doctor's arm in a grip like a vice. He said, 'Get 'er out of danger, Doctor. Get that leg off for God's sake.' Ramm's voice was hard, bitter. He'd seen the indecision in the doctor's face, the unwillingness to take any sort of drastic action, because he didn't feel capable. But, Ramm was thinking, anything's better than nothing and you couldn't go far wrong in hacking through a bone. Afterwards would be different, and Commodore Kemp would take the necessary action.

The radar aboard the big ships had picked up the approach of the second wave of aircraft and shortly afterwards they were seen, coming in on their bombing runs. The Seafires, up again from the carriers, twisted and turned as they attacked the heavy aircraft and their fighter escort. Once again the convoy had scattered outwards, once again the water was dappled with the misses, once again fires broke out aboard the ships as the bombs found their targets. More casualties – the enemy was making the most of his chances while the convoy was still within range. A few more days and they would come out from under as it were, beyond the attentions of the shore-based bombers. Then would come peace for a while if they were lucky. There would still be the threat of U-boats but to a lesser extent. There might be surface raiders, but Kemp still didn't consider them likely in view of the strength of the convoy's escort. So there might well be peace – until they entered the Straits of Gibraltar and came into the war-torn waters of the Western Mediterranean.

When the attack had again been beaten off, and the *Langstone Harbour* was proceeding safely under tow, a report came to the bridge: the amputation had been performed and the girl had come through. That was all: O'Dwyer was not committing himself further. But later, when he came to the bridge himself, he seemed a changed man, much more confident. Nevertheless, he repeated to the Commodore that the *Wolf Rock*'s facilities were somewhat lacking and Susan Pawle would be better off aboard a ship equipped with a proper sick bay.

Kemp asked the question direct: 'Is she going to live, Doctor?'

'Early days . . . but one thing's sure, and that is, she'd have a much better chance – '

'Off the ship. All right, that point is taken. I'll put it to the Flag but I can guess the answer. Finnegan?'

'Sir?'

'Report the facts to the Flag – get the medical details from the doctor. Ask for a transfer soonest possible. Indicate urgency.'

'Aye, aye, sir.' As Finnegan called for the yeoman of signals Kemp looked across toward the *Nelson*. Bringing up his binoculars he believed he could make out the Admiral standing by the guard rail of his bridge . . . a double row of gold oak-leaves on the peak of the cap above eyes watchful through binoculars like himself. Had he, Kemp wondered, the right to bring extra worry to the Admiral? He had felt obliged to meet the doctor half way but in fact he could have taken the decision himself to retain the girl aboard until conditions were easier. The Admiral had plenty on his plate, was faced daily with many decisions that could affect the conduct of the war and the lives of hundreds, thousands of men and through them their families ashore. And within the next five minutes one of those decisions, a very minor one really in the whole pattern of the war, was flashed across the turbulence of the North Atlantic.

Commodore from Flag. Do not repeat not propose endangering convoy for transfer requested. Resubmit if still necessary when weather moderates and convoy is further from danger zone.

Kemp felt rebuked. Third Officers of the WRNS loomed large in family environments but were of little account at sea.

SIX

Dr O'Dwyer poured himself a stiff whisky and knocked it back neat. It was satisfactory that he had performed the operation; but he knew that it could have been more expeditiously done. He had been clumsy and hesitant. He had been assisted by the chief steward and the Captain's steward, both of whom had looked green and sick while the grisly work proceeded. A lot of blood had been left behind when the girl had been brought clear; she may well have lost too much. Had there been the facilities, O'Dwyer would have carried out a transfusion. As it was he could only hope for the best and keep the wound clean and bandaged. He wished he had the assistance of a nurse. All the Wrens, including their First Officer, had volunteered to help and that was something, but not the same as a qualified nurse. They had to be instructed and then supervised most of the time.

O'Dwyer looked through his port at the heaving, restless seas: there was no moderation of the weather in prospect and Gibraltar, where he hoped the girl would be put ashore, was as yet some five days' steaming ahead.

Five days might prove too long.

O'Dwyer poured another whisky, this time drinking it more slowly, thinking back to the operation. He had only the basic bachelor's unspecialized degree as a surgeon; as a ship's doctor he had had to deal with broken limbs and such in the ordinary course of his duties, although in the liners he had had the assistance not only of a nursing sister but also of an assistant surgeon, usually a much younger man signed on articles at a nominal rate of pay and working his passage to, say, Australia, or homeward bound to UK to take London qualifications. Since leaving the big liners he had been lucky: in the passenger-carrying cargo ships no operations had been required until now. On the few occasions when an appendix had come up, he had been able to postpone operating until a port had been reached and the patient put ashore. Dr O'Dwyer had not operated for very many years. Never had he operated under such conditions: the threat of the unexploded bomb had been very close, though at the time his concentration on the job in hand had excluded it from his mind.

Now, just thinking about it, he sweated: that bomb was there still. He poured another whisky.

ii

In rear of the convoy the *Langstone Harbour* came on at slow speed behind the towing destroyers. Captain Horncape, dead tired and wet through, remained on the bridge for most of the time, relieved for short naps by his chief officer. Towing was a difficult business at the best of times; in such weather it was tricky in the extreme, though in all conscience there was little anyone aboard the *Langstone Harbour* could do without power if anything went adrift.

Horncape watched the towing pendants between the destroyers and his ship: they were lifting clear of the water for most of the time even though the bower anchors had been hung off and the cables shackled on to the towing wires and then paid out fully from the cable locker to bring the maximum weight on the tow. It was when the middle of the towing pendants lifted clear that the danger came: there was then immense strain on the wires and cables as they took the whole direct weight of the deep-laden ship, coming up bar taut and dripping water until they were submerged again by the next wave.

And the *Langstone Harbour* was dropping farther and farther behind the convoy: Horncape had never expected the Commodore or the Admiral to reduce speed to accommodate one ship. He was lucky to have both a tow and an escort. But as the great hulls of the merchant ships and the aircraft-carriers, and the high superstructure of the *Nelson* drew away with the cruisers into the distances of the ocean, Horncape felt a strong sense of isolation. In peacetime, you didn't worry about that, it was part of a seaman's calling. In war, it was very different.

62

He was almost asleep on his feet when he was spoken to by his chief officer.

'You're all in, sir. Let me take over.'

'I'm all right. You've not had much sleep yourself come to that.' Chief officers got no rest when supervising the long business of taking a tow, and they had their own watches to keep as well. Horncape said again, 'I'm all right, Mr Marlow. Sail got me used to this sort of thing.'

'That was a long while ago, sir.'

'Rubbish, man!'

Marlow thought: obstinate old shellback. Horncape had never been bashful as to his own opinions, which were that sail was the only real training for a seaman and that the modern product could never stand comparison with the old-timers. The Old Man was accustomed to holding forth at meals in the saloon, all about wooden ships and iron men who had now become iron ships and wooden men, about the ferocious winds and seas off the pitch of the Horn, of rotten food – cracker hash and burgoo, or biscuits filled with weevils, no vegetables and often little fresh water; of masters who had driven the crews like slaves, of coffin-ships on which the owners spent as little money as possible with the result that masts and yards carried away under stress, often carrying men with them as they plunged to the deck or over the side to be swept away forever by the roaring greybeards of Cape Horn. It all became boring; but you had, Marlow thought, to admire his guts. Even his obstinacy . . .

Marlow left the bridge, sliding down the ladder to the Master's deck and down again to the fore well-deck whence he climbed the ladder to the fo'c'sle-head for another look at the tow and the securing slips of the cables, the Blake slips taking the strain off the cable clenches in the locker below. As the tow lifted again and again, the whole weight of the plunging ship was being taken on the Blake slips and the bottle-screws. On either bow the destroyers appeared and vanished to the tremendous surge of the waves, down into the valleys to rise again and lie perched on the peaks until once again they slid down into the depths.

iii

Sub-Lieutenant Finnegan came up the ladder to the *Wolf Rock*'s bridge and saluted the Commodore who was standing as he seemed always to be standing, in the wing with his oilskin collar pulled up around his ears. 'How's it going, Finnegan?'

'No luck, sir. Still jammed fast.' There had been a hope that when Susan Pawle had been taken from under, the girder would have given a little, but this hadn't happened. The bomb remained and the engineers' cabins had been evacuated. The engineers and wrens were now redistributed amidships and in the fore part of the ship, to the discomfort of everybody.

'What's Ramm's opinion?' Kemp asked.

Finnegan shrugged. 'He really doesn't know, sir. Obviously it *could* go up.'

'None of us know,' Kemp said. More signals had been made to the Flag, asking for the views and instructions of the Fleet Gunnery Officer. The response had been unhelpful, adding nothing to what those aboard the *Wolf Rock* had worked out for themselves: try to free it without sending it up and dump it overboard and if it couldn't be freed, leave it and pray. The Admiral, once within visual signalling distance of Gibraltar dockyard, would ask for ordnance ratings to be sent off at a pierhead jump and embarked to proceed through the Mediterranean and render the bomb safe on passage. But there would, the Admiral signalled firmly, be no delay to the convoy which was sailing on a very tight schedule.

'Sitting on death, sir,' Finnegan said.

'Put a sock in it, Finnegan. No alarmist talk, if you please. It's only what civilians in the UK have been putting up with for a long time now.' Kemp gave a tight grin. 'Although I admit they do evacuate the adjacent streets and buildings!'

'That's quite a point, sir.'

Kemp was looking astern through his binoculars. '*Langstone Harbour*'s out of sight.'

'Yes, sir. She ought to be okay ... we're beginning to come to the limit of the aircraft range, I guess – '

'Yes. But the conditions are rotten for the tow.' Kemp's mind went off at a tangent. 'I wonder if old Horncape remembers my name. I – ' He broke off as he saw another figure coming up the ladder. 'Well, Miss Forrest. How's the girl?'

'Susan Pawle?'

'Who else?' Suddenly Kemp remembered: that other bomb, potentially anyway, the pregnant Wren Smith. 'Oh – yes. Well?'

64

'Third Office Pawle . . . the doctor doesn't seem inclined to say, Commodore. He won't be specific, won't commit himself. But she doesn't look too good to me.'

Kemp nodded. Jean Forrest, hatless and with her dark hair blown all over the place, looked suddenly – Kemp thought – attractive. Perhaps she was the sort that responded to emergencies, feeling herself less of a spare hand and thus showing more personality. She went on, 'Third Office Pawle . . . Mrs Pawle . . . I don't suppose you know the story, do you?'

Kemp shook his head. 'Is there one?'

'Yes, there is.' First Officer Forrest told him about the husband lost aboard a submarine on patrol, about the desperate desire to get away from the scenes of the past and the memories of shared experiences. She would, Jean Forrest said, come back to her memories in due course but currently everything was too red and raw. And now this had happened.

'Rough,' Kemp said with sympathy. 'Very rough.'

'Yes. I know it's awfully early days, but what I had in mind was remarriage – '

'*Very* early days!'

'Yes, I agree. But they do remarry – she's so young. But without a leg!'

'That's not our worry, Miss Forrest. What we have to do is get her into Gibraltar and the military hospital, that's all.' As an automatic action Kemp was continually scanning the seas through his binoculars, only half his mind on the conversation. 'Now about that other girl, the pregnant one. *Is* she pregnant?'

'I don't know. She's tending to to walk back on that . . . says she could be out in her dates, but I don't believe it. I think she just doesn't want to risk being landed at Gibraltar.'

'She's not going to be landed at Gibraltar. What about the doctor?'

Jean Forrest sighed. 'She refuses to be examined by him. Just simply refused point blank – '

'Refusing an order? What do they do to Wrens for that, Miss Forrest?' There was a twinkle in Kemp's eye. Had he been a girl, pregnant or not, he wouldn't have submitted himself to Dr O'Dwyer's investigations. 'Drum 'em out of the service, or what?'

'I wouldn't be sure – in this sort of case. I don't know . . . we don't come under the Naval Discipline Act, you know. I think one just tries to talk them out of bloody-mindedness!'

'And did you?'

'I tried but failed. As a matter of fact, I did say . . . '

'That you'd refer the matter to me?'

'Yes,' she said.

'Thank you indeed, Miss Forrest,' Kemp said crisply. 'I really don't see what a pregnancy has to do with me.'

'You'd have come up against them in the liners, surely?'

'Like hell! The Line never took women who were pregnant beyond a certain stage. You've probably no idea of the havoc caused to places like Port Said or Colombo when a ship arrives with more souls than it left its previous departure port with! The shore officials seem quite unable to cope with things like that . . . numbers that don't tally.' They talked for a few moments about the Mediterranean-Australia Line and of its chairman and then Jean Forrest excused herself: she was going below again to see Susan Pawle. She would, she said, send Wren Smith to Kemp's cabin when he gave the word. That made Kemp feel pressured: he had no recollection of having actually agreed to see the girl but had no doubt given his consent simply by his silence on the point. When Jean Forrest had left the bridge Kemp spoke to Sub-Lieutenant Finnegan.

'Pregnant Wrens, Finnegan.'

'Yes, sir?'

'More in your line than mine, I dare say. Or am I being slanderous?'

'I guess so, sir. Members of the WRNS are all young ladies, so I'm told.' Finnegan was straight-faced.

Kemp glared. 'Are you being funny, Finnegan?'

'Me, sir? Gee, sir, no – '

'All right, all right. I have a problem, and you're closer to the girl in age than I am. How do I get it out of her . . . the fact of whether or not she's pregnant? She seems in two minds on the point, probably for nefarious reasons. I don't think I need to explain further, do I? I'm sure the galley wireless has been at full blast.'

'You can say that again, sir – '

'I don't want to say it again, Finnegan. I've said it once and that's enough.'

'Yes, sir. My apologies for being a Yank, sir.' Finnegan grinned: he and the Commodore, despite the difference in age and rank, had a good understanding of one another, as apparently his own predecessor, Cutler, had had. 'I guess I've heard it all, yes. Right or wrong, though, I wouldn't know. But if you're asking my advice, sir, well, I guess I'd – I'd kind of *scare* it out of her. Threaten her with Gibraltar and a load of brass hats.' Finnegan hesitated. 'The fact is, sir, she *could* be landed at Gibraltar the way things have turned out. With that third officer.'

Kemp nodded: obviously! Sheer weariness seemed to be slowing him down mentally. Wren Smith would have ticked over that being put ashore was very much on the cards now; she would perhaps have changed her story accordingly, as Jean Forrest had suggested.

Bracing himself against the *Wolf Rock*'s pitch and roll, Kemp gave a heartfelt sigh and mentally cursed the carnal proclivities of seamen ashore in Portsmouth.

iv

'Look out for Christ's sake!'

Petty Officer Ramm roared the words out as something shifted and the bomb moved. It moved just a couple of feet, downwards and sideways. Stripey Nelson just missed being crushed by its weight of metal and high explosive, giving a startled yelp as the thing grazed past his backside. There was a searing pain and he felt blood run. Reaching behind himself, his fingers touched bare flesh. Some projection on the bomb's casing had ripped through his oilskin and the seat of his trousers, and had torn his skin as well.

Everyone in the compartment had moved away instinctively. Ramm was the first to approach the bomb again as it settled into its new position.

'Settled firmer than bloody ever,' he said. 'But I reckon it's no nearer going up. Would have done on the move if it was going to.' He looked around, pointed a finger at one of the ordinary seamen of the guns' crews. 'You. Report to the bridge, pronto. Move!' He turned to Stripey Nelson. 'What's up with you, eh? Clutching your bum like a – '

'It 'urts, PO.' Nelson explained what had happened.

67

'Right! Nip along to the quack . . . nothing's going to happen here and you might get blood poisoning or some such.' As Nelson moved away still clutching his rump, the PO yelled out, 'An' get a 'hurt certificate, remember, so after the war you can blame it on 'Is Majesty an' get a flaming pension for your piles.'

From the bridge, Captain Champney called the engine-room with the warning that the bomb had shifted a little downwards. Mr Turnberry was as phlegmatic as Petty Officer Ramm: if the bomb had settled down it was probably no more dangerous than before. The trouble, of course, was that no-one knew just how dangerous it had been, and the engine-room staff would be the first to suffer after the men who were trying to free it. Chief Engineer Turnberry had a reasonably vivid imagination and didn't need telling that if the thing *did* go up they would all be sealed right into their own coffin. And the ship's violent motion, the appalling heave and twist, plunge and lift again, wasn't helping the bomb's stability even if it was jammed as the Navy seemed to be saying. Something could give again, like it had just done.

v

Jock Campbell, chief steward, was no believer in bombs that didn't go up. True, there had been some during the various blitzes that periodically slaughtered the civvies back home, but mostly they had gone up in the end, just when everyone thought they were safe and had begun a drift back through the police cordons to rescue what they could from the debris of their homes. Or just when the heavy rescue squads were about to lift an injured person to safety from under a collapsed building. That had happened to his own aged parents in Glasgow. Campbell had pieced the story together when his ship had come in a couple of weeks later, talking to the police and firemen and rescue squads. His mother and father had been pinned down, like Third Officer Pawle, and both had been alive and apparently not injured, or not badly, and there had been every hope of getting them out. Jock Campbell's father had been heard singing, presumably to keep the old lady's spirits up, one of Harry Lauder's songs, *Keep right on to the end of the road, keep right on round the bend* . . . The end had in fact come while he'd been singing, a UXB having decided to go up after all. Afterwards, nothing had been found, just a load of debris, the old home where Jock had been born and brought up, down in the Gorbals. He'd not been back to Glasgow since. The missus and kids had been evacuated from his own marital home in Liverpool after the first of the blitzes on the port – he'd established them with a farming cousin near Wrexham.

Now, with that bomb poised aft to blow him to where bloody Hitler had already blown his mum and dad, Jock Campbell found his mind straying from the paperwork he'd set himself to do, which was largely concerned with the catering department over-time sheets there was plenty of that, what with women embarked and all, the Captain's steward for one dancing attendance not only on the Old Man but on the Commodore and the WRNS officers as well. His mind was on Glasgow as he'd known it years ago, both before he'd gone to sea and since. A teeming city, extremes of wealth and poverty, a vibrant city keeping itself afloat on a sea of whiskies and chasers. On Saturday nights the whole place seemed to get drunk, down in the Gorbals and Sauchiehall Street in the centre of the city especially. The police had been bastards, big tough men with leather faces, patrolling in pairs with long truncheons, like in Liverpool. Always in the ports the police were a different breed from those of the rest of the British Isles. They needed to be. Seamen and the inhabitants of the ports were a tough lot, hard to handle when drunk, rampaging through the Saturday night streets, looking for fights. Especially in Glasgow. *I belong tae Glasgow, dear old Glasgow toon.* . . . Shades of Will Fyffe.

Nostalgia: Glasgow would never be the same again when this lot was over, Jock Campbell reflected. Too much of it had gone already, under the high explosive and the incendiaries. The bloody Jerries would probably get the Broomielaw, the quay in the heart of the city whence so many times Jock had sailed down the Clyde to Rothesay on the Isle of Bute, Glasgow's summer playground where the clean wind blew down from Loch Striven and there was all the fun of the fair on high days and holidays. It was on board one of the Clyde paddle-steamers that Jock had met Mary MacGregor who was to become his wife. Already himself a junior ship's steward on leave, he'd been peering down the skylight at the great beams of the reciprocating engines as they lifted and dropped and turned the paddlewheels, when he'd heard the sound of a gramophone, a portable one that when not in use shut down into a handy box, very easy to carry. Looking round, he'd seen a middle-aged couple, the man with a flat cloth cap on his head, like his own dad, and the gramophone playing. Harry Lauder was singing. *Roaming in the gloaming, on the bonnie banks o' Clyde, Roaming in the gloaming wi' a lassie by my side. . . .*

Mary had been with them and Jock had been immediately drawn to her. He grinned and made some comment about Harry Lauder. 'My dad's mad on him,' he said.

It had been Mary who'd answered, returning his grin. 'So's my dad,' she said.

'And you?'

'I quite like him too,' she said.

'My dad met him once,' Jock said. That was enough: Mr Mac-Gregor was interested and they talked about Harry Lauder and the old days, the days of the last war when the young Jock had been a lad. They'd got along fine and that had been the start of it. It had been Harry Lauder who had brought Mary and himself together. After that, after a decent interval of calling on the MacGregors and getting the two families to meet so that it was all respectable there had been plenty of roaming in the gloaming when Jock had leave, plenty of the bonnie banks o' Clyde even though in the upper reaches by the great shipyards of John Brown and the others the banks hadn't been all that bonnie really. Long Sundays had been spent on the banks of Lomond-side, or walking by the Gareloch or taking again the paddle-steamer to Rothesay or further down the Firth of Clyde to Ar-drossa in Ayrshire, or across to Lamlash on Arran. That had been about the time Job Number 534 had come alive again and the shipyards had once again been busy, Jock's father going back to work after a long period of unemployment, and Mary's father too, both working on what was to become the great Cunard-White Star liner *Queen Mary*. On the day the Queen came herself to launch her namesake, Jock and Mary had become officially engaged and on his next leave from the sea they had married.

Now, Jock wondered if he would ever see Mary again. If that bomb blew the stern off they would have had it, everyone aboard. There was too much HE below hatches for anything to survive, and the convoy and escort wasn't going to stop to pick up the odd survivors. Even if the bomb didn't go up, they had yet to get through to Trinco in far-off Ceylon and there would be plenty of hostile forces around determined that they wouldn't make it.

Best not to think about it.

Jock gave himself a mental shake and concentrated on the overtime sheets. A moment later Botley's face came round the door and Jock Campbell looked up.

'Nothing to do, eh?'

'D'you mind, Chief. Just dropped in to keep you up to date, like. Course, if you don't – '

'Let's have it,' Campbell said.

'Right. That Wren.'

'Which bleeding Wren?'

'The one with the nipper up the spout – '

'Just hearsay.'

'Well, maybe. But I've just seen 'er with Harrison.'

'*Mr* Harrison to you, Botley.' Campbell rolled a blotter over some inked figures. 'Doing what?'

Botley smirked. 'Well – not doing *that*. Not likely in the cabin alleyway – '

'She up there? Wrens didn't ought to be, you know that. Only the officers.'

'I know. But it's not up to me to shout the odds at the chief officer, is it? What they were doing was, Mr Harrison was passing a bottle of gin to the popsie. They didn't know I'd seen. I just thought I'd warn you, Chief. Make out the gin stock's low, eh? Mr Harrison 'e won't part with it if it's on ration.'

Campbell said, 'Now look. I'd be a right Charlie to leave UK with low gin stocks, wouldn't I?'

'Sacrifice yourself for the unborn, Chief. Do a good turn.'

Campbell blew out a long breath. 'I know what you're on about, all right. Abortion. A bite late now – after a bottle's been passed over. Anyway, the only thing I could do is inform the skipper – *I* can't institute a ration off my own bat. Inform the skipper, and then what? Mr Harrison puts two and two together and it adds up to Steward Botley – doesn't it? I suppose you hadn't thought of that?'

Botley hadn't. He said as much, and after some thought,

71

added, 'Well, I reckon p'raps it's not our business. Like you said
... too late now. Seems a pity, though.' He left the cabin, his
yellow duster dangling down his leg. He was frowning. Abortion
... plenty of girls who'd been indiscreet or careless tried to find a
way out of their predicament when they had the know-how, true
enough. For Botley, however, things were the other way. He and
the missus wanted kids, wanted them badly. They'd tried hard
enough but always a nil result. Once, there had been a mis-
carriage, a terrible disappointment. It really hurt Botley that a
potential mother could even think of aborting herself.

vi

Dr O'Dwyer asked, 'What seems to be the trouble?' Leading
Seaman Nelson stood before him, face anguished, still clad in his
oilskin.

'Me bottom, Doctor.'

'Ah ... ' There was a strong smell of whisky and O'Dwyer,
slumped in a chair, was wreathed in cigarette smoke. Stripey
Nelson noticed a box of peppermints on the chest-of-drawers
beside the doctor's bunk, no doubt for use when the Captain
called for him. 'Can you be more precise?'

'Tore it on the projy.'

'Projy?'

'The bomb, like. Bit o' jagged metal – '

'I'd better examine you,' O'Dwyer said.

'Want me to strip orf, Doctor?'

'The affected part, yes.'

Leading Seaman Nelson took off his oilskin, dropped his trousers and pants, and turned round in a bent attitude. There was a
silence while the doctor peered at the affected part. Then he said,
'You'll have had your jabs, of course?'

'Yes, Doctor. TABT in Pompey. Couple o' weeks ago. Booster,
like.'

'Yes, I see. Then in that case ... nothing to worry about, I
assure you ... some ointment and a bandage.' O'Dwyer's words
seemed to slur a little. Stripey Nelson waited in his undignified
attitude. Nothing happened, but after a while he heard something like a snore. He looked round: Dr O'Dwyer was fast asleep.

Stripey stared indignantly. 'My arse!' he said. '*Officers!*'

SEVEN

After the bomb had shifted that little way Harrison lowered the whip of the after derrick again in an attempt to secure it with a heavy rope strop around its middle. Even if the thing couldn't be lifted clear it could perhaps at least be held in its position and made safe against another downward slide.

Petty Officer Ramm was taking charge below, feeling sick in the pit of his stomach. Something, he knew, could have happened internally when the bomb shifted. His hands shook; he was going to be clumsy but it couldn't be helped. Close up to the bomb, waiting for the descent of the whip, he found, like Jock Campbell, home thoughts crowding. Imminent death had a way of concentrating the mind on the essentials, and Ramm knew, had always known deep down, that his own first essential was his wife Greta and his small house in North End, Pompey. Never mind the others, the one-night stands as they'd mostly been, world wide. You could scarcely name a port anywhere where Ramm had been that he hadn't had a woman. Gibraltar, Malta, Port Said, even Aden. On to Colombo, Singapore, Hong Kong, Shanghai and Wei-hai-Wei, the latter known to generations of British seamen as Wee-I. Ramm had burned the candle at both ends. He could recall pay parade as a young AB when the ships' companies had mustered by ship's book numbers, junior ratings receiving their pittances from the paymaster on the flat tops of their caps held out in front of them, chief and petty officers taking it more privately in their hands; parades when his cap had shaken in his hand so badly that he'd been in danger of losing his cash. You couldn't bang all night without it having some effect,

73

and often Ramm had been glad enough to clear away to sea for recovery. That was one thing: there was another, currently more serious to his mental state: the women hadn't all been overseas. He'd had others in Chatham and Devonport – and in Pompey itself. He'd done a long spell at Whale Island, the Navy's principal gunnery school, when qualifying for gunner's mate. There had been times when Greta had gone up to Norwich to visit her mother and Ramm had been bereft. Her substitute, a girl who had then worked as a barmaid in a Commercial Road public house, had become more than just another one-night stand. The liaison had lasted. The last time they'd done it had been during his recent leave and afterwards the girl had said something that had shaken Ramm rigid.

She said, 'I know where you live, Perce.'

'You do?' He'd jumped a mile, metaphorically: he'd always been circumspect about giving anything away, on the principle that you didn't foul your own doorstep. 'How's that, then?'

She answered with another question. 'Didn't ever want me to know, did you?'

'Just never got around to it, that's all.' He asked her again how she knew.

'Followed you once,' she said.

'You bitch.' That had come out hard and almost involuntary. She didn't seem to mind too much and he hadn't said any more because he had to keep on her right side. He just said he'd esteem it a favour if she kept her distance from his missus with him going back to sea. She'd said of course she would; but Ramm had been left with a nasty thought: possible blackmail. Now the worry was of a different, but allied, kind: if his number was on that bomb, if it went up, he didn't want Greta ever to get an inkling of what he'd been up to all the past years. The barmaid from Commercial Road might do the dirty. She could think she had reason to get her own back. Ramm hadn't been entirely straight with her: vaguely he'd spoken of leaving Greta, but had always hedged when pressed. . . .

'All right below?' Harrison's voice, sounding edgy as well it might.

Ramm said, 'All right, sir, yes.'

'Coming down now.'

The whip came within Ramm's reach. He grabbed for it, took it

74

across towards the embedded bomb. The strop was dangling from its end. As Ramm moved with it, Harrison ordered the winchman to pay out more slack. Ramm detached the strop and started passing it, embracing the body of the bomb. When the strop was in position, he hauled it taut, using all his strength, put the eyes over the hook of the whip, then called up to the chief officer.

'Secured, sir. Ready to hoist.' He looked over his shoulder. 'Leading Seaman Nelson – you and six hands lay alongside the bugger and steady it as it comes clear. *If* it comes clear.'

ii

Yeoman Lambert was searching the seas astern, sweeping with his binoculars across the convoy as the ships plunged and lifted. There had been no moderation in the wind and weather. Bloody unseasonable, Lambert thought moodily. As he swept around a lamp began winking from one of the escorts on the port beam of the convoy and Lambert, reading it off, reported to the Commodore.

'Radar report, sir. Echo bearing dead astern, closing fast.'

'Thank you, Lambert.' Kemp levelled his glasses astern and almost on the heels of the radar report there was more flashing from the convoy's rear. Again Lambert read and reported: a ship was overtaking; it looked like a British destroyer.

Finnegan said, 'Must be *Burgoyne* or *Hindu*, sir, standing by the *Langstone Harbour*.'

'But dammit – they're towing!'

They waited, somewhat uneasily, Kemp debating whether or not to sound the alarm. But neither the destroyer that had picked the vessel up on its radar, nor the Flag, seemed worried. And within the next few minutes a ship appeared astern of the convoy and began signalling.

Lambert said, 'Identification signal of the day, sir.'

'Make the acknowledgement,' Kemp ordered.

'Aye, aye, sir.' A moment later Lambert said, 'All correct, sir. *Hindu*, sir. Signal following ... *Hindu* to Flag, both towing pendants parted, starboard cable torn out of vessel under tow. Master reports casualties. Propose returning to stand by but weather too bad for me to put doctor aboard. Message ends, sir.'

'Thank you, Yeoman.'

Lambert hesitated, signal clip-board in his hand. 'Any signals, sir?'

'No signals, Yeoman. Nothing we can do. Stand by for the Flag to repeat *Hindu*'s signal for information.' He added, 'The Admiral may have orders for us – but I doubt it.'

Kemp's doubt was proved correct: the convoy formation was to be preserved . . . and the *Langstone Harbour* left to wallow out of control, Kemp added to himself. With the starboard cable gone, there would be no possibility of again passing a double tow; if one of the destroyers succeeded in passing a fresh tow at all, it would be a single one and the *Langstone Harbour* would drop farther and farther astern of the convoy. And with her, Jake Horncape. Kemp wondered what had happened in Horncape's life through the years, whether he had married, whether he had a family. Kemp remembered through the mists of time that Horncape had sworn that he would never marry, preferring the freedom to enjoy the sea and the world without encumbrances or backward thoughts of home; but so many youthful seafarers had said and still said the same kind of thing and mostly they ended up married. . . . Kemp often thought that a woman was a fool to marry a seaman, his own wife included. It was no life at all, hanging around the ports waiting for a ship to come in, or waiting in the loneliness of an empty home for the sailor to come back from the sea. Until children came along, anyway; and then it was the father who suffered, growing away from his family as it came to maturity. Kemp himself had seen little of his sons in their formative years, he had been the stranger who turned up roughly every three months, stayed for a week, upset the routine, and then vanished again. The constant good-byes were a strain on both husband and wife, though husbands were so busy once they'd rejoined their ships that they had little time to brood. Mary, Kemp reflected, hadn't had much time to brood either: when their sons had gone off to their preparatory schools, old Granny Marsden had replaced them with her complaints and her ubiquitous walking-stick, needing a good deal of looking after from the start.

Now well astern of the convoy, Captain Horncape also spared a thought for the wife that unknown to Commodore Kemp he had acquired twenty-five years earlier when he had forsaken sail for steam and was on leave in London, London in the days of the last war. No *Luftwaffe* then, but the zeppelins had come over and dropped their bomb loads ... great sausage-shaped monsters gliding across the skies, laying eggs. It had been during a zeppelin raid that Jake Horncape had proposed to his wife, then known as Nesta Norris the Darling of the Music Halls. She had not been very successful on the halls; and the night before rejoining his ship, Jake, besotted and feeling sorry for her, not wanting to go back to sea leaving her, as he'd put it to himself, adrift without an anchor, had popped the question. He'd been her anchor for a number of leaves past and she was starting to depend on him. They married in a register office the day before the news broke of the battle of Jutland, the first and last meeting of the Grand Fleet under Sir John Jellicoe and the German High Seas Fleet. A somewhat indecisive battle in which both sides claimed victory: and the same could have been said of Jake Horncape's marriage.

They had fought through the years and neither could be said to be the winner. Nesta Norris, who on becoming Nesta Horncape had retired young from the music hall scene, had not retired from being everyone's darling. There had always been someone around when Jake came back on leave to the two rooms they rented in Whitechapel, someone who had to be thrown out, sometimes metaphorically, sometimes physically, while Nesta giggled coyly and then became the repentant, loving wife. Deeply in love, Jake couldn't resist her and always forgave, even when men, often young enough to have been in uniform, called with their straw boaters and blazers and looked awkward when they were met by the husband; or older men, gallants who twirled in embarrassment at waxed moustaches resplendent beneath dyed hair well oiled down.

'Just friends,' Nesta used to say. 'Old pals from the halls, nothing more than that, darling. You forget I was a bloody star.'

A star that had never really waned. Jake Horncape, wedging his heavy body against the lurch and roll and sag of his probably doomed command, thought about his last leave, just before the convoy had left UK. As so often in the past, he had arrived home unexpectedly, home being then on the outskirts of Southampton, and had found Nesta, now aged fifty-one, on the point of hopping into bed with a chief engineer from the P. & O. There had been a flurry of underwear and the chief engineer had departed with muttered apologies and a red face. He had been a portly man with a gut like a balloon; but he had at least been P. & O. as Nesta, pouting prettily, had said. Not for the first time, Jake had threatened divorce but Nesta had just said, 'Oh no, darling, you wouldn't,' and of course he knew he wouldn't. He was still besotted . . .

Captain Horncape looked down through a vision of Nesta towards his fo'c'sle. By now it had been cleaned up: when the starboard cable had been torn out from the cable clench, that fo'c'sle had looked like a battlefield. Horncape's chief officer had been standing in the eyes of the ship at one moment, the next his headless body had rolled aft past the broken slips to bounce down on top of the windlass below in the fore well-deck. The flying cable had also taken the bosun and ripped away his left leg which for a time had remained jammed beneath the port cable where it led down through the hawse-pipe. Another seaman, still alive but only just, had been crunched flat by the cable's end as it whipped up from the navel pipe before vanishing into the seas ahead. The damage to the ship herself was only superficial: smashed bulwarks and guardrails, and the gaping holes where the starboard bitts, the Blake slips and the bottle-screws had been torn straight out of the deck plating.

'Captain, sir?'

Horncape turned. His second officer reported, 'Holes plugged, sir, but seeping. Crew accommodation being pumped out –'

'Pumps coping?'

'Yes, sir. The hands are going to be a bit wet, though.'

A bit wet. Horncape remembered the days in sail. He said shortly, 'They'll get used to it, lad. How about the cable locker?'

'Not too bad, sir. Under control.'

'That's good. You'll be aware you're acting chief officer now, Phillips. You'll make sure the cargo's all right. I don't want any seepage into the holds while we're lying broached-to.' He added grimly, 'Just keep in mind those poor, starving buggers waiting for us in Malta!'

'If we ever get there,' Phillips said.

Horncape glared. 'We're going to get there, Mr Phillips, make no mistake about that. What are those hands doing down for'ard, loafing under the break of the fo'c'sle?'

'Waiting to take up the new tow, sir –'

'Waiting my backside, Mr Phillips! Get 'em up there ready! I'm not having the bloody RN making signals about unreadiness aboard my ship. Get down there and take charge.'

Phillips turned about and went down the ladder. Captain Horncape stood with his hands behind his back, body braced against the fore screen of his bridge. The ship was behaving like a pregnant bitch, without power, broadside to the wind and sea, beginning to develop a list as the water poured continually over her exposed port side and found its way below. If they found themselves unable to button-on again to the destroyer, then they'd had it. The ship wouldn't live for ever under the pounding she was getting.

iii

'She's coming!'

Ramm, sweating profusely beneath his oilskin, had felt the bomb give a small movement together with a grating sound as the metal scraped against the smashed girder. Stripey Nelson was alongside him, staring with a fixed expression at the bomb's awful closeness and muttering away about something or other. Ramm snapped at him to shut up: Ramm's ear was once more against the bomb, listening. He didn't know exactly what for: probably a tick. The bomb *could* have a clock mechanism that had gone temporarily wrong and if it had then it might start up again. Ramm knew his own shortcomings: he was a gunner's mate and thus an expert, or supposed to be, on the mechanics and firing of the guns themselves. That didn't make him an expert on bombs but he was all the *Wolf Rock* had.

Very, very gradually the derrick went on hoisting under Harrison's direction. Slowly the bomb lifted. Things moved around it: the girder sagged as the bomb began to come clear and there was a shout of pain from one of the seamen.

'What's up, Barton?'

'Me foot, PO –'

'Fuck your foot, keep quiet. Take it to the quack when you've finished here.'

Leading Seaman Nelson said, 'Fat lot o' good –'

'Shut up, Nelson. Just bloody shut up!' Ramm was shaking

badly now. So far, so good. So near and yet so far. He looked upwards, past the bomb's tail fins: the deck was one hell of a long way up and even suppose the whip could lift the thing clear, the strop might slip and down the bugger would come again, crushingly.

The derrick's clatter stopped suddenly. Ramm almost had a heart attack. 'What's up, up top?' he called.

'Fault in the steam winch. Hang on.'

Ramm said despairingly, 'Oh, for fuck's sake!'

iv

'I'm going down,' Captain Champney said when the report reached him. Kemp went with him, leaving Finnegan on the bridge to deal with any signals that might come from the Flag. Going aft they found a couple of the Wren ratings with PO Wren Hardisty, walking up and down. Miss Hardisty saluted smartly.

Returning the salute Kemp asked, 'Exercise?'

'Yes, sir. Keep the girls occupied.'

'Very commendable,' Kemp said. Miss Hardisty seemed pleased. Kemp moved on aft, thinking unwelcome thoughts: he already had the other WRNS officer dead below decks. In the prevailing weather conditions there could be no question of a sea burial; she must be carried on and perhaps the body could be landed at Gibraltar if the Admiral approved the transfer to hospital of Susan Pawle.

EIGHT

The steam winch had started up again: a minor fault, soon rectified by Mr Turnberry's second engineer brought up post-haste from the engine-room. The lift went ahead: the bomb came clear and was hoisted, swaying, through the hole in the deck-head, watched by Ramm and the gunnery rates, now standing clear of the drop after remaining to act as steadiers if the strop should slip while the bomb was still within reach. When it was clear above the poop, Kemp ordered Ramm's party out on deck and followed up himself, having a word with Captain Champney on the way.

'The derrick'll take it clear enough, I think, Captain. Out over the water.'

'Yes. But how are we cast off the strop? Might be better to lower to the deck, then roll it overboard. Or drop it from deck level. The strop could be reached and cast off by a man on deck.'

Kemp turned to Petty Officer Ramm. 'What do you think, Ramm?'

The gunner's mate pursed his lips. 'Tricky, sir. I dunno . . . it just could go off on contact. Also there's the scend o' the sea, sir –'

'Yes, quite. I appreciate the risk.' Kemp turned again to Champney. 'The farther off, the better – bearing in mind your cargo. The derrick can lift it a good deal farther out and not only that – it can be lowered gently, not dropped.'

'And then let go?'

Kemp nodded. Champney asked, 'How, for God's sake?'

Kemp said, 'A man on the end of the whip.'

'Perched on the bomb itself?'

81

'That's about it. The only way.'

Champney blew out his cheeks and shook his head slowly. 'And the man? A volunteer?'

'I'll not ask for volunteers,' Kemp said. 'I'll go myself.' He gave a tight grin. 'I'm still pretty agile. And don't forget, I did my time in the old square-riggers. It'll be child's play.' He added, 'Do you mind if I give my own orders to your winchman, Captain?'

'It's your life,' Champney said, shrugging.

It was the lives of them all, Kemp thought but didn't say so, if the bomb did happen to go up. He would be a little closer, that was all. Just a split second before the rest. As Kemp made his arrangements with Ramm and the handling party and the man on the steam winch, Captain Champney went back to the bridge. The ship would need careful tending while the bomb with the Commodore sitting on it was hoisted outboard. And Kemp would need to judge his own moment, the moment of cast-off, dead right. The right moment would be, Champney thought, when the *Wolf Rock* was in the trough of the sea rather than on the crest of a wave that could if luck was against them hurl the bomb back aboard again, a second drop that might well send it up. In the trough, the bomb should sink as the ship herself came up on the next crest, should sink beneath the bottom plating. In the meantime the engine should be so used as to carry the ship as clear as possible of any explosion below the water and at the same time to protect the screw. Champney called the engine-room on the voice-pipe and told Turnberry the position. Then, using his megaphone, he called down to Kemp aft.

'I'm keeping the engine on full ahead, Commodore. But the moment you cut away, I'll stop her. All right with you?'

Kemp waved back. 'All right, Captain.

Champney went himself to the engine-room telegraph and pulled the handle over, for'ard then aft, twice repeated, before setting it on Full Ahead, the emergency signal for Turnberry to give her all he'd got. The extra power could be felt almost immediately, and the speed came up. Champney went into the bridge wing and looked aft. The bomb with the whip now slack had been laid gently on the deck, and Kemp was climbing on to it, getting a foothold on the metal surface, holding fast to the whip with both hands. As Champney watched, Kemp freed one hand to signal to the winchman, and very slowly the whip tautened as the winch took up the remaining slack. Ramm and his gunnery rates got round the bomb, steadying it as the lift came on. Champney felt his fingernails dig hard into his palms, and sweat ran down inside his collar. The ship was lurching and the seas were as high as ever: the *Wolf Rock* was heading into wind and sea which kept her as steady as was humanly possible, but in such conditions total steadiness was an unrealistic hope. Water was coming over the fo'c'sle head to stream aft, thundering past the island superstructure, swilling around the bomb on its passage to the washports.

As the strain came on the whip, the bomb and Kemp began to lift. Slowly, gently, higher and higher . . . clear soon of the guard-rails, buffeted by the gale that slewed them out sideways, starting a terrifying swing. High still; and then a signal from Kemp as he clung to the thin whip of the derrick, and the men on the guys started hauling the arm of the derrick outwards as the clatter of the winch ceased.

With the bomb, Kemp hung poised over the water's turbu-lence, some ten feet clear of the ship's side, rising and falling as the ship herself rose and fell to the sea's violence. Then another hand signal and the winch started up again, and the whip's load was lowered, coming close to the surface – so close, soon after, that both bomb and Commodore vanished for long moments beneath the waves, to reappear again as the water fell away. Kemp's hand was on the strop. He held a seaman's knife, blade open and ready. Then, as once again he came clear and visible, he was seen to make a clean, hard, decisive cut, the moment chosen exactly right as the water fell away beneath him, fell away but not too far, and as Champney rang the telegraph to stop, the bomb dropped a matter of no more than a foot, and disappeared be-neath the water. The ship moved on under her own impetus, the bomb now safe from the spin of the screw. Kemp made his final hand signal and was swung back aboard. Dripping water, his face pale, he went straight to the bridge.

'Finnegan?'

'Sir?'

'Make to the Flag, from Commodore, bomb disposed of overboard. Will not now require dockyard assistance from Gibraltar.'

83

Kemp stripped off in his cabin, had a hot bath run by Botley, then a tot of whisky. He felt deathly tired all of a sudden: the strain told more when you were not so young, some of the resilience both mental and physical left a man. He called the bridge and told Champney he intended turning in for a spell but would be obliged if he was called at once should his presence be needed. Then he crashed down in his bunk, flicked off the light, and was asleep within seconds. A dreamless sleep, virtually total unconsciousness: when he woke it was a moment or two before he remembered where he was and that the threat of the bomb had gone. The motion of the ship told him that the foul weather was with them still. He rang for Botley: when the steward entered his cabin, Kemp learned that he had slept right through the night and that it was now breakfast time.

'Big eats, sir?' Botley enquired.

'Yes. I'm reasonably hungry. And plenty of coffee. Hot and strong, Botley.'

'Aye, aye, sir.' Botley set down the tray of morning tea and departed. Kemp sat up in his bunk, lit a cigarette and drank the tea. He wondered if Champney had been on the bridge all night. Probably not: there was no need for the ship's Master to work as it were watch-and-watch with the Convoy Commodore. And obviously there had been no alarms or excursions, or he would have been called. Something to be thankful for.

Breakfast came: corn flakes, fried bacon and eggs, toast and marmalade, the hot, strong coffee he had asked for. After it Kemp felt a new man; he shaved and dressed and went up to the bridge to be met by the ship's chief officer and Sub-Lieutenant Finnegan.

'Morning, Finnegan. Had your breakfast?'

'Yes, sir.'

'Nothing to report, I gather.'

'Nothing at all, sir. Quiet as you like, all night. There's just one thing, though. Not what you'd call operational, sir.'

'Oh?' Kemp lifted an eyebrow. 'What *would* I call it?'

'At a guess, sir, I'd say you'd call it a bloody nuisance.' Finnegan paused. 'First Officer Forrest, sir. About Wren Smith. The pregnant one,' he added helpfully.

'Thank you, Finnegan, I'm not too old to have a memory. What is it now? Twins?'

Finnegan said, 'You told Miss Forrest you'd see Wren Smith, sir –'

'So I did. Well?'

'She asks when it'll be convenient, sir.'

'Damn and blast! It's never going to be convenient – but don't tell Miss Forrest that, Finnegan.'

'No, sir.'

'All things being equal, I'll see the girl at . . . ' Kemp looked at his wrist watch. 'Four bells, Finnegan. In my cabin.' He added firmly, 'Chaperoned.'

Dismissing pregnant Wren ratings from his mind, Kemp took up his binoculars and stared across the restless, heaving sea. The station-keeping was still not too good; but allowances had to be made on account of the appalling weather. Even a well-practised battle squadron, with all the ships having more or less similar tonnages, speeds and handling characteristics, would have had its work cut out to maintain decent station. But once the weather improved, Kemp would have his yeoman of signals busy, clacking out gentle, or not so gentle, reproofs from the Commodore if a better showing was not made. The Masters wouldn't like it: they were always an independent-minded lot. Kemp gave an understanding grin across the water: basically, he was one himself. How long, he wondered, was this wretched war going to last? Would he, when at last it was over, be too old to take up his peacetime command again, and sail the seas in tranquillity along the old route to Fremantle, Melbourne and Sydney? Not that it had always been tranquil: the weather was with a seaman in peace as well as war, and both crew and passengers could pose problems for the Master, the final arbiter of right from wrong, the autocrat who was in control of everything aboard and whose judgment had to be that of a seabound God.

Which led him back to Wren Smith again.

iii

Kemp went down to his cabin at a little before four bells. Champney was on the bridge again and Kemp had repeated his request to be called at once if needed but otherwise not to be interrupted, though in fact he would have welcomed any diversion from what

85

he believed would prove an ordeal. Wren Smith might manifest one of any number of female characteristics: she might be weepy, she might be brazen, she might be loquacious, she might need to have every word dragged out of her. How did one handle a pregnant Wren? Kemp remembered Finnegan's advice, more or less tongue in cheek Kemp suspected: use threats, the threat of a landing at Gibraltar; it was true that sympathy would be misplaced in the circumstances. In Kemp's view pregnancy was a natural enough thing and one that made women even harder to handle than when they were not pregnant, but the Navy was the Navy and it didn't like problems of pregnancy of unmarried women.

Sharp at 1000 there was a knock at Kemp's door and Botley appeared.

'First Officer Forrest, sir,' the steward announced.

'Thank you, Botley, ask her to come in.'

'Yes, sir.' Botley withdrew. Miss Forrest and PO Wren Hardisty came in, the latter unexpected by Kemp. Between them came Wren Smith. Tarty, was Kemp's first thought, but currently a shade bedraggled and apprehensive, and very pale faced. Dark hair, long, seemed stuck to her cheeks. There was a kind of cockiness as well as apprehension in the girl's expression. Kemp had got to his feet as the women entered and since there were not enough chairs for them all to sit down, he remained, as they did, standing. Kemp felt awkward: the standing position was too reminiscent of Captain's Defaulters aboard a warship and he had not intended such an atmosphere to prevail.

'Wren Smith, sir,' Miss Forrest said. Kemp noted that the First Officer was going to be formal. She rattled off an official number – Defaulters again.

'Ah,' Kemp said. 'Well, young lady. I – er – gather you're in trouble.'

'Not really.'

PO Wren Hardisty said, 'Address the Commodore as Sir.'

'Oh, all right. Sir.'

Kemp said, 'Let me put it more directly. I understand you're pregnant.' He paused, wishing Jean Forrest would help him out. 'Have you anything you wish to say?'

'No. Only that –'

86

PO Wren Hardisty came up again. 'Address the Commodore –'

'All right, all right, PO,' Kemp interrupted. 'We won't stand on too much ceremony. Go on,' he added to Wren Smith. 'You were saying?'

The girl's voice was defiant now. 'I made a mistake. Me dates. I'm not due yet.'

'You mean you're *not* pregnant, is that it?'

She nodded. 'Sorry if I've made any trouble. I just made a mistake, that's all, sir. It isn't any crime anyway, to get a – to get caught, like –'

'No, no – not a crime. Just a blasted nuisance in the middle of a vital convoy.' Kemp, feeling disadvantaged, was growing angry. There were so many more important matters to worry about. He went on, 'I'm told there is a distinct possibility you *are* in fact pregnant –'

'I'm not. I told you, I –'

'Kindly don't interrupt me, Wren Smith. I repeat, you're being a nuisance, and if you're trying to conceal a pregnancy . . . have you any idea of the consequences, if I permit a pregnant Wren to be on-carried to Trincomalee, rather than land her in Gibraltar or Malta for passage home to UK? I tell you one thing: you'd be sent back on the first available ship – even from Ceylon. And the C-in-C British East Indies Fleet isn't going to be pleased about a pregnant Wren taking up valuable passage space unnecessarily. Do I make myself clear? I wish to know, here and now, what the facts are.'

'I'm not bloody well pregnant!' Wren Smith said, and burst into tears.

Kemp blew out his cheeks, and caught Jean Forrest's eye. He said, 'Over to you, Miss Forrest. And, I think, Dr O'Dwyer.'

As the women left his cabin, Kemp reflected that he hadn't handled the interview particularly well. Also, he was still far from certain of his ground in ordering a Wren to submit herself for examination by the ship's doctor. Nevertheless, he felt he had enough justification, since there was that distinct possibility that there might have to be contact with Gibraltar in spite of the bomb having been disposed of: there was still Susan Pawle to be considered and in Kemp's view the base hospital in Gibraltar was the place for her to be attended until she could be returned to the UK. Before Gibraltar was reached, Kemp needed to know Wren

Smith's condition. Later that day, O'Dwyer carried out his examination but the results as he reported them to the Commodore were totally indecisive. If, as the girl had first stated, she had missed her first period, she *could* be pregnant; but far from necessarily since there were other conditions that might lead to this. In any case, it was far too early to make a diagnosis, and the ship did not carry any facilities for pregnancy testing. O'Dwyer added it as his opinion that if indeed the girl had missed her first period, and perhaps despite her denial her second, then her condition would certainly become diagnosable by the time the convoy reached Trincomalee.

'You mean there'd be no disguising it?' Kemp asked.

O'Dwyer nodded. 'That is so.'

'Damn and blast!' Kemp said for the second time. 'Now, the other girl, Mrs Pawle. How's she doing, Doctor?'

'As well as can be expected. The wound's keeping clean, no infection. Physically, she'll mend I believe, though she really must be landed the soonest possible –'

'That'll be up to the Admiral,' Kemp said. 'Let me have a full report, will you, and I'll send a signal to the Flag. Then *Nelson*'s PMO can support the request.' He paused. 'You said, physically. What's her mental state?'

O'Dwyer shook his head, a gesture seemingly of doubt. 'I can't really say. No-one loses a leg without some mental trauma, of course. She's very weepy and doesn't want to talk.' He added, 'I understand she's been recently widowed – and now this on top of it.'

'Yes. It's a damn tragedy for a girl. For anyone, I suppose, but a girl with a wooden leg's a particularly pathetic sight. Bound to have a lasting effect.' They talked a little more; O'Dwyer thought Susan Pawle would probably be invalided from the WRNS, which in itself would be bad mentally. When the doctor had left his cabin, Kemp pushed the port open: there had been a strong aroma of whisky, and Kemp fancied O'Dwyer had been hopeful of an offer of a glass. Kemp went back to the bridge, back into the tearing wind and the sea's spray that was still drenching the decks, the weather still too bad to conduct a sea burial of the dead Wren officer.

Later that day, as once again the skies darkened into night, Captain Champney indicated that the convoy was approaching the position for the turn eastwards for Cape St Vincent and the entry to the Mediterranean. 'About an hour to go, Commodore.'

'And then we bring the wind and sea almost abeam,' Kemp said. 'Life just gets worse, doesn't it!'

'It'll be uncomfortable,' Champney agreed. 'In the case of the *Langstoné Harbour*, when she makes the turn, it'll be bloody dangerous.'

Kemp nodded; he had Jake Horncape much on his mind. Anything could be happening aboard the freighter with its injured crew members still presumably without medical attention from the doctors aboard the towing destroyers – with no improvement in the weather since the last report, no boat could yet hope to live in the mountainous waves.

As the hour ran down to the alteration time, Yeoman Lambert reported the expected signal from the Flag: the convoy would turn on the executive and would steer a course 090 degrees. When the executive was flashed, Champney brought the *Wolf Rock* onto the new course. Immediately conditions became worse, with the weight of the wind and sea some three points on the starboard bow – almost abeam, as Kemp had said. The ship laboured badly, lurching into the troughs, climbing again and once more sliding down the great water sides. Below, Chief Steward Campbell, warned in advance, had checked his storerooms and spaces to ensure so far as possible that everything was secured, but nevertheless heard unwelcome sounds of breaking crockery coming from the galley and pantries. In the engine-room Mr Turnberry, on the starting platform for the course alteration, felt his feet slide from under him and grabbed for a hand-wheel to support himself. He listened to the crash of the seas sweeping past the engine-room bulkheads, thin sheets of metal that alone stood between the men below and the raging tumult outside. In the makeshift sick bay Jean Forrest sat by the side of Susan Pawle, reaching out to hold the girl's shoulders, steadying her against the increased motion. Susan was as pale as death. Jean Forrest had a suspicion she was going to die; there was no apparent will to live. Even Gibraltar with its proper medical facilities . . . and Kemp had told her that in any case Gibraltar lay three days' steaming ahead yet.

Petty Officer Ramm made his night rounds of the gun positions. The old 6-inch aft of where the bomb had gone down was manned in cruising stations by two of the gunnery rates; on the bridge, one hand kept the watch, handy to go to any of the close-range weapons, Oerlikons and pom-poms, as required if there should be a sudden alarm. Which wasn't in the least likely on a night like this, Ramm thought. He'd seldom seen such weather, not apart from once getting caught in a typhoon on the China coast when he'd been an AB in the old *Sussex*, one of the high freeboard cruisers, 10,000-tonners, that had rolled her guts out in anything at all of a sea. That typhoon had been something to remember; Ramm, cold and wet now as then, preferred to forget it and remember something nicer: Gibraltar, pre-war when the combined Home and Mediterranean Fleets had met for their annual manoeuvres, the battleship *Queen Elizabeth* wearing the flag of the Commander-in-Chief Mediterranean and the *Nelson* that of the Commander-in-Chief Home Fleet. Big ships – battlecruisers as well as battleships, aircraft-carriers, cruisers, destroyers, submarines. All the pomp and circumstance, all the bullshit of the peactime Navy, made a man feel mighty important when he went ashore in his white uniform with the blue badges of a leading seaman rated as a director layer which Ramm had been by that time. Bronzed, fit, athletic, swaggering out of the dockyard by the Ragged Staff Gate, past the Trafalgar cemetery and the Naval picquet house, along Main Street in the scented air of dusk, towards Casemates where the pipes and drums of a highland regiment beat out for the ceremony of The Keys when the Land Port into the garrison was shut nightly ... it gave Leading Seaman Ramm romantic backing; and it pulled the birds, all right! Not that he needed help, mostly. In Gibraltar Ramm had a kind of up-homers, which was the Navy's term for a cosy family atmosphere away from home, a temporary mum and dad, preferably with a good-looker for a daughter, who would feed and generally cosset a sailor on shore leave. Ramm's Gibraltar up-homers didn't include any mum or dad, just a Spanish girl named Francisca, with swelling tits and a willing nature. She was in fact a widow, her husband, a picador, having been killed by a bull in the bullring at La Linea, the frontier town on the Spanish side of the border, beyond No Man's Land, and she was around five years older than Leading Seaman Ramm which he didn't mind a bit because she was experienced and thus exciting. She had taught him quite a lot over the years of his visiting Gibraltar either with the Home Fleet on those manoeuvres or when serving in the *Warspite* in the Med. Sometimes Ramm thought he had begun to live only after meeting Francisca, the first meeting having taken place in a night-dark alley near the Cathedral when she had been roughly handled by a drunk AB and had sought Ramm's assistance. Very fortuitous.

Happy days, Ramm thought as he lurched along the after well-deck of the *Wolf Rock*, making for'ard towards the bridge. Very happy days, and what had become of Francisca now? Probably still doing it, Ramm supposed; he was philosophical about it because he had to be. He'd never imagined Francisca led a sheltered life when he wasn't in Gibraltar, any more than he did himself when he was elsewhere. Still thinking about past dalliance, Ramm went through the door into the midship superstructure and started up the ladder leading to the deck officers' accommodation beneath the Master's deck. As he reached the head of the ladder a cabin door opened and someone looked out: Mr Harrison.

'Good evening, sir,' Ramm said.

'Good evening. Er . . . ?'

'Just night rounds of the guns,' Ramm said. He noticed an edginess in Harrison's manner, as though he didn't wish to have Ramm around. Ramm, knowing he was an awkward sod at the best of times, didn't shift. He said, 'Weather's getting worse on the new course.'

'It would, wouldn't it?' Harrison snapped.

'Well, yes, sir, it would, that's true enough. Doesn't make life any easier, though. Know when we're due through the straits, do you, sir?'

'Three days, near enough.'

'Ah. May get better weather then, with any luck. Should do, any road. Though the Med can be bad at times. Cold and wet too.'

Harrison, looking decidedly strained, was on the retreat back into his cabin when Ramm's persistence was rewarded. He heard the sound of the door at the foot of the ladder opening and he heard a foot on the steps.

He looked down. There was a WRNS rating coming up: the

91

one the buzz was about, the one with the suspected bun in the oven. Ramm said, 'What's all this, eh?' From the corner of his eye he saw Harrison's firmly closed door. 'Wrens not allowed up 'ere, officers' quarters. All right?'

'I – I –'

'Just turn about and bloody scarper. Or else. Get you bloody court-martialled, would this, if the Commodore got to 'ear. Get you chucked out. Me, I'll turn a blind eye this once. Now get.'

Wren Smith got, fast, without another word. Ramm turned away, gave a Churchillian sign at the Chief Officer's cabin door, and climbed to the bridge. All knowledge was useful; the time might come when he could benefit by it. And grateful Wrens who'd been shown mercy by a petty officer might, who could tell, be amenable. Ramm reckoned he was still good-looking, with a trim figure and no fat.

NINE

Next morning, in his exposed position in rear of the convoy, Captain Horncape aboard the *Langstone Harbour* had made an urgent signal by lamp to the destroyer *Hindu*, standing by still as an unencumbered escort to the freighter under tow of the *Burgoyne*. One of the injured men was in a bad way and Horncape believed he would die unless medical attention came quickly. Initially advice was sought by signal, but the medical facilities aboard the *Langstone Harbour* were virtually non-existent and to comply with the advice of the surgeon lieutenant in the destroyer was impossible. Horncape reported as much and after some delay a further signal came back from the *Hindu*: her Captain would attempt to put the doctor aboard by breeches buoy. The risk was great and all hands knew it: the destroyer would have to approach the freighter dangerously close and the chances of collision would be high, calling for expert handling of both ships. In the meantime there was much to do in setting up the taking of the ropes for the passage of the breeches buoy across the gap between the ships.

Second Officer Phillips, acting Chief Officer, would be in immediate charge. 'Have you set up a breeches buoy before?' Horncape asked.

'No, sir –'

'Then you'll have to learn fast. I doubt if any of the fo'c'sle hands have done it either.' Horncape's bosun, one of those injured, his leg-stump being kept clean and bandaged by the chief steward, was in no condition to leave his bunk. Quickly, Horncape ran through the drill. A rocket trailing a half-inch heaving line would be fired from the fo'c'sle of the destroyer across the *Langstone Harbour*'s decks and this would be laid hold of and secured, then hauled in. This heaving line would have attached to it an endless fall rove through a tailed block which Phillips would make fast to either the foremast or the mainmast, depending on whereabouts in the ship the heaving line was caught. Next a heavy hawser would be bent to the whip and sent across, being made fast some two feet higher than the block. From then on, it would be work for the destroyer: the breeches buoy, an affair of canvas with holes for the occupant's legs, would be secured to the whip, the doctor would be lifted into it and then be sent across to the *Langstone Harbour* by pulley-hauley on the part of the destroyer's seamen.

'The dangers are obvious,' Horncape said. 'Parting of the hawser as the ships lift and plunge – that's just one. If it parts with the doctor embarked, it'll be a case of finish. He's a brave man. All right, Mr Phillips? I'll be watching . . . but my first concern's the ship herself. Do your best, lad.'

ii

With Jean Forrest, Kemp went down to see Susan Pawle. She lay like a zombie, eyes sometimes closed, sometimes open but not seeming to focus on anything, just a blank stare. As O'Dwyer had said, she was weepy: a slow trickle of tears without any sound. Kemp tried to talk to her, gently, tried to be encouraging whilst knowing there was precious little if anything to be encouraging about. Even apart from that, from the essential hollowness of what he tried to say, he was not at his best with young women, no more so with Susan Pawle than he had been with Wren Smith and her very different problem. The father of sons only, he had no daughter-relationship to fall back on. Going back on deck with the WRNS First Officer, he voiced his misgivings.

'She doesn't want to live. She's not making any effort.'

'No, I agree, Commodore. It's not surprising, is it?'

'No, it's not. But she must be got out of it.'

Jean Forrest looked at him sideways as they reached the open deck and the gale's force, a quizzical look. 'How?' she asked.

Kemp shrugged. 'We must think of something, that's all I can say.'

94

'It's my worry, Commodore, not yours. You have the convoy to think about. I'm a spare hand, a passenger. Leave it to me.'

'All right,' Kemp said. 'I'll do that. But if you want to talk about it, you can – any time within reason. I mean –'

'The convoy – yes, I know.'

They went in through the door to the midship superstructure and up the ladder at the bottom of which Petty Officer Ramm had intercepted Wren Smith. Outside his cabin door, Kemp paused. He said, 'You're tired, Miss Forrest. Just about all in by the look of you. A shot of whisky wouldn't do you any harm. Come in.'

She said gratefully, 'Well . . . thank you, Commodore,' and went in through the door which Kemp was holding open. Kemp gestured her to a chair and rang for Botley. 'I suggested whisky,' he said. 'There's gin if you prefer it, Miss Forrest?'

'Yes, I think I would,' she answered. Botley came and the drinks were brought. Jean Forrest seemed to relax, some of the lines of strain disappearing. She was really quite good-looking, Kemp thought, and wondered why she had never married. Over the drinks, he found out the answer. They chatted, initially about her uncle and the Mediterranean-Australia Line, and then the talk flowed as it were backwards. She spoke of her days in Blenheim Palace doing War Office liaison duties but she didn't mention the married brigadier. It did come out, however, that she was one of those women among so many of her age-group that had become engaged to a young officer in the last war and had lost him in action. In Jean Forrest's case she had been a little over seventeen years of age when she had become engaged, towards the tail end of the war, and her fiancé, an infantry subaltern not long out of Sandhurst, had been killed only a matter of days before the Armistice.

Kemp was pondering whether or not to offer her another gin when there was a knock at his door: O'Dwyer.

'Yes, Doctor?'

'I have the full report you asked for, Commodore. For the Admiral. On Miss Pawle's condition, and the desirability of –'

'Yes, thank you, Doctor.' Kemp took the report and scanned it briefly: the prognosis didn't look good at all and it ought to convince the surgeon commander aboard the flagship; the Admiral might be a different kettle of fish. Kemp made no offer of a drink to O'Dwyer: the doctor was well capable of supplying his

95

own needs to excess and Kemp wasn't going to encourage him, even though he must have appeared impolite. Jean Forrest finished the remains of her gin and left the cabin with the doctor. Kemp read the report through again and then started to draft a signal to the Flag, adding that he still had the body of a Wren officer for disposal. After some thought he made an alteration, indicating that he *already* had the body of *one* dead Wren officer, hoping the Admiral would get the reference and take the hint. The signal ready for transmission, he took it to the bridge and passed it to the signalman of the watch. The Aldis clacked out through the overcast and the blown spume and was acknowledged from the *Nelson's* flag deck. The reply came within the next ten minutes. *Commodore from Flag, your 1036, weather reports indicate deteriorating conditions in the straits and I have reports from Admiralty of strong Italian forces likely to move out from Taranto to intercept. In these circumstances I do not repeat not propose to delay the convoy off Gibraltar.*

'So that's that,' Kemp said to Finnegan.

'A case of over to you again, sir.'

Kemp gave a hard laugh. 'What can I do about it? The plain facts are that one girl's life can't stand against the safety of the convoy. I see the Admiral's point, of course. He's hoping to get through before the Italians get down past Sicily, but I don't reckon there's much hope of that. Those Italian battleships have a damn sight more speed than we have.'

'They still won't hurry to meet the *Nelson*,' Finnegan said. 'A token show of force, mabye.' Kemp didn't respond; the Italian fleet had not so far been noted for any real desire to engage against heavy ships but this time they might muster their courage and make an all-out attempt, backed by the German JU87s and 88s from the Sicilian airfields, to stop the convoy in its tracks. How would the *Langstone Harbour* make out, limping along with her fragile escort, under tow? Malta stood in desperate need of her cargo; Mussolini would never let her pass into the Grand Harbour of Valletta.

Kemp sent down to Jean Forrest, asking her to come to the bridge. He informed her of the Admiral's signal and she seemed shattered at the lack of concern, the fact that Susan Pawle had not even been referred to in the reply. It was, she said, heartless and abominable.

96

'It doesn't surprise me,' Kemp said. 'The Admiral bears a hell of a responsibility. So many ships, so many men. All those troops.' He waved a hand away to the port quarter, towards the troop transports coming along through the spray and the immensity of the waves, lifting and plunging, rolling, their masts and funnels vanishing from time to time in the troughs. 'A fact of this bloody war, if you'll excuse the language, Miss Forrest.'

'It *is* a bloody war,' she said, and turned away. Kemp called her back. He saw the sparkle of tears in her eyes: she was perhaps remembering again that other war, and the news that would have come from the Flanders front. He said, 'One moment, Miss Forrest. There's something I have to do now, since there's to be no contact with Gibraltar.'

'Yes, Commodore?'

'The girl that died.'

'Sea burial?'

Kemp nodded. 'We'll have to. We'll have to accept the weather. You know what seamen are like.'

'Do I?'

Kemp coughed. 'Superstition. More perhaps in the merchant ships than in the RN. The old hands especially, of course, and the *Wolf Rock* has a number of them.' He paused. 'To be frank, they don't like being shipmates with corpses. I'm sorry, but there it is. We're moving into a good deal of danger.'

'Yes,' she said. 'Yes, I do understand. When's it to be?'

'I'll have a word with Captain Champney and I'll let you know. The sooner the better in my view, Miss Forrest, since it's got to be done.'

'You'll take the service?'

'It's Captain Champney's prerogative but I doubt if he'll want to exercise it.'

'I hope we don't have it twice, Commodore.'

'Miss Pawle? I pray we don't. But we may have many more, once we're into the Mediterranean, you know. *Mare nostrum*'s a turbulent area now.' Kemp paused. 'How's the doctor coping?'

'Reasonably well,' she said. 'So far as I can say, anyhow.'

'She's being kept out of pain?'

'Oh, yes. But I doubt if you can go on for ever, administering morphine or whatever it is. I just hope he doesn't overdo it. He's not particularly compos mentis at times.'

97

'So I've noticed. However, we have to trust him – no choice, is there? We're lucky to have a doctor at all, unlike poor old Jake Horncape back there.'

There was always someone at Susan Pawle's bedside, one of the Wren ratings if not Jean Forrest. PO Wren Hardisty, when her duties as the girls' ramrod permitted, sat and talked even though she knew she was not being listened to. Miss Hardisty had once in the long ago been a children's nurse, a nanny in an aristocratic household, and to her now the sick Wren officer was another of her charges, like the old days, when often enough she had sat by the bed of a child with measles or chicken-pox or some such, and had talked without being always listened to. Cook, in those days, had called her Rambler Rose, Rose being her Christian name. She rambled now, aboard the horrible discomfort of the *Wolf Rock*, heaving about like an oversprung pram in the deep ocean. She talked aloud, and knitted as she did so, a long woolly scarf, comfort for the troops to be sent home from Trincomalee if ever she got there alive.

Petty Officer Ramm, passing the door of the cabin where Susan Pawle lay, heard a monotone coming through the curtain and paused to listen. He recognized Miss Hardisty's voice, a loud one. He retailed what he'd overheard, later, to Leading Seaman Nelson.

'Funny,' he said. 'Proper old rat bag I always thought.'

'PO Wrens are, usually, GI.' Stripey Nelson risked a joke. 'Sort of female gunner's mates. . . . '

'Put a sock in it, Leading Seaman Nelson. What I was going to say . . . I peeped in like, and there she was, old battleaxe, yacking away to that poor young girl who wasn't taking a blind bit o' notice far as I could see in a quick gander. All about some bloke called Tom Perkins, who I gathered was a gardener. Ripped 'is 'and on a rose bush . . . got tetanus and kicked the bucket.'

'Go on?'

'That's what I heard her say, more or less. Horse shit, used as manure for the flaming roses . . . has tetanus in it.'

Stripey stared blankly. 'What's that got to do with anything?'

98

'Don't know. Maybe the old girl's round the bend, I dunno. Point is . . . ' Ramm creased his brows in an attempt to put his thoughts into words. 'I reckon she was being sort of kind. Motherly, that's it, motherly. Not what you'd expect of her, marching round the bloody deck chasing them girls.'

'P'raps she's a snob, sucks up to the officers.'

'Could be.' Ramm moved to the ship's side, to leeward, closed one nostril with a thumb and blew hard down the other, clearing the channel without recourse to a handkerchief. Looking over the side as he did so, he forgot all about PO Wren Hardisty and her odd behaviour: being flung about by the waves' movement was a corpse. Bloated and disintegrating, but definitely a corpse. Left from some earlier convoy under attack, obviously. Equally obviously, beyond all human aid. But, years of service routine making him react automatically, Petty Officer Ramm made a report to the bridge just the same: corpse overboard. When Commodore Kemp got the report, he shuddered, knowing what he had to do later that day. But the dead girl would go to her committal decently, sewn into a canvas shroud, lead-weighted at the feet. She would surely sink and not be left as a grisly, untidy reminder on the face of the ocean. To make sure, if necessary, Kemp would bring up his revolver from the safe in his cabin, and put a few shots into the body before it disappeared.

Below, Miss Hardisty talked on, reliving her own past. Tom Perkins had indeed been a gardener at the big house, and had been carried off by agency of the germs that lurked in horse manure and became transferred by some weird chemistry to the thorns of rose bushes. Miss Hardisty had wept for many a long month: she and Tom had started walking out together, blessed by the master and mistress – there was nothing clandestine and definitely no hanky-panky of the sort that had led Wren Smith into trouble and deceit. Miss Hardisty would never have dreamed of doing anything like that, no more would Tom Perkins, who was an upright man. Thereafter Miss Hardisty had left her employment, her growing-up charges no longer in need of a nanny in any case, and, vowing to remain a spinster, had become a shop assistant in haberdashery, advancing to manageress over the years. The war had taken her into the WRNS; her father had been a chief stoker serving under Admiral Beatty in the last war so the WRNS was an obvious choice.

She said all this, or much of it, to Susan Pawle's unresponsive ears. And in the end, the result of several such talkative visits earlier, persistence got through. She found that the officer was staring at her and seemed to react.

Miss Hardisty asked, 'Feeling better, ma'am?'

'Not really.'

Miss Hardisty clicked her tongue. 'Poor mite ... ma'am. I dessay you're glad of company. There's been one of us here all the time you've been sleeping, ma'am.'

Susan, Miss Hardisty saw, was trembling. She asked, 'Is it the pain again, ma'am?'

'Yes.' Susan spoke through clenched teeth.

'I'll get the doctor.' Miss Hardisty got to her feet, the knitting dangling.

'No. Don't go. Not yet. Where are we?'

'The ship, ma'am? Not far off Gibraltar now.'

'Gilbraltar ... will they put me ashore?'

'I can't say, ma'am. I just don't know.' Miss Hardisty knew, all right, she'd been told the Admiral's reply to Kemp's signal.

'What's going to happen to me?'

'I don't know that either, ma'am. I wish I could help, I do really.'

The ship rose and lifted, rolled, plunged, a sickening motion: at times the curtains over the port seemed to stand almost at right angles to the deck and the bunk where the girl lay. Susan rolled with the motion, held from falling out by the bunkboard. She was crying again now, not sobs, but a drift of tears down the white cheeks. 'Will I be invalided, do you think, PO?'

Miss Hardisty sighed. 'That I don't know either, ma'am, I'm sorry.'

'I don't think I could take that. I want to carry on ... for Johnny's sake. He was a submariner.'

'Yes, ma'am. Oh, I'm *sure* you'll be all right. There'll be plenty of appointments once you're up and about, while the war lasts. Never say die, ma'am, that's my motto. Now I'm going to get the doctor. I won't be long, ma'am.'

She left the cabin. She found Dr O'Dwyer out on deck, eyes bleary and bloodshot, mouth slack. He was taking deep breaths, using the Atlantic gale to clear his head, Miss Hardisty thought with disgust.

100

She said, standing square with her hands behind her back, 'The young lady, sir.'

'H'm?'

'Third Officer Pawle, sir – '

'Oh, yes. How is she?'

'Poorly. In pain again. It's very distressing.'

'You're asking for another jab?'

'It seems the only way, sir. I mean, if you agree, of course. But I was thinking, though it's not for me to say, I know that . . . '

'Yes?'

Miss Hardisty had been thinking along lines similar to Jean Forrest. 'Is there any danger in too much morphine, sir?'

O'Dwyer laughed, a croaking sound. 'That depends on what you mean by too much. Too much – just like that – yes, there would be danger. Too much means – a fatality. Miss Pawle hasn't had too much.'

'But,' Miss Hardisty persisted, 'there might come a time, mightn't there? I mean . . . what happens then?'

'That time hasn't come yet. We shall see that it doesn't.'

It was, she thought, an unsatisfactory answer and it indicated to her that the doctor didn't know. She went below with him and stood by while he administered the morphine and remained while Susan drifted off into her drugged sleep again. Soon after that she was relieved by Wren Smith.

'You,' Miss Hardisty said grimly when the girl came into the cabin. 'I don't know as I ought to leave *you* with the officer.'

'Why ever not, eh? I'm not contaminated, am I?'

'Some would say you were, Wren Smith. And do your jacket buttons up, girl, try not to look like a walking scran-bag.' Miss Hardisty left the cabin and as she dropped the curtain back into place across the door she heard Wren Smith's verdict loud and clear.

'Silly old bitch, needs a man herself.'

She halted, scandalized and hurt. Then she moved away: she had to pretend she hadn't heard. The remark had gone deep, and her face had lost its colour. It was so unkind, so unfair. She thought of Tom Perkins, gone for many years but never to be forgotten. A gentle man, and decent. Miss Hardisty's work in the haberdasher's had filled something of the gap, now filled by her responsibilities as a PO Wren. That thoughtless remark that had come through the curtain with an intent of being overheard brought back the gap very strongly: what would she do when the war was over and she faced demobilization? Middle-aged and crusty, loved by none, stripped of her petty officer's status, just another ageing civilian looking for rehabilitation in a world in ruins, the aftermath of war. There would of course be thousands, millions, like her. Women who had lost husbands or fiancés. Like her, but not quite the same. In Wren Smith's terms at all events, she had never had a man.

iv

Aboard the *Langstone Harbour* Captain Horncape had watched the preparations for sending the breeches buoy across. It had been a tense operation, with the destroyer being at times flung towards the freighter's side, collision being avoided by good seamanship and a fair dose of sheer luck. Horncape's second officer was on the cack-handed side and the operation had taken a good deal longer than Horncape would have wished; but at last the ropes had been secured, leading across the water between the plunging ships, and Horncape had seen the destroyer's doctor being put into the legs of the breeches buoy, one hand clasping a steadying line above his head, the other clutching the bag of medical gear that he would need once aboard. With the Naval seamen tailing on to the rope rove around a big block, the breeches buoy with its human cargo began to move out over the warship's deck, out over the turbulent waves that rose between the ship like gigantic waterspouts. The haul was slow; everything depended for success on the pulley-haulers being able to walk back in time should the scend of the sea fling the ships apart and bring sudden and undue strain on the rope spanning the gap.

From time to time the doctor was invisible in the blown spume off the wave crests, from time to time his body was submerged in the rising waves themselves. Horncape gripped the teak bridge rail like a vice, knuckles standing out white, lips moving in prayers for the doctor's safety. In those agonizing minutes all was forgotten except the operation in hand, no thought for the enemy that might be lurking beneath the seas, waiting to attack in better weather, no thought for the forthcoming passage of the

102

Western Mediterranean and the hoped-for arrival in the Grand Harbour.

Then Horncape heard the high shout from Phillips, second officer: 'That bloody strop . . . the eye's opening!'

Immediately, Horncape left the bridge, sliding down the ladder and doubling for the after well-deck and the mainmast. As he went he saw two seamen, men who seemed to be all thumbs and no fingers, trying to rig a back-up strop and to seize the end of the main rope to the mast before the strop went.

Too late: Horncape could only watch in horror as the eye of the strop opened right up under the strain of the breeches buoy, the rope came clear in a fraction of a second and the end whipped back to drop over to seaward of the after guardrails. When the heavy spray cleared for a moment, there was no line stretched between the ships; a tangle of rope drooped from the sheaves of the block aboard the *Hindu*. There was no sign of the breeches buoy itself or of the doctor. Everyone was looking down into the water, uselessly enough. Even if a body was seen, it could never be brought aboard either ship. Captain Horncape put his head in his hands, seeing what could have happened before the destroyer's captain had had time to stop his engines, needed for close manoeuvring, the doctor's body, drawn into the whirl and wash of the screws, shredded into mincemeat by the great blades.

Second Officer Phillips faced Horncape. 'I don't know what to say, sir. It –'

'Say nothing, lad. Not your fault . . . except that it would have been better if you'd checked that strop before using it. Basically, it's to be laid at poor Marlow's door, I fear.' It was the chief officer's job to overhaul the deck gear and see it fit for use at all times.

Later that day, after an exchange of signals between the *Langstone Harbour* and the *Hindu*, the course of the tow was altered to the east in accordance with the instructions from Naval Control in the Clyde.

TEN

Past the great eminence of Cape St Vincent currently not visible to port behind the night's darkness and the heavy overcast of continuing foul weather, past Cape Sagres and Cape Santa Maria, below the Gulf of Cadiz for Cape Trafalgar and Tarifa Point, the convoy and its escort steamed on, the aircraft carriers taking seas across their flight decks as their bows pitched under. From the bridge of the *Wolf Rock* Commodore Kemp studied the lights along the Spanish coastline as Cape Trafalgar was raised on the port bow of the convoy.

'German agents in plenty over there,' he remarked to Captain Champney.

'As ever. Franco may have kept his country out of the war, but . . . ' Champney shrugged. 'They see everything, those bloody Nazi agents. All movements of shipping. Compositions of convoys and strength of escorts, the lot. Straight back to Berlin. Even though it's night.'

Kemp nodded. The overcast might help this time, but there was not much security in a night passage when the weather was fair since the phosphorescence of the ships' wakes would be seen clearly and there was always a luminosity over the water even in the darkest night. Black silhouettes would give the game away, sure enough. This time, unless the overcast did give them some security, the German Naval Command would know within the next hour or so that the convoy with its capital ship escort was on passage through the Gibraltar Strait. That news would go as quickly to Mussolini and his battle fleet waiting in the port of Taranto. There was just a hope that the aircraft carriers of the

Mediterranean Fleet had been sent on a foray against those Italian battleships, flying off their squadrons of elderly stringbags, but if this was so, then there had been no cyphered confirmation from the Admiralty, or at any rate no such indication from the Flag.

Ahead of them now around Tarifa was the glow of light from the Rock of Gibraltar: the rock had never been subject to the blackout regulations, since in any case it would have stood out under the lights from neutral Algeciras and La Linea. Then, as the leading ships of the escort, with the *Nelson* behind, came round Tarifa Point to make below Gibraltar Bay and enter the Mediterranean proper past Europa Point, a signal lamp started flashing from the signal tower in the dockyard.

Yeoman Lambert reported, 'Calling the Flag repeated Commodore, sir.' He read off the signal, a brief one. 'From Admiral commanding Gibraltar and North Atlantic, sir. Force H is ordered to join escort.'

'Force H! Well, that's something we didn't expect! Must be on account of the Taranto business,' Kemp said. The news was heartening. Force H, based on Gibraltar and consisting of the battleship *Rodney*, sister ship of *Nelson*, the battleship *Malaya* and the aircraft carrier *Formidable* with their escort of twelve destroyers, would be a very welcome addition to the convoy's defence. A few minutes after the yeoman had read off the signal, Champney, looking through his binoculars, saw the movement of the great shapes out from the dockyard.

'Coming through the breakwater now, Commodore,' he said.

It was an encouraging sight, but it was also an indication of the expected strength of the enemy.

ii

Aft by the 6-inch gun, Petty Officer Ramm had watched the occasional lights along the distant Spanish shore inwards from Cape Trafalgar, along with Stripey Nelson. 'Makes you think,' he said.

'What of, GI?'

'What of?' Ramm's tone was scornful. 'Of your bleeding namesake, Leading Seaman Nelson. Of England's glory. Of the whopping of the Frogs and dagoes, all them years ago. The great Lord Nelson . . . who else? Pity you aren't more like him an' all.'

'Never 'ad the chance, GI.'

Ramm didn't respond: in his mind's eye he was seeing the great ships of the line with their massive areas of square white sail, the gun-ports with the cannon pointing through – the *Victory* had had a hundred and six of them – the gunners sweating and running red with blood along the gun-decks, the hammock netting on the upper deck filled with the seamen's hammocks as some protection against splinters and cannon-balls and sniping from the enemy rigging as the fleets came together for a fight to the death, some of the ships dismasted with their rigging and yards trailing down into the water, some of them on fire and burning furiously to the waterline, the officers with their cocked hats and epaulettes standing by the diminutive figure of their admiral on the *Victory*'s quarterdeck as the British fleet blasted its way into the history books and the nation's hearts. Petty Officer Ramm saw other things as well: Lord Nelson ashore in Naples, having his way with that Lady Hamilton and never mind the husband. Ramm's thoughts were still with women as the *Wolf Rock* brought Gibraltar abeam: more precisely, with Francisca.

'So near and yet so far,' he said aloud.

'Oh?'

'Never mind, Leading Seaman Nelson, keep your thoughts on the ship.'

Stripey grinned in the darkness. 'Like you, I s'pose, GI?'

'Yes.'

'Not 'arf,' Stripey said. Then he saw the movement of the heavy ships, the great bulk of the *Malaya* and the *Rodney* coming out behind the destroyer escort. 'Battle-wagons!' he said. 'Coming with us, I wonder?'

'If they are,' Ramm said, 'and I reckon they are, then we're in for something big.'

iii

As the convoy moved on past Europa Point with no shore contact, Kemp was thinking back to the previous day when despite the weather the canvas-shrouded body of Third Officer Anne Bowes-Gourley had been sent overboard from a plank rigged in the after well-deck. He had read the committal service. That had been a heart-rending business. To have to watch the body of a young woman slide from under the White Ensign provided by Yeoman Lambert from the Commodore's flag outfit, had been something he would have wished never to do. Women should not, in Kemp's view, be part of war but in this war that had become inevitable. Plenty of civilian women had died in the bombing raids on the ports and other big cities – Wrens too, in Portsmouth and Devonport.

Mercifully there had been no need for Kemp's revolver: the body had been well weighted by order of Peter Harrison, who had anticipated difficulty in the heavy waves, and she had sunk quickly. All the WRNS draft except for Susan Pawle had been present, standing wet and sad in the rain and the spray. Many of them had been in tears, including Jean Forrest and PO Wren Rose Hardisty. The girl had been only twenty-one or thereabouts. Her parents wouldn't know yet; in due time Kemp would write to them, offering useless words of sympathy; so would Jean Forrest. After the simple, agonizing service Kemp had personal words with each of the girls and then once again took Jean Forrest to his cabin and gave her, not gin this time, but a strong shot of whisky, no water at all.

He raised the question of the parents. They had a right to know. He said, 'The report's gone by light to the Flag, of course – I saw to that. We can only assume the Admiral will pass it to the tower at Gibraltar.'

She nodded. 'Do you know when the next mail will leave the ship, Commodore?'

'Port Said I should imagine. There's been no word from the Flag about putting it ashore at Gibraltar.'

'No, I suppose not. No contact.' Jean Forrest sounded very bitter. 'That girl ... Susan Pawle. It's criminal really. At times I wish we still had that bomb aboard, then the Admiral would have had to lie off to embark the bomb-disposal people.'

'Ifs and buts,' Kemp said shortly. 'No use dwelling on that, Miss Forrest.'

'There are plenty of things it's no use dwelling on.' She was thinking of the Blenheim brigadier. He'd been a so-and-so, of course, but she'd liked him and he had brought something to her rather lonely life: with the onset of real war, after the so-called phoney stage, all social life had been broken up, old friendships ended as men were called away, new links to be forged, so many things changed, all the outlooks different, everyone busy with war work of one sort or another. Jean Forrest had unashamedly enjoyed sex and the brigadier had been good at it; which thought made her ashamed when it came to dealing with Wren Smith now about to be carried on from Gibraltar with her personal problem. Where was the difference between herself and Wren Smith, except that Wren Smith hadn't been very clever about it? The moral issue was precisely similar; but morals had largely gone by the board now. It was a case of here today and gone tomorrow, and enjoy life while you could. Drink and sex were largely the means of wartime enjoyment and there were plenty of entrepreneurs to meet the demand. Little drinking clubs had sprung up everywhere where there were officers of the three services – London's West End where the office admirals and generals hung out, Southsea for the Portsmouth-based ships and establishments, Plymouth for Devonport, Rochester and Gillingham for Chatham. Edinburgh, Glasgow, Liverpool, Salisbury, Colchester, Aldershot . . . some people were coining it, all part of war, some lost and others gained.

'A penny for 'em?' Kemp's voice broke into her thoughts; he was smiling kindly across the cabin. 'Things it's no use dwelling on,' he prompted.

'Oh . . . nothing really, Commodore.' She had summed Kemp up from the moment of first meeting over his breakfast table in that Glasgow hotel: she needed a shoulder to cry on but although he seemed a kindly man his wasn't the right shoulder in the circumstances of her own particular bereavement, the so-and-so brigadier. John Mason Kemp, Commodore RNR, late senior Master in the Mediterranean-Australia Line, was the faithful sort. Jean Forrest doubted if since marriage he had ever slept with any woman other than his wife, and that despite the long and frequent partings and the easy proximity of women afloat between Tilbury and Sydney, all inhibitions cast aside in so many cases as they met the hothouse atmosphere of a great liner. Floating gin palaces-cum-brothels, she'd heard them described as. In peacetime; not any longer. Now they were all hired transports on charter to the War Office, like those currently in company. She said, 'Just home thoughts, that's all.'

Kemp nodded understandingly. 'We used to call it an attack of the channels.'

'Channels?'

'Yes. It used to come on homeward bound. On the outward run you were looking ahead to Australia and somehow you didn't think backwards too much. But the moment the ships left Fremantle homeward, the whole crew seemed desperate to get home quickly, couldn't wait to see the English Channel and the good old White Cliffs. Then a spot of leave.'

'Then back to Australia again.'

'That was the pattern, yes.'

'Not much of a life for a married man.'

'Well – no, I suppose not. But I wouldn't have changed it, never thought of leaving the sea. The sea gets into the bloodstream, I think! And seafaring people. They're about the only sort I really get on with.' Kemp gave an embarrassed cough. 'I refer to men, Miss Forrest. The ladies . . . well – '

She laughed. 'It's all right, Commodore, I know what you mean. How did Mrs Kemp take the absences? It's harder on the wives, I'd have thought.'

'Yes, it is. My wife grew accustomed, I suppose.'

There was a twinkle in her eye. 'You never exactly asked her?'

'Well – no, I don't think I did. She knew what she was in for, marrying a seaman.'

'Yes.' Jean Forrest thought: how like a man, never raise questions that are best left unanswered. Just expect the wife to accept. Even Kemp, it seemed, had his selfishnesses. Again, like any man. She finished the whisky and set the glass down on a table beside her chair. 'Thank you, Commodore. That did some good.'

When she had gone, Kemp went back to the bridge, back to the never-ending gale. The wind had backed a little now, and the convoy, on its easterly course, was once again steaming directly into it.

iv

Passing Gibraltar the *Nelson* had reported to the signal tower that the *Langstone Harbour* was coming along astern, her engine useless, in the tow of *Burgoyne* with *Hindu* standing by. The assistance of an ocean-going rescue tug had been requested to take over the tow. The Flag had made the point that the stricken ship was urgently needed in Malta and should be allowed to continue through the straits with her destroyer escort rather than be deviated into Gibraltar for repair. Once she had discharged those vital foodstuffs, she could undergo engine repairs in the Grand Harbour, where the Navy maintained all necessary facilities.

'She'll never make it,' the Admiral commanding in Gibraltar said. 'On her own, virtually! Two destroyers against Musso's battleships – and the U-boats!'

'Or what's left of them, sir,' his Chief of Staff said.

'H'm?'

'They'll have met *our* battleships and aircraft carriers by that time.'

'You mean they'll do a bunk?'

'That's what I mean, sir. They've done it before. I believe an arse-end Charlie would have a pretty fair chance.'

'Well, it's undoubtedly true that Malta needs that cargo. No use holding it here until we can find another ship to carry it on. I wouldn't care to be aboard that freighter, though, a damn sitting duck.'

Nor would the Chief of Staff, a captain RN who had done his share of seagoing in the past. But the cargoes had to be got through and it was the merchant ships and crews that had to take them. Dangers were the daily ration now, the norm. You just carried on regardless. If you had to give certain orders that led to men's deaths, you just shrugged it off and forgot about it. If you didn't, you'd go round the bend. No use brooding; once the Admiral signified his assent to the rescue tug the Chief of Staff would put it all in hand and authorize the tower to call the freighter when she appeared around Tarifa Point and tell her she was not to enter.

The Admiral asked, 'What do we know about the ship, Barnett?'

The Chief of Staff gave him the bare details: tonnage, hold capacity, speed when the engine worked.

'Who's her Master?'

'Captain Horncape, sir.'

'Horncape, what an extraordinary name. Very well, Barnett, see to it, will you. Tug and so on. Now.' The Admiral turned his attention to other matters. 'It's late but since I've been called . . . have a word with my secretary in the morning, Barnett – the

110

question of the guest list for that French admiral's visit, the dinner . . . '

v

By dawn the convoy was east of Gibraltar, and moving now into the danger zone. Signals went from the Commodore to his charges, reminders of the need henceforward to be extra vigilant as regards lookouts and guns' crews. The weather was still foul but the reports indicated an improvement expected within the next twenty-four hours. U-boat attack would be unlikely in the currently prevailing conditions but was to be expected when the weather moderated. And over all would be the threat from the German dive bombers as the convoy moved within range of the airfields in Sardinia and Sicily.

A few more hours yet of comparative safety, Chief Officer Harrison thought as he paced the bridge in the morning watch, the four to eight, together with Kemp who seemed never to sleep. They chatted as they walked; Harrison found Kemp somewhat heavy going, one of the old guard, rigid with liner discipline and a career background of sail and the rounding of Cape Horn, something that Peter Harrison was glad to have been young enough to escape. When Kemp had been a young man, it had been more or less obligatory to take one's certificates of competency in sail, in the square-riggers: second mate, mate, and master. Seven years minimum of hell, terrible weather, filthy food and very long voyages. And definitely no women until that long voyage was over, except sometimes for the Master's wife which in effect added up to the same thing. Masters' wives were mostly grim in any case, often more autocratic than their husbands. No life for such as Peter Harrison, who liked the fleshpots and all that went with them.

Coming off watch he washed and shaved and had his breakfast in the saloon. Then he went below to the chief steward's cabin. He had established, some days earlier, an understanding with Jock Campbell, not without some surliness initially from the chief steward.

'Got your own cabin, Mr Harrison. Why involve me?'

'My cabin's kind of . . . out of bounds. There are two people

111

with large, prying eyes and big ears. I refer to First Officer Forrest and that bloody man Ramm, who I think is jealous. Any help you can give, I'd be much obliged. If you follow?'

'I think I do, sir, yes. But you're asking plenty, asking me to connive – '

'Not connive. Certainly not. Just ease the way a little, that's all.' Harrison grinned. 'I'm not pinching the stores or asking you to smuggle booze ashore for me, am I?'

'Yes, well.' Jock Campbell sucked in a deep breath and blew it out again. You met all sorts at sea and some could be nasty if you didn't meet them half way. Take Mr Harrison, now: one day, and probably quite soon, he would have his own ship as Master. He, Jock Campbell, might well find himself as Captain Harrison's chief steward, and then what, if he'd already fallen out with him? You had to have an eye to the main chance, after all. Campbell preferred an easy life, liked to keep on good terms with those around him, and in particular those above him. An ill-disposed Master could turn life into a variety of hell if he wanted to, and there was something about Harrison that said loud and clear that he was one who would do just that. Jock Campbell decided to compromise with his conscience. Mr Harrison, he said, would find a key on his keyboard and he, Campbell, would turn a blind eye . . . the key was that of the linen store and no-one ever went in there unaccompanied by the chief steward himself. Jock Campbell, with his end-of-voyage bonuses ever in mind, kept a very careful check on his stocks and made the necessary issues himself.

So this morning everything was arranged ahead. Peter Harrison, entering the chief steward's cabin, said, 'Good morning, Mr Campbell.'

'Good morning, sir.'

'The blind eye if you don't mind.'

Campbell said nothing; grinning, Harrison took the key from its hook and left the cabin. Making along the working alleyway one deck down from the chief steward's cabin, he reached the linen store, let himself in, locked the door behind him, and waited for a knock. Five minutes later it came; Wren Smith was admitted and the door locked again.

She looked worried. 'You sure this is all right?' she asked.

He nodded. 'All arranged. What's the trouble?'

112

'I've not got long,' she said. 'That old bag Hardisty, snooping on me most of the time . . . '

'You gave her the slip?'

'Yes. Just about.'

'Stop worrying,' he said, and took her in his arms. He kissed her. He could scarcely wait now; nor, he knew, could the girl. Harrison felt a momentary twinge about the naval rating from Portsmouth, waiting for her in Trincomalee; but he dismissed the twinge easily. The girl was easy meat and promiscuous, like so many women at sea; and being already pregnant, or so she believed, he had no worries on that score. Afterwards, Harrison and Wren Smith left the linen store separately.

ELEVEN

Petty Officer Ramm emerged from the cabin he shared with Yeoman of Signals Lambert. He was not in the best of moods. During the night indigestion had hit him; his stomach felt as sour as a dustbin that hadn't been emptied for weeks. Also, he was worrying about his wife Greta and the proximity to her of the barmaid from Commercial Road, Pompey. Some time after the arrival in Trinco, the mail from UK would catch them up. There was no reason, really, to fear that mail; no reason why the barmaid should have shopped him in the interval since he'd left Pompey to rejoin Kemp's staff. But it was a continual, nagging worry and henceforward he would fear every incoming mail.

Walking along the alleyway with his worries and his indigestion, intending to go up on deck for another check around the ship's armament that would shortly be in action, he witnessed an interesting sight: Wren Smith emerging through a hatch in the deck, a hatch that Ramm knew led down to the working alleyway where the various store-rooms and such were situated, a place where Wren Smith, or for that matter any other member of the WRNS, had no business at all to be.

Seeing Ramm the girl looked confused and startled, as well she might. Guilty conscience, Ramm thought. He said nothing to her as she scuttled past him. But he waited, a sardonic look on his face, sucking at a hollow tooth. His wait was rewarded. Up the hatch came Peter Harrison. Harrison, seeing him, looked as confused as Wren Smith.

'Good morning, Mr Harrison, sir.'

'Morning, Petty Officer Ramm.'

114

Very formal, Ramm thought. Harrison smiled. 'Checking round below,' he said.

'Yes, sir, I see. Routine, is it?'

'That's right.'

'Very necessary I'm sure, sir. What with the damage aft an' all.'

'Yes – yes, exactly. I – '

'Did you,' Ramm enquired innocently, 'see any sign of that Wren Smith while you was below, sir?'

'Wren Smith? Good heavens, no. Why d'you ask?' Harrison paused. 'Is she missing?'

'Missing, sir? Oh no, sir. Only a little up top, that's all, sir,' Ramm said, and tapped with a finger at his forehead. Harrison seemed to get the drift: it had been a crazy risk for a Wren rating to take and if anything came out the heavens would fall on her. On him, too.

He said, 'You seem to have set yourself up as a sort of moral guardian, Petty Officer Ramm. If I were you, I'd watch it.'

'Yes, sir. I could say the same to you, sir, but then it wouldn't be my place, would it?' Ramm turned about and walked away, left-right-left, every inch the gunner's mate, arms swinging, aware of Harrison's angry stare behind him. Ramm thought, let him bloody sweat. He won't do it again. Much too risky: he wouldn't know how far Ramm meant to take it, either. As Ramm came out on deck he saw PO Wren Hardisty walking, or lurching, up and down the after well-deck. Her morning constitutional: Ramm had seen her at it every day so far. They exchanged good mornings; Ramm had a strong urge to report what he'd seen, but he overcame it. He overcame it for two reasons: one, he'd sinned himself and had the worry that Greta was going to find out one day soon about the close-to-home sins in Pompey, and it didn't do for the pot to call the kettle black in case it brought nasty luck; and two, he was going to sin again before long, and he knew very well who with, and there was no point in alerting Ma Hardisty so that she would stick to Wren Smith like a leech.

ii

Astern of the convoy, the *Langstone Harbour* came round Tarifa Point in the daylight hours behind the ocean-going rescue tug

115

that had met her south of Cape St Vincent. Word had already been passed to Captain Horncape from the tug that he was not to enter the dockyard but was to continue through to Malta for discharge of his cargo. But as soon as he was round Tarifa into Gibraltar Bay he made his own signal to the shore-bound Admiral indicating that he had casualties aboard, men who needed urgent hospitalization and he proposed to lie off the mole in calmer water and await a launch from the dockyard.

The response was fast: within twenty minutes a Naval picquet-boat was on its way out between the arms of the breakwater, with a surgeon lieutenant in the sternsheets and four sick-berth attendants carrying Neil Robertson stretchers. Some fifteen minutes after that the two injured men, strapped into the stretchers, had been carefully carried down the accommodation ladder into the picquet-boat on their way to the military hospital, where naval as well as military personnel were admitted. The naval doctor had shaken his head over the loss, as now reported to him, of the surgeon lieutenant from the *Hindu*. Horncape asked him the question direct: had he, Horncape, done the right thing in asking for a doctor to be sent across in such dangerous conditions?

'Well, it was the destroyer's responsibility. They could have refused.'

'That wasn't quite what I asked, doctor. I'm sure you understand.'

The surgeon lieutenant nodded. The two casualties had in the event lived without the attentions of the doctor from the *Hindu*. But whatever the Board of Trade had to say about it, masters of ships were not medics and it was right enough to err on the side of safety. And why add to Horncape's worries? He was no longer young and had worries enough when commanding a ship without viable engines, bound through to the Sicilian Narrows and Malta, along one of the war's most dangerous waterways. The surgeon lieutenant said, 'Yes, I'd say you were quite right, sir.'

'A doctor *would* have made a difference?'

'I think so, yes. The prognosis . . . they've got here all right, but with medical care en route – well, they'd have had a better chance on hospitalization.'

Horncape was much relieved. The *Hindu*'s doctor had been on his conscience ever since the breeches buoy had gone for a bur-

116

ton; to have to live with the thought that his death had been totally unnecessary would have been to spend the rest of his life in a kind of hell. From his bridge wing, Horncape watched the picquet-boat making across the bay and in through the break-water, its bowman and sternsheetsman standing smartly fore and aft with their boathooks, their white uniforms standing out in the early sunlight creeping over the Rock of Gibraltar. As once again the tow was resumed behind the rescue tug that would take him all the way to Malta, with the destroyer escort standing by to act as their sole defence, Captain Horncape heard the bugles from the one remaining capital ship in the dockyard, heard the beat of drums and the resonance of the brass as the band of the Royal Marines played for Colours and the White Ensign rose slowly up the ensign staff on the quarterdeck. God save the King. A mist came to Horncape's eyes as his ship moved towards Europa Point: all over the Empire, or such of it as was still free of the enemy, similar ceremonies would be taking place aboard the ships in port. But it would be a long time before such sounds were heard again in Hong Kong and in Singapore and if things con-tinued to go badly in the Mediterranean, then the bugles, the drums and the brass might yet be silent in Gibraltar and Malta as well. As regards the latter, the old *Langstone Harbour* might bring some temporary succour, help to keep the flag flying over the brave little island a little longer.

Captain Horncape would use every endeavour to reach the Grand Harbour.

iii

Dr O'Dwyer's whisky-laden thoughts went back across the years and he grew maudlin. Once he had been a keen young medico; that had been before the last war, when Edward VII had been on the throne and life had been gay and full of promise. On qualify-ing from his medical school, a London hospital, he had gone straight into practice as assistant to two elderly partners in the East End of London. The prospects had been quite good: one if not both the partners would be retiring in the not too distant future and even though the practice was not a lucrative one, young Dr O'Dwyer would at least be senior partner quite quickly.

They had been days of hard work, with not much pay as an assistant although he got free board and lodging in the senior partner's house. Dr O'Dwyer had done his rounds on foot or by the omnibus, carrying his black bag and an air of importance with him. Always by the end of a long day he was very tired. The senior partner's house had been a dreary place, he remembered, the senior partner's wife a frugal one and something of a drudge, as dreary as the house, a taker of messages for the partners, mistress of just one general living-in servant who seemed never to keep the rooms properly dusted and was a poor cook. There had been a daughter so negative that Dr O'Dwyer could not now recall her name. She was in her thirties and unmarried and of a consumptive appearance and she sat around the house all day doing nothing to help her mother. She had seemed to resent the young O'Dwyer, who was a vigorous young man and well set-up, popular with the young women upon whom from time to time he attended and whom he most studiously avoided at all other times, having taken to heart the warning of the senior partner at his first interview.

'No hanky-panky, O'Dwyer. You know what young women are.'

'Oh yes, sir, indeed – '

'Your medical school will have impressed that upon you, naturally. Let me impress it further.' The old man had leaned forward in his chair and with a shaking hand had tapped O'Dwyer on the knee. 'One word – *one word* – out of place and you'll be in trouble. So many of them are like that – troublemakers, you see. Never allow them an opportunity. Never carry out an examination without a chaperon, a mother, a sister, an aunt. Even then, if they're so minded, they can make accusations of impropriety. Lies, you see. Often their presence is worse, if they care to lie.'

'So what does one do, sir?'

'You use your brain, O'Dwyer. You sum them up. I shall give you a list of those to beware of – they're best avoided. Tell them to go to the hospital – never examine them. Once the undergarments are off, you're in danger. A doctor's life's a minefield, O'Dwyer, and you must bear that in mind at all times. You can be brought before the General Medical Council at the drop of a hat – and should your name be struck off, your career's at an end.'

O'Dwyer had heard all this before; but having the points made by a practitioner actually in the field as it were impressed him deeply. He had best have a care; and he did. He kept examinations of females to a safe minimum, thus learning little of the female form during his early medical experience. Pregnancies and suspected pregnancies were referred to one or other of the partners. There were, of course, other women, those who were not patients, and these had been encountered mainly in public houses where Dr O'Dwyer was wont to relax after the day's work and before reporting back to the discomforts of the senior partner's house.

These meetings were not long in being brought to the senior partner's attention: spies abounded, it seemed, and a doctor was to some extent a local public figure.

'Don't do it, O'Dwyer. Too risky, man! Contain yourself for heaven's sake, we simply can't risk the practice being brought into disrepute – '

'But they're not patients, doctor – '

'Ah!' An admonitory finger was raised. 'Not patients *now*, I agree. But suppose they become so? Where will you be then, may I ask?'

Once again young O'Dwyer had taken the good advice. Too weary at the day's end to go far afield to where the inhabitants were outside the practice boundaries, he had taken to smuggling the odd bottle of gin into his room. He grew in upon himself, depressed, overtired, underfed. And the partners didn't die. O'Dwyer, the perennial assistant, sought other practices but without success. When the war had come along in 1914 his country needed him and he joined the RAMC with a feeling of great relief. In France there were women who would not be patients, and there was wine. There were also guns and mortars and German soldiers with rifles and bayonets ... Captain O'Dwyer was caught up in the first battle of the Somme.

He left his field ambulance and ran from the distant sound of the German machine-guns.

Then the heavens opened on him. They didn't shoot doctors for cowardice, he discovered, although he was in fact threatened with the firing squad and spent weeks in dreadful anticipation. He was cashiered, discharged with ignomiry, back to civilian life in the middle of a great war. By this time he was ill, his nerve

119

shattered, and he had taken to drink, much more than the odd bottle of gin. Even so, doctors were scarce now, and he found a practice in a town, a manufacturing town in the West Riding of Yorkshire where they were not too fussy. He disguised his past by making out he'd been unfit for military service following a long illness during which he had been unemployed. He did his work reasonably well and was never too drunk to hold a surgery or make visits: he had learned how to hold his drink and not let it be seen. But there came the time when he forgot the good advice tendered by the old doctor in London's East End, and the sudden yielding to desire was due to the drink. It was not the drop of a hat that almost brought him before the General Medical Council; it was the drop of a knicker. He would never have got away with it had not his new senior partner, for the sake of the practice, compromised his soul by a lie that he too had been present at the examination, and had threatened the girl concerned with the courts for trying it on. But Dr O'Dwyer was given the sack. Thereafter he had developed a hang-up about women and their dangers. Drink was safer. When the war was over, Dr O'Dwyer did the sensible thing: he became a ship's surgeon. Drink at sea was both cheap and plentiful: after deduction of his percentage as a ship's officer, a bottle of gin or whisky cost him three shillings and sixpence. The duties were not onerous. Ship's crews were mostly very healthy, so were the passengers in the liners: really sick people didn't travel. Also it was lucrative: a good salary and in addition he was able to charge fees for cabin visits when passengers were seasick, or constipated, or suffered from diarrhoea after passage of the Suez Canal for instance. On top of that was the free first-class accommodation, the excellent meals and the services of a personal steward, and two nursing sisters in the sick bay who did most of the doctor's work for him. So the habit of drink had grown, with so much time on his hands.

Now, aboard the *Wolf Rock* passing to the east of Gibraltar towards the Sicilian Narrows and the German dive bombers Dr O'Dwyer reached out once again for the whisky bottle. His hand shook and some was spilled: no matter, it was still cheap enough. Dr O'Dwyer gave a hiccup and then heard the tap on his cabin doorpost.

'Come in,' he said hoarsely.

The curtain parted. It was First Officer Forrest.

'Good morning, Miss Forrest.'

'Good morning, doctor.' She looked at him critically. He was dressed in white shirt and trousers, no jacket, and the shirt was dirty, the collar rumpled, the tie askew. She saw the bottle of whisky, not much left in it, and the refilled glass. She said, 'I've come about Mrs Pawle again.'

'Yes, I see. It's not ... not my fault she wasn't landed in Gibraltar.'

'I know that, doctor. I'm not blaming you for that. But she's still your patient and I don't believe she's doing very well.'

'The wound's clean.'

'Yes,' she said. She felt inclined to say, how do you know, you've scarcely looked at the girl. 'My girls have done that for her, washing and bandaging. It's the morphine I'm worried about – oh, I know the pain has to be dealt with, but surely there's a limit to the number of injections you can give? Surely there's some alternative, isn't there?'

'Aspirin,' he said half-heartedly.

'Aspirin! The stuff you take for a hangover. Really, I – '

'No, no, no. Aspirin is an analgesic, you know. It can be a help.' O'Dwyer stirred himself, sat a little straighter in his chair. Miss Forrest was quite attractive and she was asking his help. She was depending upon him. She had, he saw, a very good figure for a woman of her uncertain age. His gaze became a trifle fixed in the region of her breasts. 'I'm not at all sure Mrs Pawle isn't malingering a little – '

'Malingering! A leg – '

'Yes, yes, I know. Terrible for her, of course. And I'm sure the pain's been real enough, at any rate earlier on. But it should have eased by now, you see. I'm not sure her trouble's not psychological. To some extent, that is. I know her history, of course. Very tragic, the loss of her husband. And you say the wound's clean ... there's no – no – '

'Suppuration.'

'Yes, suppuration. No gangrene. Quite clean. But the loss of the husband is causing ... or may be causing ... ' O'Dwyer's voice trailed away. Jean Forrest believed he was rambling a little and his gaze was becoming more fixed. There was something like a leer.

She said sharply, 'May I ask what you're looking at, Dr O'Dwyer?'

'What? Oh – nothing, really.'

'Then kindly look somewhere else.'

'Most certainly, yes.' The eyes turned away, a hand reached for the glass. Some of the liquid trickled down the doctor's chin. He wiped it away with the back of his hand. 'I'm sure you need not worry about the patient. We'll get her up as soon as the weather's better, get her on deck in the fresh air. I believe that'll help, both mentally and physically. In the meantime, we'll stop the injections and try aspirin. At least it's worth a try . . . '

He dropped his glass. He bent to pick it up. When he straightened, Jean Forrest had gone.

iv

Kemp studied the chart with Captain Champney and Chief Officer Harrison, their attention on Sardinia. Finnegan was looking over their shoulders. 'Cape Spartivento,' Kemp said. 'We'll bring it due north at dusk tomorrow – right, Captain?'

Champney nodded. 'If the convoy maintains its speed, yes.'

'It will.'

'So dusk tomorrow – '

'Is when we must expect attack. Though it could come before, of course. The weather's moderating . . . lucky for the enemy, is that! Not for us. Finnegan?'

'Sir?'

'Have you the latest forecast?'

'Yes, sir. I was going to report . . . wind decreasing, expected to be no more than light airs by dawn.' Finnegan added, 'The barometer's rising already. So's the temperature.'

'Yes.' Kemp yawned, stood back from the chart and stretched. They were all in white uniforms now, the Dress of the Day signal having come from the Flag to the escorts, repeated Commodore for information, at 0800 that morning despite the fact that at that time the weather had still been bad. The Naval mind was rigid where dress was concerned. East of Gibraltar, between certain dates of the year, Naval personnel shifted into whites. All the officers' caps now bore white cap-covers. Kemp asked, 'How's the gunnery practice going, Finnegan?'

'Ramm's keeping 'em up to it,' Finnegan said, and grinned.

Ramm was being a bastard, and Finnegan reckoned he knew some of the reason: Ramm was suffering frustration. Finnegan had noted the way the gunner's mate looked at Wren Smith whenever she came into his line of sight, all randy. For her part Finnegan didn't believe she was interested; she had better game, and the name of the game was Peter Harrison. Not much escaped Sub-Lieutenant Finnegan. And he believed Wren Smith was doing the ship some good via her effect on Petty Officer Ramm: the more he took his frustrations out on the guns' crews, the more shit-hot they were likely to be in their handling of the guns, and the safer might be the *Wolf Rock*.

Maybe.

'Any special orders, sir?' Finnegan asked.

'Just one for now,' Kemp said. 'A signal, to all merchant ships from Commodore: we are now twenty-four hours off Cape Spartivento. Extra lookouts should be posted from now and all guns' crews warned to be ready for action with instant response required. When attack comes all Masters must remember that no ship should stop or reduce speed to pick up survivors. Speed and the cohesion of the convoy are vital. All right, Finnegan?'

'If you say so, sir.'

Kemp lifted an eyebrow and his face hardened. 'Just what is that supposed to mean, Finnegan?'

'Why, sir, just that the bit about not picking up survivors kind of gets me. That's all.'

'You'll keep your opinions to yourself, Finnegan.'

'Yes, sir.' Finnegan tore off one of his curious salutes, right forearm brought across his body horizontally with the hand vertical in front of his nose ... Kemp held onto his temper. The customs of the United States were often maddening to a middle-aged, dyed-in-the-wool British convoy commodore. But America was by this time indispensable to the war effort and had they not joined in after Pearl Harbor the end might well have come for Britain. Men, ships, tanks, munitions, aircraft, the United States supply line had been magnificent. Finnegan was all right, too; he was simply young, something that the years ahead would rectify. Feeling unusually huffy Kemp left the chart room and walked out to the bridge wing where Yeoman Lambert was sending his signal by blue-shaded lamp to the merchant ships in company, all of them moving more steadily than before and keeping very good formation, as Kemp was glad to see.

123

After an all-round look through encroaching darkness Kemp went below meaning to go to his cabin to snatch an hour or two's sleep. But he by-passed his cabin and made his way out on deck for a word with the 6-inch gun's crew aft of the now tarpaulin-covered wreckage of the deckhouse over the engineers' accommodation.

In the after well-deck he encountered the PO Wren. She stood smartly at attention and he shook his head at her.

'No need for formality, Miss Hardisty.'

'Oh – no, sir.' She was confused, flattered that the Commodore not only remembered her name but addressed her as though she were an officer. 'I mean yes, sir. I'm sorry, sir.'

He smiled, stood before her with his arms behind his back. PO Wren Hardisty thought he looked quite magnificent with his square, weathered face and solid figure, and the broad gold bands of rank on his shoulder-straps. 'What's the news of Mrs Pawle?'

'Oh, she's poorly, sir, still very distressed. It's only natural, I know that, but it worries me to see her.'

'You've all rallied round, I'm told. You've all helped her a lot.'

'Well, we've done what we could, sir, not that it's much, poor young lady. What's going to happen to her if we get hit, the good Lord alone knows, and – '

Kemp said, 'Don't worry about that, Miss Hardisty. She'll be a first priority I promise you. And don't forget, we have a strong escort – the more so now Force H is with us. We're going to come through, never doubt it.'

'Oh, I don't, sir, not really.' Rose Hardisty stiffened herself, brought her shoulders back, a PO Wren four-square to anything the combined machinations of Hitler and Mussolini could throw at her. She remembered her late father, the chief stoker who had served under Admiral Beatty and had been at the battle of Jutland in Beattie's flagship, HMS *Lion*, a great battle-cruiser. She remembered the yarns he used to spin about that war, all the dangers he'd faced, and faced them bravely without a doubt. Then she remembered something else, something she'd heard whispered about Wren Smith and her carryings-on. It was not the province of a PO Wren to speak directly to the Convoy Commodore, she knew that, it ought to go through First Officer Forrest in the proper service manner, but Commodore Kemp was talking to

124

her and he seemed kindly and it might be a good opportunity, one that might not recur. So, impetuously and with good intent, she indulged in indiscretion. She said, 'There is another worry, sir. That Wren Smith. She – '

'That's been gone into already, Miss Hardisty. There's no more I can do about it.'

She rushed on. 'Not about landing the girl, no, sir, I realize that – not until Port Said anyway. But I believe she's been carrying on with that Mr Harrison and – '

'Indeed.' Kemp's tone was frosty.

'So I understand, sir, and – '

'Hearsay, Miss Hardisty. And don't bring the galley wireless to *me*. At this moment I do not propose to concern myself with the morals of your young women and the ship's Chief Officer. If they wish to – ' Kemp broke off: he was furiously angry and the less he said the better. He strode away, his face formidable in the gathering gloom of the Mediterranean nightfall, cursing beneath his breath, cursing predatory ship's officers and eager young women. It had been one thing aboard a liner in peacetime; it was quite another aboard the Commodore's ship in a troop convoy moving towards what would almost certainly be bloody action with much loss of life. And the PO Wren had had no damn business to bring it to his attention in such a manner: something a male petty officer would never dream of doing. There were the proper avenues; but probably it was hard to impress the proper avenues on Wrens. Nevertheless the attempt should be made. He would have a word in due course with First Officer Forrest. Currently there were more important things to think about.

Rose Hardisty watched him go, blaming herself for her stupid temerity. He had been provoked, she believed, almost into uttering the forbidden word, the word that Petty Officer Ramm and many of the other men used with such abandon. That wouldn't be at all like Commodore Kemp in the normal way. Rose Hardisty felt her face flush a deep red and she turned and went for'ard towards the midship superstructure and then down a hatch towards where the Wren ratings had been re-berthed from the engineers' accommodation. Just like a male PO, she could relieve her feelings by finding fault with the junior ratings even where no fault existed. What else was the point in being a petty officer and taking all the responsibility for your subordinates, the buffer

125

between the commissioned officers and the rest? Rose Hardisty knew that the embarked naval ratings, as well as many of her own brood, regarded her as an interfering old bag, fat and forty and never had a man – that rankled still and would go on rankling – and there were times when she decided to live the part. This was one of them. And if Wren Smith was wise she'd stand clear of any more provocation, button up her pinny and keep it buttoned.

PO Wren Hardisty's current intentions came to nothing when from the *Wolf Rock*'s bridge Yeoman Lambert reported a shaded blue signal lamp flashing from the *Nelson*, after which things moved swiftly towards a lurid red hell.

TWELVE

'Aircraft reported, sir, coming in ahead. Flag's increasing speed, sir.'

'Finnegan!'

'Here, sir.'

'Get down to Mrs Pawle's cabin – she's going to be your responsibility in action.'

'But I'm needed – '

'Do as you're told, Finnegan. Ramm's perfectly capable of taking charge of the guns.' Kemp turned to Captain Champney, who had already sounded the action alarm. 'As much speed as you can muster, please, Captain. Yeoman, make to the convoy, am increasing speed to maximum. Act independently to avoid imminent attack by aircraft but keep within the overall escort pattern.'

'Aye, aye, sir.' Lambert hurried to his signalling projector thinking the bastards had turned up a lot earlier than expected, maybe because of the improving weather allowing them to get off their Sardinia-based airfields. In the moment of coming danger Lambert, as always in this perishing war, found his thoughts turning homeward to Pompey and the wife. If she could see him now . . . but just as well she couldn't. She'd bust a gasket with worry; she had always worried about him when he was out of her sight, even when he went to post a letter and might get mown down by a Corporation bus or something. Doris should never have married a sailor, not really she shouldn't, but Lambert didn't know what he'd have done without her. Or what she would do without him if anything happened on this or any future convoy – and never mind that unfortunate discovery on his recent leave. The war seemed to stretch away into his future, no let-up, no peace ever again, world without end.

Below in the engine-room Chief Engineer Turnberry wasn't worrying about the shore and things or people left behind: his mind was filled with his engines, as were his ears. The racket was horrific as more oil fuel was fed into the furnaces and the single shaft turned faster to thrust the *Wolf Rock* on and help to keep her safe from the coming attack. The engines would stand so much and no more, which was a fact of sea life that no deck officer seemed ever to appreciate.

Champney had rung down personally: 'Flag's just reported surface vessels as well as aircraft. I'll want all you've got, Chief, and then some more.'

'She'll not take it for long, Captain.'

'For long enough, she will.'

'How long's long enough, for – '

'You've had your orders, Mr Turnberry.' Champney had slammed back the voice-pipe cover: there was to be no argument. Turnberry cursed but carried on, grinning to himself after a moment. The Old Man knew he, Turnberry, always argued the toss, stood up for his engines, which he regarded as human, and knew, too, that there was usually an element of exaggeration in what Turnberry said. Yet there was truth in it: engines were not made to withstand speeds over the statutory maximum other than in short bursts. And they didn't want a buggered-up engine. At the same time they didn't want to take a bomb. Or a projy from the Italian Navy.

Turnberry watched the revolution counter: just a few more and then that was it. Never mind the orders, he wouldn't go beyond what he considered the danger point.

He stood on the starting platform, glances darting everywhere as the revolutions increased and greasers stood by, probing now and again with their long-necked oilcans, keeping all the bearings running sweetly. All in order.

But not for long.

ii

When the aircraft were heard overhead Rose Hardisty had already mustered her charges in what First Officer Forrest said was

128

the safest place, as safe as possible from bombs while at the same time as handy as possible for abandoning ship if they had to, a place decided upon by discussions between the Commodore, Captain Champney and Jean Forrest after the boat had become jammed: the alleyway outside the chief steward's cabin, one deck down beneath the deck officers' accommodation and with a hatch handy for an exit to the upper deck. They were mustered here when the first wave of dive bombers came in and there was a near miss on the port side of the *Wolf Rock*, a little aft of the engine-room. Below, Chief Engineer Turnberry was thrown violently from the starting platform as the ship lurched to starboard. The noise of the close explosion had been terrifying, everything had started to judder and ring with the concussion, and Turnberry's first thought was that the ship's side and with it the engine-room bulkhead to port must surely have been breached.

But no: no water came in. Turnberry, picking himself up while his ears recovered from temporary deafness, believed that not even a seam had been sprung, which was quite a miracle in his view, or maybe the near miss hadn't been as near as it had felt and sounded. The voice-pipe from the bridge was whistling at him: the Captain again.

'All right below, Chief?'

'So far, yes – '

'No damage?'

Turnberry said, 'No damage in the engine-room. I'm going through to the boiler-room for a look-see, but I reckon all's well.'

'Report as necessary, Chief.' Champney replaced the voice-pipe cover. Turnberry clicked his tongue; no need to tell him to report as necessary, of course he would do so. He went through to the boiler-room and as he'd expected found everything in order. In the meantime his second engineer was carrying out a check round the double bottoms beneath the engine-room deck plating. More thuds came as Turnberry went back to the starting platform, more near misses but not quite so near as that last one. Second Engineer Guthrie came up from the double bottom, through the hatch, his overalls covered in oil and filth: the double bottoms were no nice picnic area.

'All right?' Turnberry asked in a shout over the engine racket.

'All right, Chief. No seepage that I could find.'

Turnberry nodded. His face had tightened up after that big

crump: it wasn't his first time under attack, far from it, but each time it grew worse. One day, a man's chances must run out. They said a cat had nine lives; maybe the same applied to human beings. Turnberry reckoned he'd had a good many of his nine if that was so. He remembered some of the Russian convoys, the long, hard slog through to Murmansk or Archangel with supplies for Joe Stalin, who'd never seemed particularly grateful for the risks run by British seamen, RN and merchant service, as they fought both the Jerries and the appalling winter weather when everything froze on deck – rigging, anchor gear, guns, the decks themselves like skating rinks, all under tons and tons of ice with the naval gunnery rates constantly chipping away at the armament to try to keep the barrels and breech blocks clear. Every time a sea had come over, it had seemed to freeze in the instant of hitting the deck. One thing about an engine-room: you kept warm whilst on watch. That was the only advantage – that, and the fact you were safe from shrapnel and shell splinters. That apart, engine-rooms were mantraps if anything happened. The tracery of steel ladders that ran up to the air-lock and the exit to the engineers' alleyway enforced a single-file track to the open air. And it was the chief engineer who by virtue of his position had to be the last out.

Turnberry often thought about that, having no wish to die. If he died now, it would be a very inconvenient time. Things were happening in his private life. Just before sailing from the Clyde his wife had gone into hospital for a serious operation, a hysterectomy. At best there would be a long convalescence. His daughter aged fifteen was on her own; no viable grandparents to help out – his wife's parents were dead as was his own father, and his mother was suffering from early senile dementia and had to be supported in a private nursing home that was costing the earth. A breadwinner lost at sea would be no help to anybody. And the buzz had it that Adolf and Musso were determined to stop this convoy getting through. Somewhere out there, Turnberry was convinced, there was something – a bomb, a torpedo, a shell – with his name clearly upon it.

In the meantime, Champney was flinging the *Wolf Rock* all over the show, turns to port and starboard under full helm, the engine-room seeming at times to turn turtle, but so far no alterations to the revs, the telegraph remaining on Full Ahead. Turn-

130

berry looked up at the clock behind the starting platform: five minutes since that first close shave, just five minutes that had felt like a lifetime.

Sub-lieutenant Finnegan, carrying out his orders to stand by Susan Pawle, looked down at the bunk. A girl with one leg made a different shape beneath the blanket from the normal in Finnegan's experience. He felt embarrassed, tried not to look, but found his eyes drawn to it. He tried to make reassuring conversation, though Susan appeared half doped and very drowsy.

'It's going to be okay, ma'am.'

'Yes.'

'I'm here to look after you. Commodore's orders, ma'am.'

'Thank you.' She stirred herself a little and tried to smile, but it didn't work out. 'I hate being a burden.'

'No burden, ma'am.' Finnegan looked across at Rose Hardisty who, having mustered her flock, had turned them over to First Officer Forrest and come to be with Susan Pawle, resuming her old one-time role as nanny. She had got to her feet when the Commodore's assistant had come into the cabin, but he'd waved her back to her chair where she sat, Finnegan thought now, like a warder in a women's gaol, heavy-faced, stolid, all tits and bum. 'I don't want to be in the way, ma'am – '

'Oh, you're not, sir, and please don't you call me ma'am, just PO, sir.'

'Like Petty Officer Ramm?'

'Yes,' she said. 'And do talk to the young lady, sir, and cheer her up, she can do with a young gentleman's company.'

Finnegan grinned and said, 'Why, okay then.' He racked his brains, trying to think up something that wouldn't be trite or flippant. Half his mind was on events up top; the sound of the dive bombers could be heard clearly, the scream of aircraft engines at full throttle, the rattle of the close-range weapons and the loud crack of the 6-inch as Petty Officer Ramm did his best to keep the Jerries away with his bursting shrapnel.

He looked down again at the girl. Her eyes were wide, and they were very blue, a deep blue that could for all Finnegan knew be

131

Irish. Her mouth was trembling and the long, dark lashes below the blue eyes were wet with tears. He felt immensely sorry for her. He said awkwardly, 'Mind if I sit beside you, ma'am?'

'No. And my name's Susan,' she said.

'Okay, ma'am, Susan.' He sat on the bunk, close up against the single leg, his rump uncomfortable on the bunk board. 'Mine's Frank. Frank B. Finnegan from the good old USA.'

She asked which state.

'Montana,' he said. 'Cow country. Far from the sea. Too far. I've always dreamed of going to sea. Used to go over to Frisco, watch the ships. Dad, he spends his life in the saddle. You like horse riding, that's the place.' He came to a stop, red in the face. He'd been talking just for the sake of it, trying to do as Rose Hardisty had suggested – cheer her up. But you didn't cheer a one-legged girl by talking tactlessly about horse riding. He tried, clumsily, to cover up. 'I mean, well, you don't have to ride, not if – '

'All right,' she broke in. 'Don't bother. I'll get used to it. I never wanted to ride anyway.' Again she tried to smile and he met the attempt with a friendly grin.

'Guess I'll keep my big mouth shut,' he said. 'I've often been told it's too goddam big for my own good. By Commodore Kemp among others. But I guess he's gotten used to me now, we get along fine. He's a great guy.' He grinned again and added, 'Mostly.'

'Why has he sent you here?' she asked directly.

He said, 'Why, I told you ... Susan. To look after you.'

'You mean see that I'm taken to a boat if – if anything happens.'

'Well, maybe, yes, but nothing's going to happen. We have a darn big escort, and now we have Force H as well, out of Gibraltar. Plenty of destroyers as well as the big stuff. Any Eyetie submarines, they're going to be depth-charged to hell and back again, ma'am, take my word for – ' Finnegan broke off; he could have killed himself, felt the furious vibrations coming from Rose Hardisty, heard the PO Wren's sharp intake of breath. How could he have done it? He'd heard the girl's history, the submarine that had failed to return. He muttered, 'Jeepers creepers. Gosh, I'm darn sorry. Said I had a big mouth ...'

'It's all right,' Susan said bleakly. He saw that her lips were trembling. He'd brought it all back. 'I've got to get used to it. The war's going to go on, and I'm going to hear people – talk like that. I'm going to hear it on the news broadcasts and read about it in the papers.'

He said nothing; just sat there, Rose Hardisty's gaze on him as though he was something nasty brought in by the cat.

Susan Pawle said in a sudden and surprisingly harsh voice, 'I want to talk about it. No-one has. They won't. They keep off it. And I do want to talk about it. Do you mind?'

'Of course I don't mind,' he said gently. 'You talk all you want, ma'am, Susan.'

She talked, as outside the attack continued and every now and again the *Wolf Rock* shook like a dog coming out of the water, her plates reverberating to the shock waves of bombs and depth charges as the German aircraft came in again and again and the destroyers went into their attacks on the Italian submarines that had prowled out from Cagliari. She spoke of Rothesay on the Isle of Bute, of drinks in the lounge bar of the Victoria Hotel, of the Wrennery established in a requisitioned house named Tigh-na-Mara on the shore of Rothesay Bay, of those parties in the ward-room of the *Cyclops*, the depot ship; of long walks around the island, of expeditions up the Kyles of Bute or across Inchmarnock Water to Arran and the little town of Lamlash beneath Goat Fell. She spoke of boat trips up to Lochgilphead and along Loch Fyne to Inverary, of Mediterranean-blue water washing the shore beneath the great, historic pile of Inverary Castle, seat of the Dukes of Argyll, chiefs of Clan Campbell ... and with all this her memories of Johnny Pawle came out, and Finnegan formed a vivid mental image of a tall, goodlooking, fresh-faced lieutenant RNR, Kemp's own service, who had come from the Union Castle Line into the wartime Navy, and had gone on that last patrol with a smile and a kiss and a promise of many, many more rambles in the future and when the war was over a return to the Union Castle liners, sailing at set intervals for the Cape, with a cottage somewhere in the country near his home port of Southampton.

And she talked of the other, harsher things: she revealed her nightmares, her torments, her mind filled with underwater explosions, tearing pressure hulls, escaping fumes, flooding compartments, shattered bulkheads, men flung this way and that, the boat nose-diving to the bottom, the claustrophobia, the feeling of panic that must never be shown by the officers above all others, the deaths by being blown apart or from slow suffocation, the grisly corpses floating in their steel coffin until they became skeletons to last until the end of time. Johnny Pawle, lieutenant RNR with a lifetime ahead of him, just bare bone, moving to the scend and surge passing over the sea bed.

Finnegan listened, never interrupting. Rose Hardisty listened too; her Wrens, and Petty Officer Ramm, would perhaps have been astonished if they had seen her cheeks wet with tears.

iv

'Got the bugger!' Ramm said in a loud shout, a shout hoarse with a sense of localised victory. 'Well done, Stripey!'

Stripey Nelson, gunlayer on the 6-inch aft, reached behind his white anti-flash gear and wiped sweat from his face with a filthy handkerchief and tried to look modest. Of course, it had been sheer luck and he knew it, but he might as well make the most of it. He had caught the Stuka at the end of its dive and had pressed the tit at precisely the right moment and the Stuka had simply disintegrated, there one second, gone the next and its crew with it.

'Dead-eye Dick, that's me, GI,' he said. Ramm didn't respond, already the 6-inch was loaded again, a projy nicely up the spout. With the gun now elevated to its HA firing position, Stripey Nelson blasted away into the night sky, trusting to luck, more or less, that the resulting shrapnel bursts would bring down another Jerry. There was light all around as the anti-aircraft batteries of the cruisers and capital ships kept up a continuous fire. Stripey's namesake along with her sister battleship *Rodney* looked like the centre of a firework display as tracer from the close-range weapons spread in all directions and the gun-flashes from the heavy ack-ack lit sky and water in their vicinity. The cruisers, extended towards the surface ships, were in action of their own. The merchant vessels, doing their own dodging man-oeuvres as ordered by the Commodore, were all intact still. A bloody miracle, Stripey Nelson thought when he had a moment to look and think. There wasn't in fact much time and only a matter of moments later there was none at all: a Stuka came suddenly out of the darkness, falling like one of its own bombs.

Just before it came out of its dive slap above the stern of the *Wolf Rock*, its cannon opened, laid well and truly on Stripey Nelson's bulky figure, and Stripey died with a series of bullet holes running the length of his spine; as he died the six-inch itself and all the rest of its crew disintegrated as a cannon shell took the ready-use ammunition waiting in the racks to go into the breech. The Commodore's ship was racked with what sounded below decks like a gigantic explosion. To Chief Engineer Turnberry this was the one with his name on it, though it hadn't yet killed him personally. He had shouted the order for the engine-room personnel to get up the ladders when he was called by the bridge.

'Captain here, Chief. What's it like?'

'No damage here. What's it like up top, that's the bloody point?'

'A shambles on the upper deck aft but we're all right, no penetration of the after holds. Bosun's running out the fire hoses – I believe we'll last. Keep the speed up, Chief.'

Turnberry grunted irritably as he replaced the voice-pipe cover. Keep the speed up, indeed! After that last one speed was definitely his own first priority, just so long as the engines responded without protest. He sent the engine-room hands back to their posts.

On the bridge Kemp was joined by his assistant. Kemp said, 'You had certain orders, Finnegan.'

'Yes, sir. But when I heard – '

'Stay with her, sub. You can do nothing for the gun's crew now. We're short of a 6-inch – that's all. Mrs Pawle's – '

'That PO Wren can cope, sir. Tough as old boots.'

'Possibly. If necessary, you'll carry more authority. So go back to that girl. How's she taking the explosion?'

'Pretty badly, sir.'

'I'm not surprised,' Kemp said. Turning away from Finnegan, he looked astern. Matters had gone well for the convoy so far, less well for the escort. Three of the destroyers attached to Force H had been hit by the dive bombers; two had gone down, one was drifting with her after guns blown right out of their mountings and with a heavy list to starboard. She had signalled that her rudder was useless and one shaft was out of action. The Vice-Admiral commanding Force H could not at that moment spare a ship to take up a tow but a signal would be made to Gibraltar

135

asking for an ocean-going rescue tug to be sent with the utmost despatch. With the fleets engaged, there was no point in maintaining wireless silence and in the main transmitting rooms of the warships the Safe To Transmit boards were in position. Soon after the signal had gone to Gibraltar, there was a massive explosion on the port beam of the convoy and flames shot into the sky.

Lambert reported, 'Cruiser, sir.'

'Can you identify?' Kemp asked.

'Not yet, sir, but I don't reckon it's one of ours. Eyetie, sir. Not one I recognize any road.'

Within the next few minutes confirmation came from the *Nelson*, steaming majestically in the centre of the convoy, giving the vital troop transports the close protection of her batteries: an Italian cruiser had indeed blown up whilst being engaged by the 15-inch guns of the *Malaya*. Kemp caught Champney's eye and read the unspoken question: he nodded in reply and Champney flicked on the tannoy in the wheelhouse.

His voice boomed out along the decks and alleyways of the *Wolf Rock*. 'This is the Captain speaking. An Italian cruiser has just been sunk.'

There was cheering from the men on deck, with an extra one from Petty Officer Ramm. That, he said to himself, helped to even up the personal score, one Eyetie cruiser for Leading Seaman Stripey Nelson and the rest of the 6-inch crew. Currently, Ramm was supervising the clearing-up operation along the upper deck, along with the ship's bosun, Tod Ridgway. In fact, things were not too bad considering, as Ramm remarked.

'Could have done a lot more damage, Bose. Structurally, that is.' He looked around, not able to see much except when the nearer gun-flashes brought some light to the scene. There were human remains, legs and arms, and there was a stench of burned flesh. At one moment Ramm slipped on something greasy: a pool of blood. Tod Ridgway, reacting fast, saved him from a tumble over the side. The guardrail had been blown away in the explosion, and the sea yawned ready. Ramm said, 'Jesus Christ, eh! Near one, was that.' He knew well enough that the ship wouldn't have stopped to pick him up. He watched the hose parties still at work, making sure, although the fire after the explosion had been nipped smartly in the bud. With all the explosive cargo under hatches, there was a clear need to keep the decks cooled down. More than anything else, Ramm wanted a fag. When he saw that the bosun didn't need his further assistance, he made his way for'ard to the bridge, where the close-range weapons were keeping up their fire whenever a target came within their capacity. They were, Ramm thought sardonically, doing bugger-all good though you never knew what a lucky shot might do. He thought ahead, to after the action, if there was an after. There would be a scooping-up operation to do, if anything remained to be given some sort of sea burial. In point of fact, the hoses would already have disposed of most of the carnage.

As Ramm reached the bridge there seemed to come a lull in the general racket, a quietening of the guns. Kemp saw the PO's approach.

'Well, Petty Officer Ramm. Someone on the 6-inch did a good job.'

'Yessir. Leading Seaman Nelson, sir.'

'Casualties?'

Ramm said, 'No survivors, sir. All gone when the ammo went. Including Nelson.'

'He'll be mentioned in my report. For what good that'll do him.' Kemp brought up his binoculars and scanned the sea all around. 'I think they're pulling out. For now, anyway.' All the Seafire squadrons had been flown off from the *Indomitable* and the *Formidable* and appeared to have swung the action in favour of the convoy. The Stukas had had enough, and the heart had been taken out of the Italians by the loss of the cruiser and, as reported by Captain (D) within the next few minutes, the loss of no less than three of their submarines, sunk by the depth charges from the destroyer escort.

'A fair night's work,' Kemp said to Champney. With no losses to the convoy itself, it could be considered a kind of victory. But there was a long way to go yet. As the aircraft-carriers turned into the wind to begin the operation of landing on their squadrons, Kemp had a word with Captain Champney and then passed the order for the remnant of his guns' crews to stand down from first degree of readiness and resume cruising stations. Kemp himself remained on the bridge, head sunk into his arms folded on the rail of the fore screen. He was thinking about the casualties: all those men from the 6-inch. There would be letters to be written to the next-of-kin, a job that Kemp hated. No words of his could ever hope to compensate . . . the words, always in his own handwriting, must seem hollow. Killed in action . . . died for his country . . . they should be proud . . . never let his shipmates down, fighting to the last.

A load of guff? Only up to a point, for the words would be true enough. But sometimes Kemp doubted the sentiments behind them. War was a bastard, never did any good, just shifted the power balance for a few years after it was all over, and then you started preparing for the next time, so that more good men could die for their countries on both sides. The same throughout history, and no reason, really, why it should ever change.

Kemp was still on the bridge with Champney when the first light of the dawn stole over the eastern horizon, bringing the sun's rays peeping over a calm blue sea with a brilliance of colour, reds and greens and golds shot with orange. No enemy in sight: like a peacetime cruise had it not been for the twisted wreckage aft, the metal burned black, the wooden deck charred, and of course the casualties. And the great camouflaged shapes around the *Wolf Rock*, steaming now in the orderly rows of the convoy formation, the battleships as steady and as large as blocks of flats, their White Ensigns streaming in a light breeze added to by the wind made by their own passing, the St George's Cross of the Admiral flying from the *Nelson*'s foremast as a challenge bold and flaunting to those who would interrupt the convoy's passage through Mussolini's *mare nostrum*.

THIRTEEN

There was a knock at Jean Forrest's cabin door. 'Who is it?' she called. She was in her dressing-gown, meaning to go along to the bathroom set aside for the WRNS officers' use. Even with the weather warming up now, she kept her door shut, not trusting to the curtain.

'It's me, ma'am.'

'Oh. All right, PO, come in.'

Rose Hardisty entered. Jean asked, 'Is it important?'

'It's about Third Officer Pawle, ma'am.'

'Yes?'

'She's complaining of funny feelings, ma'am. In her leg. Pain, ma'am. The one that's off.'

'I believe that's quite usual, PO. There's a name for it. Sympathy pains, I'm not sure. It's nothing to worry about.'

'Yes, ma'am. I've heard it happens. But does it really? I mean –'

Jean Forrest gave a short laugh. 'It certainly doesn't mean Mrs Pawle's hallucinating or anything like that. There's nothing mental in it – not in that sense anyway. It can go on a long time, I think.'

'Yes, ma'am. Well, I'm relieved to know that.' She still looked worried. 'It's that Dr O'Dwyer, you see. He's not up to it, not really he isn't. Though of course it's not for me to say. But there doesn't seem to be much use asking him anything. And though I shouldn't say this either, ma'am, he does smell of whisky most times.'

'A seafaring failing, Petty Officer Hardisty. If I were you, I wouldn't talk about it to anyone else, and –'

139

'Oh no, ma'am, no, I wouldn't ever dream of doing such.' Rose Hardisty looked shocked at the suggestion. 'Only to you, ma'am, feeling it my duty in a manner of speaking.' She paused. 'I remember when I was in service there was trouble about Barker, Barker being the butler, ma'am, and inclined – '

'Yes, all right, PO. Is there anything else?' Jean Forrest lifted her sponge-bag into a more prominent position, hoping the hint would be taken. There was a stickiness about sea air that urged her towards a bath.

'Just Third Officer Pawle, ma'am.'

'But you've already – '

'Yes, ma'am. But I was going to say, apart from those funny pains, she's better. In herself if you take my meaning, ma'am. Brighter like. I'm ever so glad to see it.'

'The depression lifting?'

Rose Hardisty nodded. 'That's it, ma'am, yes. And it's all that Mr Finnegan. The American,' she added in a somewhat wondering tone as though being American was something out of the ordinary. 'Commodore Kemp's – '

'Yes, I'm aware of Mr Finnegan, PO. What's he done?' There was just a hint of somewhat sardonic naughtiness in Jean Forrest's accompanying smile and PO Hardisty, recognizing it, flushed. It was, she thought, out of place, considering, though of course you never knew with Americans, who she understood were overpaid, over-sexed and over here.

She said, 'He hasn't done anything, ma'am. Just talked to her, that's all. He's just a gangling boy, really, ma'am, though I say it as perhaps shouldn't, but he does seem to understand. He drew her out . . . or not that, quite. I don't know if you follow. She said she *wanted* to talk to someone. To him, ma'am. That Mr Finnegan.'

'Uh-huh. Well, it's her way, perhaps, of coming to terms . . . it's very natural I think. Really we should have known.'

'Ma'am, I didn't think it – '

'All right, PO, I'm not blaming you, far from it. *I* should have known. It often helps, to talk. Talk things out.' Jean Forrest was thinking again about the Blenheim brigadier and her own need for a shoulder to cry on. Yes, she should have thought; in bereavement one's friends so often shied off the subject, mainly out of embarrassment but also, Jean fancied, from some notion that

140

they would be intruding, a notion that grief was a very private thing. That was fairly conventional these days although once it had not been the case at all, the bereaved had worn deepest black and had been encouraged to mourn, Queen Victoria having been perhaps the best known example of mourning widowhood. Conventional now to do the opposite, but not necessarily right. On the other hand, Susan definitely hadn't seemed to want to talk about anything, had in a sense been turning her face to the wall. Or bulkhead, now that they were at sea ... thinking of their current situation, Jean Forrest asked if the Wren draft was being kept occupied.

'So far as possible, ma'am. Physical training on the upper deck, but that has its problems, ma'am.'

'Such as?'

Rose Hardisty answered primly. 'That PO Ramm, ma'am. He has a funny look in his eyes sometimes.'

'Lecherous?'

'Yes, ma'am, I think so. He stands about and watches ... when they bend down mostly. But other times on deck too.'

'Sailors are like that, PO. I suggest you take a leaf out of the book of the usual run of men divisional officers and order something like a kit muster from time to time – that'll keep the girls busy and out of sight for a while.' Jean Forrest got to her feet, dismissingly. As Miss Hardisty turned to leave the cabin, the First Officer said, 'By the way, I believe Dr O'Dwyer means to get Mrs Pawle out of bed soon.'

'*Out of bed*, ma'am?' Rose Hardisty stared in disbelief. 'Why, that's – '

'It's the modern idea,' Jean Forrest said, slightly tongue in cheek since Dr O'Dwyer didn't seem the sort to keep up with modern trends even supposing he'd heard of them. 'Get them mobile. I expect there's something in it. But there aren't any crutches aboard the ship. She's going to need support. Something else to keep the girls occupied.'

She went off to her bath.

ii

Many hours steaming astern, the crippled *Langstone Harbour* came along behind the ocean-going rescue tugs. A warning had

141

come from Gibraltar that ahead of her track the main body of the convoy with Force H had come under combined German and Italian attack; and Captain Horncape had been expectant of action at any time after leaving Europa Point behind to the westward. The escorting destroyers, *Hindu* and *Burgoyne*, had gone to first degree of readiness, with all guns' crews closed up behind the gunshields, with the signal staff and Asdic cabinets fully alert to spot the enemy's approach, all lookouts scanning the sea's surface for the tell-tale feather that would indicate a submarine at periscope depth.

Captain Horncape remained on his bridge, dead tired, almost zombie-like, steadying himself against the ship's roll by wedging his body into a corner of the bridge wing. Every now and again he fell asleep standing up, coming to with a jerk and a guilty feeling after no more than a couple of seconds. Age, he decided, was catching up with him; the war had come along at a time when he was past his ability to go for long periods without sleep. There was a lack of energy, too. His mind drifted from the war, from the alarums and excursions of the sea, crossing the miles of ocean back to his home on the fringe of Southampton, back to Nesta his wife whom he loved dearly. Age had not dimmed her capacity to enjoy the delights of the bedroom, far from it; but so often, after coming home from sea, he had been tired, unromantic and not as eager as he ought to have been, which had explained the chief engineer from P. & O. among others. (It had rankled that he was an engineer, one of the black gang that were spoiling the sea's cleanness with their filthy smoke.) A couple of times a week was the most he could muster now and the more Nesta tried to nag him into further action, the less willing he became to have his much needed sleep interrupted.

Captain Horncape, detesting the onset of age, wished he were young again. All he could do now was to grow even older, each wartime day a little tireder than the day before, on and on to the inevitable conclusion of mankind, senility and doddery legs, full of niggling complaints and a mind that looked backwards rather than into a negative future.

Twenty-five years of marriage. Their silver wedding day would in fact be the very day the *Langstone Harbour* was due to enter the Grand Harbour of Valletta with her life-saving cargo. There had been no celebratory party in advance, before Horncape had sailed from the Tail o' the Bank: like most seamen, he was superstitious and the party would be held when one day he got back to UK. But on the day itself Nesta would be having a few friends in for such drinks and food as could be mustered in wartime, and he wished her well. His thoughts would be with her, but not too closely after bedtime.

During the early hours of next day the crow's-nest lookout reported a vessel coming up astern: this was identified as another ocean-going rescue tug, making to the east with a big bone in her teeth. As she passed the *Langstone Harbour* signals were exchanged, the matey chit-chat of the sea, no hard information. But as the day wore on there was another sighting, this time from ahead, and the crippled destroyer passed them Gibraltar-bound behind her tow and this time gave Horncape interesting and very satisfactory news of an action involving the convoy. The assault had been met and overcome and the convoy was intact, or had been when the destroyer had parted company.

'Luck's with us,' Horncape said to his acting chief officer. 'The way's been cleared for us, it seems.'

So far. After their mauling the Italians probably wouldn't mount another attack immediately on the heels of the last one. But there was still a long way to go to Malta and its half-starved garrison.

iii

'Kit musters,' Steward Botley reported to Petty Officer Ramm. 'For the Wrens, like.'

Ramm stared. 'Kit musters, eh. How do *you* know?'

Botley said, 'I have my ways and means, Mr Ramm.'

'Bloody bat-ears.'

'I s'pose that's one way of putting it, yes. Not my fault if some people 'ave loud voices, is it?'

'When's this caper going to take place, then?'

'I didn't establish that, Mr Ramm.'

'Listen out again, then. Bung your lug against the key'ole.' Ramm went on his way to his cabin, thinking about kit musters for Wrens. He'd never before associated kit musters with the female sector. It would be a real lark, would that! Everything laid out: bras, knickers, suspenders, petticoats, sanitary towels, pantie-girdles such as he'd seen on the counters of Marks and Spencers and the Landport Drapery Bazaar in Pompey. Things, some of them, that the missus didn't wear. French knickers, perhaps . . . but then he'd heard that the Wrens wore regulation knee-length bloomers, navy blue in colour. Taxi-cheaters, he believed they called them. Hard to get a hand under.

Ramm gave a sudden chuckle. Old Ma Hardisty would bust a gut if she found a french letter or one of those douches that his missus used. It would be worth his while finding some excuse or other to get in on the act, turn up unexpectedly when all the gear was laid out for inspection. Some lark!

A bloody shame Leading Seaman Nelson wouldn't be there to share the laugh with him. Old Stripey had had his drawbacks but now Ramm missed him more than he'd ever thought he would. In his shared cabin, which was fitted with a wash-hand cabinet, Petty Officer Ramm washed and shaved, staring intently at his stubble and his long, lined face, and then went up on deck for a tour of the ship's armament and a little chasing of the hands. When he emerged from the midship superstructure and looked down into the fore well-deck he stopped and stared and said, 'Lor' love a bloody duck!'

Third Officer Susan Pawle, on her one leg, was being led past Number Two hatch, making towards the break of the fo'c'sle, slowly and very hesitantly, between the ship's surgeon and the Commodore's assistant, that Finnegan. Ramm made a clicking sound with his tongue and shook his head from side to side. What a thing for a girl to have to go through life with. Or without, to be precise. It was a pathetic sight, Ramm thought. She was in a dressing-gown and underneath was a pyjama leg, just the one, like a stork asleep with its head tucked under its wing feathers. To add to the simile she had her head down, staring at the ground as she hopped along between her two supporters. When the small party turned about to come aft again, Ramm believed the girl was crying. Or had been: her face, pretty really, was a mess, all streaked. He saw that when she looked up and happened to catch his staring eye. Ramm's leathery face would have shown a flush if it had been capable of doing so. He looked away at once. Poor girl, he thought, being stared at like something in a circus.

He went down the ladder, into the well-deck and straight up to her. He saluted and said, 'Well done, ma'am, if I may say so. Glad to see you're better. Very glad I am.'

She smiled at him, a somewhat wobbly smile. 'Thank you, PO. I appreciate that.'

'You're welcome, ma'am. Anything you want, you just ask.'

She thanked him again; he gave another salute and marched away towards the fo'c'sle, very formal, doing his gunner's mate's left-right-left, boots banging the deck as he went. He was a little surprised at himself: the 'ma'am' had come out quite spontaneously and naturally and he reckoned it had been the first time in his life he'd ever called a woman ma'am. He'd never come up against any WRNS officers before, not to address personally. He wondered what his missus would think. What she would say. Greta had always been a bit of a bolshie, no time for class distinctions. She'd once been a skivvy in one of the private hotels in Southsea, along the sea front, places full of mouldering old colonels and their wives, the latter sitting round the lounges in a circle, like a lot of old trout. They had been very snooty towards Greta and she had seethed underneath. That had been before she'd become Mrs Percy Ramm, but she had never forgotten. One day, she'd said after war had broken out, there would be a big change. That would come with the peace; Socialism would take over and rub the noses of the nobs in the dirt. She couldn't wait for it. Ramm had not agreed. He was a basic conservative who knew where his own best interests lay. Petty Officers in HM Fleet were persons of importance, and once you started sodding up the hierarchy from the top, it wouldn't be long before you sodded it up all the way down. If people like Greta had their way, he could see himself ending up eating his meals in a broadside mess instead of the comparative dignity of the PO's mess.

Greta, eh.

His worries returned, the worries about the popsie in the Commercial Road pub. Women were funny, very unpredictable. He'd made the mistake of calling her a bitch that last time, when she'd said she'd followed him home. She might be brooding on that; she could have come to the conclusion, the correct one, that he had no intention of ever leaving his wife.

145

'Well, Finnegan. How's she making out?' Kemp had been watching discreetly, from the wheelhouse.

'Shaky, sir.'

'Of course. She's probably scared to death of lifting that one leg off the ground, never mind the support.'

'I reckon that's right, sir. She was shaking like a leaf.'

Kemp was scanning the convoy, feeling in his bones that the current peace couldn't possibly last. The Axis powers wouldn't be content with an abortive attack, the score was going to be evened up before much longer. Lowering his glasses he said, 'Miss Forrest told me you'd worked a minor miracle, Finnegan.'

'Me, sir?'

'Yes, you. Just by talking.'

'Listening, sir. There's a difference.'

'Yes, I appreciate that, Finnegan. The ready ear.' Kemp paused, then added, 'She's an attractive girl. No doubt she'll marry again one day.'

'One day maybe, sir. Not for a long while, I'd say.'

Kemp nodded thoughtfully. After a moment he said, 'That leg. The medicos can work miracles these days, I believe. Look at Group Captain Bader for instance. Two wooden legs, and still flies. It takes guts but it can be done. She'll be all right.'

'Well, I sure hope so,' Finnegan said with palpable sincerity and feeling. Then he grinned. 'Sir, I guess you sounded as if you were reassuring *me*, not Mrs Pawle herself. I – '

'I just happen to be talking to you, Finnegan, not to Mrs Pawle.'

'Why sure, sir, but – ' Finnegan broke off, still grinning. 'You're not matchmaking, by any chance, are you, sir?'

Kemp gave a gruff laugh, somewhat embarrassed. 'Good God, Finnegan, not with you at all events! Poor girl's got enough on her plate without that.'

Finnegan said solemnly, 'Sir, I guess that sounds unkind, really unkind. Maybe Wren Smith's more in my line.'

Kemp turned to face his assistant, his expression hardening. 'Not funny, Finnegan.'

'Sorry, sir.'

'That girl has problems too. So, by God, because of her, have I!'

Finnegan's face was expressionless as he said, 'They won't blame you for it, sir. You don't have to worry.'

Kemp glared, then relaxed. He said, 'Get out of my sight, young Finnegan, you're becoming offensive. Go and do something useful for a change. Work your charms on Miss Hardisty.' As the sub-lieutenant saluted and left the wheelhouse, Kemp reflected sardonically on young officers with his assistant particularly in mind. He was good at his job, and he was a young man of courage; had he not been, he wouldn't have joined in the war before his own country had become involved after Pearl Harbor. He was keen and reliable and painstaking in his duties, very conscientious. But with women? Kemp's memory took him back to his previous assistant, also of the RCNVR, also American. Young Cutler. . . . A young woman called – he remembered – Roz. In the Station Hotel at Oban, with a convoy forming up in the Firth of Lorne . . . he'd had to chivvy Cutler towards the drifter that was waiting to take them off to join the convoy. Roz had been a little tight and he'd heard her, clearly, refer to him, Kemp, as an old fuddy-duddy who was jealous because he was past it. It had been fairly obvious that she and Cutler had spent the previous night together. He recalled another in Cape Town, one whose name now escaped him, an admiral's daughter of the 'twin-set and mummy's pearls' variety whom he'd met with Cutler quite by chance, and he'd bought them a drink in a hotel. She'd been very charming, had made a pretence of being overcome at meeting a convoy commodore, and had uttered the classic comment that daddy always said the convoys were aw-'fully important. Kemp could still shudder at that. He recalled also that the family home was in what she called Bodders, which being interpreted was Bodmin in Cornwall.

There had been others, quite a number. All very natural for a young sub undergoing his first experiences of the sea life and all that went with it. To seamen, women always had loomed large: Kemp himself hadn't held back, though it had not been quite so free and easy when he'd been a young man. They didn't hop into bed quite so readily as now, they had mostly wanted at least a promise of marriage first, except of course for the scrubbers that were always plentiful in the world's ports. The one trouble with young Cutler had been that he couldn't help flirting – an old-fashioned word that made Kemp realize his own age – and Finnegan was in many ways a replica of Cutler. Young officers in wartime . . . Susan Pawle was very vulnerable to being led up the garden path. That could happen however recent the loss of her husband. There was a long way yet to go to Trincomalee and the final splitting-up of the convoy and she could come to rely on Finnegan if he cared to manipulate her heartstrings.

That must not be allowed to happen. Not that it was any of his business, of course, unless and until it interfered with the conduct of the convoy. But John Mason Kemp, who had two sons but not the daughter he and Mary had always wanted, felt himself thinking along fatherly lines towards a helpless girl who was at a very critical stage of her life.

He sighed and resumed his vigil, the eyestraining business of watching sea and sky for anything that might have escaped the lookouts or the probing antennae of the radar and the pings of the Asdics as they swept ceaselessly around the orderly lines of ships. He wondered how things were aboard the big transports, the ex-liners of peacetime days. There had been some exchange of signals between the Masters and the Commodore, mainly but not wholly concerned with the conduct of the convoy and the problems of station keeping. Reading between the lines of some of the strictly non-operational signals, Kemp had suspected the occasional disagreement with the army as represented by the OC Troops aboard each of the transports. These latter were mostly good fellows but the army could be difficult and was often stodgy, bound up with regimental codes and practices and whatnot. They seldom took very well to sea life, and to being under the command of the Master. The sea was to them a thing apart, an alien environment that rolled and pitched and caused even regimental sergeant-majors, and colonels, to be seasick at embarrassing moments. The strangeness could lead to friction at times. The soldiers, or anyway the officers and NCOs, chafed at inactivity and the lack of opportunity for exercise; and the break in the infantry training programme, the training that to be effective had to be continuous, was unwelcome, especially so when action lay ahead of them, most likely, quite soon after the disembarkation at Alexandria.

Kemp knew something of their orders: they would be backing up the Eighth Army, newly under the command of General Sir Bernard Montgomery, said to be an unconventional and pernickety officer. So far things had not gone well for the army in the western desert and Montgomery was to be the new broom. He had already started sweeping: a number of senior heads had fallen. Those troops out there, rolling gently in the blue water of the Mediterranean, would probably find themselves striking out across the Libyan sands, possibly towards Tobruk and its German garrison, almost as soon as they had disembarked.

If they reached Alexandria in the first place: Kemp believed now that the earlier attack on the convoy had been something of a feeler. The main weight of Mussolini's navy had not yet appeared from Taranto as expected. His feeling of unease had increased, was increasing faster as the convoy came nearer to Malta, nearer to the Sicilian Narrows that lay between Cape Granitola at the western tip of Sicily and Cape Bon in Tunisia.

Captain Champney came up the ladder to the bridge. He said, 'You've been a long while on deck, Commodore.'

Kemp shrugged. 'Can't be helped.' He grinned, a tired grimace. 'We've all been brought up to long vigils, Captain.'

'A couple of hours' sleep wouldn't come amiss. Why not take the chance while – ' Champney broke off as a lamp began flashing from the *Nelson*. It was the masthead lamp, making an all-round signal, to all escorts and merchantmen. Somehow, it had the appearance of urgency. The yeoman of signals began reading off the message. Half a minute later he reported, his voice breaking the fraught silence between Commodore and Master.

'From the Flag, sir, addressed all ships. Prepare for action against main body of Italian Fleet observed by our reconnaissance aircraft thirteen miles ahead and closing at maximum speed estimated twenty-seven knots. Message ends, sir.'

'Thank you, Yeoman. Acknowledge.'

'Aye, aye, sir.'

Lambert turned away to his signalling projector. Kemp did the sum in his head. He said to Champney, 'Twenty-seven knots, speed of convoy fifteen, closing speed forty-two knots. What do you make it, Champney?'

'Fifteen minutes. Then we'll be inside their range.'

Kemp nodded. 'Action stations, if you please, Captain!'

His face grim, Champney went into the wheelhouse and pressed the alarm. As the rattlers sounded throughout the ship, more signals came from the Flag. So far no submarines had been picked up by the Asdics – they might yet come, but for now the threat was the heavy Italian ships, the battleships and cruisers, and very likely more Stukas from the German airfields in Sicily. The heavy ships of the escort – *Nelson*, *Rodney* and *Malaya* together with the cruisers plus the three aircraft-carriers astern of them – would form the line to lie between the enemy and the convoy. The destroyers would remain with the convoy which was to come under the sole and direct orders of the Commodore responsible for its safety.

Kemp passed his immediate orders to all merchant ships: *Convoy will scatter*.

FOURTEEN

'Buggeration,' Petty Officer Ramm said in some annoyance: he had been foiled by the action alarm. Miss Hardisty had taken Jean Forrest at her word and had lost no time in ordering a full kit muster by all Wren ratings. Their kit, smalls and all, was to be laid out neatly in rows with the owners standing beside their property, the muster being held in the alleyway outside the chief steward's cabin. Petty Officer Ramm would contrive a passing visit. Or would have done if it hadn't been for Musso.

The Wrens had started straggling along carrying their armfuls of gear when the alarm had sounded. There was then total confusion as the word came from First Officer Forrest to get the girls into their action quarters. A good deal was dropped and taken on deck by an unkind draught of wind whistling through from a hatch. Knickers, navy pattern, flew into the air accompanied by bras and other things. PO Wren Hardisty, purple in the face with embarrassment as she saw Ramm looking, a grin on his face, before he went off at the double towards his guns, ran about in an attempt at salvage until a shout from the Commodore on the bridge told her to get below immediately.

'Never mind the undies, Miss Hardisty. Life's more important than girdles!'

'Yes, sir.'

Miss Hardisty fled, a large bottom wobbling. Petty Officer Ramm, from his position now by the close-range weapons on monkey's island, caught a glimpse of a stocking hanging from a stanchion. What a bloody lark, he thought, it beat the old Coliseum in Edinburgh Road in Pompey by a mile. Wrens . . . and not a chastity belt among the lot.

One more signal came from the Flag as the Commodore watched his charges scatter on their separate courses: *action imminent*. As Lambert made his report to Kemp the telephone from the crow's-nest burred and Captain Champney answered.

He said, 'Ships in sight ahead, hull down.'

'Thank you, Captain. Are we up to full speed now?'

'Yes.'

'I'll be doing a good deal of manoeuvring. Helm, not engines. Though frankly there's not a hell of a lot of point unless we come under attack from the dive bombers. You can't predict the fall of shot from surface vessels.'

'Speed the best protection,' Champney said.

'That's it. Just bugger off, to be frank! Sounds cowardly, but it's prudent.'

Champney nodded. He, like Kemp, was thinking of the packed troop transports now on their westerly courses to head them away from the heavy batteries of the Italian battleships. The Flag had signalled that the attack was believed to include the *Giulio Cesare* carrying ten 12.6-inch guns and the almost new *Vittorio Veneto* of 35,000 tons with 15-inch batteries, plus an as yet unknown number of heavy cruisers of the First Division of the Italian fleet. The heavy gun-batteries could cause havoc among the transports. Captain Champney had never served aboard liners, but he had enough imagination to appreciate the horrific scenes that could result from a hit on a big troopship crammed to the gunwhales with soldiers out of their element. Officers and NCOs who had only just about learned port from starboard, fires starting, electrics thrown off the beam, darkness along the troop-decks and alleyways adding to the confusion. Those troopships were vastly overcrowded, something like five thousand brown jobs each where in peacetime they would have carried around fifteen hundred passengers at the most. True, soldiers were a disciplined bunch but even military discipline could crack when the floating world that contained it was basically unfamiliar. A badly listing ship, with the water rising to one side until it lapped the lower promenade decks, the troopdecks starting to flood if the heavy shells had fractured the watertight doors or blown holes in the side plating, and a rush of men desperate to claw their way up to the open air ... Captain Champney was glad enough to be where he was.

'*Opened fire, sir!*' This was a shout from Lambert, whose binoculars were trained aft towards the British battle line and the enemy beyond, and had picked up the ripple of flame that had come from beneath the towering midship superstructure of a battleship now identified positively as the *Vittorio Veneto*. A few moments later there was a curious whine and a rush of air, right overhead. Kemp and Champney ducked instinctively, and moments later great columns of water rose from the sea around four cables'-lengths ahead of the *Wolf Rock* and a little on the starboard bow.

'Ranging salvo,' Kemp said as he straightened. 'Somewhat over but the gunnery's not bad. Let's hope our chaps are as good.'

Lambert heard this and, though he offered no comment, he didn't rate the Eyetie gunners as highly as the Commodore: they would have been ranging on the British battleships for a start, not the convoy itself, and Lambert reckoned they were not over but a bloody sight too far over, for there was now a considerable gap between the *Wolf Rock* and the Flag. The ships of the convoy, obeying the scatter order from the Commodore, were all over the place, making for all points of the compass other than easterly. Lambert wasn't too worried: there was plenty of British weight between him and the Eyeties and he didn't for one moment believe the Eyeties would break through. And now the British battleships were in action, the great 16-inch batteries of the *Nelson* and *Rodney*, eighteen guns all told, plus the *Malaya*'s eight 15-inch guns, blasting away in a Guy Fawke's-night of flame and smoke.

But it wasn't just the Eyeties: now the Stukas were coming in, great buzzing dragon-flies coming down from the north-east, coming in at speed, getting into position for their dive-bombing attacks.

Kemp said, 'That's the strategy. Surface ships to engage each other, the Stukas to attack the convoy. Musso trying to knock the lot off.' He called up to monkey's island above the wheelhouse. 'Petty Officer Ramm!'

Ramm looked down over the guardrail. 'Sir?'

'Don't waste your ammunition, Ramm. I know the temptation, but hold it till they're within range.'

'Aye, aye, sir.' Ramm withdrew, sucking his teeth. Gunner's mates didn't need to be told the obvious but he knew Kemp had a point. In the last attack the close-range gunners had certainly blasted off long before their fire could be of any use. It was a human enough failing but Ramm had already had words with his gunnery rates about it and he had them again now as he stood by the Oerlikons.

'You. Able Seaman Cardew.' Cardew, a three-badgeman, was now Ramm's senior rating in place of Leading Seaman Nelson. 'No pooping off too soon, right?'

'You know me, GI,' Cardew protested.

'Yes, I bloody do, which is why I spoke. So hold off, Commodore's orders, right?'

Cardew nodded. 'Whites o' the buggers eyes, I s'pose.'

'That's it.' Ramm left monkey's island, clattering down the vertical ladder to the starboard wing of the bridge. Able Seaman Cardew, beery face a startling red in its surround of white anti-flash gear, uncomfortably tight in the Oerlikon harness because the beer had also attacked his stomach over the years to the extent that he was known as Beer Gut, peered into his sights and leaned backwards, elevating his gun as the first of the Stukas suddenly dipped its nose and came down flat out in a horribly hostile shriek. It looked like a personal attack on the Commodore's ship. As the *Wolf Rock* altered away under full starboard helm, Cardew acted in a self-preservative way and squeezed his trigger. The tracer went upwards, arcing uselessly, and there was a crescendo of a roar from the gunner's mate below.

'I said, holding your fucking fire, Able Seaman Cardew!'

'Sorry, GI.'

'You'll be fucking sorrier if you do it again, fat sod.' Ramm seethed: next thing, the Commodore would be after him again. Kemp was, but for a different sin. As Captain Champney handled the ship, doing his best to throw off the Stuka, Kemp, looking round, said, 'Petty Officer Ramm.'

'Sir?'

Kemp said no more but gestured towards the starboard ladder. Ramm, following the gesture, became aware of First Officer Forrest. He said stolidly, his face expressionless, 'Sorry, ma'am. Heat o' the moment, that's all.'

'That's all right, Petty Officer Ramm, I've heard worse. You can be thankful I'm not PO Hardisty.' By this time the Stuka had reached the end of its dive and the din had grown to a shriek like all the devils of hell in concert. As the Stuka came within range and dropped its load a hail of fire went up from the close-range weapons. Concussions reverberated throughout the ship: a very near miss. The Stuka lifted unhit, going up as vertically as it had come down. The *Wolf Rock* steamed on, constantly altering course, leaving a twisting wake to stream astern.

'Miss Forrest.'

'Yes, Commodore.' She went across to join Kemp. Kemp's face was frosty.

'Get below, Miss Forrest. Unless you've something to report.'

'I haven't, Commodore. I just thought I could be useful. Write up the action log . . . or something.'

'Very good of you. The bridge today is no place for women and the action log is taken care of. Get below, and – '

'But I – '

'I was going on to say, that's an order.' Kemp turned his back. He was furiously angry, scarcely trusting himself to say anything further. The bloody woman, he thought, coming up just at the crucial moment in a dive-bombing attack, putting herself in danger when the orders for all WRNS personnel were to remain below when the ship was under attack. Discipline, in Kemp's view, began at the top, and Jean Forrest was OC Wrens – a fine example! Damn the woman and damn all Wrens too, there'd been nothing but trouble with them. . . .

A moment later Wrens and anger were forgotten: two reports reached Kemp, one from the masthead lookout and the other from the yeoman of signals: beyond the line of battle astern, a big fire was burning, smoke and flames rising thickly from one of the Italians, a cruiser. More immediate to the Commodore was Lambert's report of a trail of smoke rising from the engine-room casing of one of the troopships of the convoy, right between her two funnels. As Kemp trained his glasses on her, a signal lamp began flashing from her bridge.

Lambert read the message. 'From *Orduna* . . . bomb hit amidships and fires starting, sir.'

Kemp nodded. For now there was nothing he could do; but if that transport was forced in the end to abandon, then the *Wolf Rock* would play her part. General orders or not, Kemp would this time stand by to pick up survivors. So many helpless troops. . . . He tried not to register that there was anything personal in that decision: the fact remained that the *Orduna* had been one of the

155

ships on the pre-war Australia run, a ship of the Orient Steam Navigation Company, friendly rivals of the Mediterranean-Australia Line on the long haul to Sydney, and Kemp had known a number of Orient Line officers, including *Orduna*'s current Master who had remained in command after the outbreak of war. He and Kemp had met at the convoy conference in the Clyde, the first time since the days of peace. They had found much to yarn about but little time to indulge in reminiscence: the war had called. But Kemp and Captain Pope were old friends, and old friends stuck together.

Kemp sang out to Yeoman Lambert. 'Make, good luck to you all and may God be with you.'

'Aye, aye, sir,' Lambert said, thinking that there was some basic inconsistency in that friendly signal: if you invoked the good offices of the Almighty, it was a bit of an insult to invoke luck at the same time, but never mind. As he clacked out the Commodore's signal the next air attack was seen coming in. Then distantly there was an immense explosion as the stricken Italian cruiser blew up, sending debris high into the sky.

'One down,' Kemp said, 'but God knows how many more to go.' He had scarcely uttered the words when one of the attacking aircraft opened up with its cannon and shells spattered the bridge. One of the *Wolf Rock*'s close-range gunners fell limp in his straps, head lolling and blood spurting from his neck. The rest of the bridge personnel were lucky: something had glanced off Kemp's steel helmet and that was all. Kemp and Lambert went across and lifted the dead man from the gun and Peter Harrison, Officer of the Watch, sent a messenger down for the doctor. Kemp looked around for Sub-Lieutenant Finnegan, then remembered his own orders: Finnegan was standing by Third Officer Pawle. Kemp reckoned he was getting even older than he'd thought. In the meantime luck was with the *Wolf Rock*: another near miss and then the Stuka seemed to go out of control. It may have been hit: afterwards, Able Seaman Cardew claimed that it had. Whatever the reason, the German took the water off the *Wolf Rock*'s port side and disintegrated. Nothing was seen of the pilot.

Kemp levelled his glasses on the *Orduna*: the smoke was rising thickly and a lick of flame was now visible, coming up from the engine-room casing and starting, Kemp fancied, to spread for'ard towards the bridge. He could see the troops falling in along the embarkation deck, already mustering at their boat stations, just a precaution. And perhaps more than that: troops were better out of the way of the seamen, who would be running out the fire hoses. Or should have been. A moment later a signal lamp started flashing and Lambert read off the message.

'Commodore from *Orduna*, sir, have lost electric power, fire hoses inoperable.'

'God Almighty,' Kemp said. He gripped the bridge rail hard, staring at what could be a doomed ship, with fires below raging out of control and never mind the firescreen doors, they wouldn't be enough to save her. He swung round on Champney, 'Captain, you have hoses, powerful ones. And electric power still.'

'Yes, I have. What are you suggesting?'

Kemp said, 'Can you lay alongside, and pump into the engine-room casing?'

'We're lower in the water than the *Orduna*, Commodore. I doubt if the hoses would lift water high enough. In any case, it'd be no more than a piddle compared with what's needed below.'

'It's all we can do,' Kemp said harshly. 'We can try, can't we?'

Champney shrugged. 'We can, but it would do no good at all. And remember my cargo, Commodore. If we're too close to her when she starts a real blaze, the holds could take fire. It's too much of a risk.'

'But – '

'My ship, Commodore. My responsibility.' Champney met Kemp's eye firmly. 'I'll not mention lives . . . we're all at risk, all the time. But that cargo's badly needed.'

'So are the troops, Champney, so are the troops!'

Champney said patiently, 'Yes, they are, and if I thought there was any point in the risk it'd be different. But there's not. We'd be of much more use standing by to pick up survivors if it comes to that.'

Kemp, his mouth tight, turned away and paced the bridge wing. He forced himself to see that Champney was right. He had wanted to make a gesture, wanted to show Pope in the *Orduna* that he was ready to help . . . but gestures, useless ones if Champney was right, had no place in war. To take any risk with ten thousand tons of valuable war material, with all those girls and the fifty-odd seamen and engine-room and catering staff aboard the *Wolf Rock*, would be too much. Old friendships must never be

157

allowed to cloud the judgment of the Convoy Commodore. Kemp turned and went back to Champney.

'You win, Captain. You're right. I was wrong.'

Champney said, 'It was a natural thought. But it would never have worked. Don't imagine I don't understand, though.'

Kemp said nothing: seamen did understand one another, and Champney had been exercising a proper responsibility of command. Kemp stood and watched helplessly as the fires spread aboard the *Orduna*, and as the attack on the convoy continued without any let-up while the merchant ships moved farther from the embattled warships astern. The screaming noise from the Stukas as they came in again and again tore at men's nerves: Lambert, dodging down behind the bridge screen as the bombs fell and again the cannon and machine-guns stuttered into brief action, found his whole body twitching as though he had been shot already. Petty Officer Ramm, knowing he was lucky to be still alive, moved about the upper decks exhorting his close-range weapons' crews, feeling blood run down his left side from a wound he'd been scarcely aware of at the time. Coming back from aft towards the bridge ladder he saw Dr O'Dwyer descending, shaking like a leaf but moving fast. Moving for safety, Ramm thought angrily.

Ramm stood in front of him, blocking his way. Before he could speak, O'Dwyer said, 'He's dead.'

''Oo's dead, sir?'

'The man at the Oerlikon. On the bridge. There was nothing I could do. He was dead. Dead I tell you!'

'Yes, sir, I heard you the first time. Doing anything about shifting the body, are you, eh?'

'That'll have to wait.' O'Dwyer pushed past, his face working. Ramm let him go. Going for the whisky bottle, he reckoned. Ramm gathered saliva and spat on the deck. Useless bugger . . . climbing again to the bridge, Ramm thought about the dead. His question about shifting the body had been intended to needle O'Dwyer; you didn't in fact shift the dead while the ship was still in action, any road when they weren't gumming up the works and getting in the way of the living. Ramm had been through the Med before now, the last time on a Malta convoy run aboard a cruiser of the escort. The hull and upperworks had been peppered full of holes by the ferocious onslaught of the Jerries and

Eyeties and the dead had been everywhere, so much so that they'd had virtually to be shovelled away from such guns as were still capable of firing. Afterwards it had been the most horrific sight Ramm had ever seen, what with blood and guts all over the show, several legs and arms, heads rolling in the scuppers. Just thinking about it now made him turn green. He climbed on for the bridge, wondering if the dead gunner would still be in the straps. He wasn't; someone had lifted him down and the body lay on the deck of the bridge wing, beneath the gun that another rating was manning. The firing had been resumed, for what it was worth. Above Ramm's head, the Seafires from the carriers were in action; that at least was something. Ramm saw the Commodore staring to starboard through his binoculars: the *Orduna* was well ablaze now, and a shower of sparks was billowing from the engine-room casing, carried on some sort of up-draught. As he watched, Ramm saw the movement of troops into the boats already swung out on their davits from the embarkation deck, and saw a number of men leap over the side into the sea as the Carley floats began moving down the slides.

Captain Champney leaned over the bridge screen and shouted down to the bosun who was carrying out an adjustment to the ready-rigged fire hoses. Tod Ridgway lifted a hand in acknowledgement. 'Sir?'

'*Orduna*'s preparing to abandon, Bosun. Have hands ready with the jumping nets, both sides.'

Another wave and Ridgway started mustering the seamen and casting loose the big rope-mesh jumping nets, dropping them down the ship's sides for swimmers to grapple and climb and be helped aboard. Below decks, word reached Jock Campbell, chief steward, that the *Wolf Rock* was about to embark survivors, numbers unknown but as many as possible. This news threw him into a degree of panic unconnected with thoughts of danger as the *Wolf Rock* reduced speed to move in among swimming men and then, most likely, would lie stopped to become a sitting duck like the *Langstone Harbour* had been until she'd been taken in tow. Campbell's thoughts were those of any chief steward faced with an inundation of persons who would need to eat and sleep and would thus take up space, of which there was none. None, that was, in any comfort. This was an emergency; Jock Campbell relinquished the key of the linen store to his second steward,

159

registering that Mr bloody Harrison and Wren Smith had had it now, no more fornicating among the mattresses and sheets. The linen store would be needed as an extra accommodation unit until such time as the troops could be disembarked, probably at Alexandria or possibly Malta depending on the Commodore's decision. Food was going to be tight and there would have to be rationing if Malta wasn't on the cards . . . that was just one of Campbell's headaches. Another one did concern danger: with troops aboard, the *Wolf Rock* would become even more of a target for the buggers attempting to stop the convoy in its tracks. He had a moment of doubt, of terror as to his own survival. The din from up top was appalling, shattering: it was the grandfather of all attacks he'd ever known since the start of the war and it wasn't only the Stukas. Botley had come down with news that the convoy was now under fire from an Italian heavy cruiser that had sneaked round the flank of the main British line-of-battle, the armoured protection between the merchant ships and the Italian fleet. Botley had added that the destroyer escort was moving at speed to intercept and that was some comfort to Jock Campbell as he wrestled with his accommodation and catering problems with half his mind. A good proportion of the rest of his mind was back home in UK with Mary his wife, safe, or so he prayed constantly, on that farm near Wrexham. If ever she went into Liverpool, maybe to look nostalgically at their pre-war home . . . it didn't bear thinking about, all those Nazi air raids, flattening the docks, bringing fire and death to the city. Hitler was a bloody sod. So was Musso . . . the bullfrog of the Pontine Marshes as Winston Churchill had once called him.

iii

As the survivors from the sinking *Orduna* waved and shouted across the water, Captain Champney took the *Wolf Rock* in as close as possible and then stopped his engine: revolving screws could churn men up, thrash them into strips of bloody flesh. The risk in lying stopped was great but had to be accepted. Kemp had been adamant: he was not going to leave them to it. As the Commodore's ship drifted closer the men in the boats and Carley floats and those who were swimming sent up a ragged cheer. By this time the great liner appeared to be white-hot almost from stem to stern; flames licked up around the bridge and took the woodwork of the wheelhouse; soon it would be a bonfire. Now the masts were ablaze, and fire licked through the big windows of what had once been the first-class lounge and the Tavern bar aft by the swimming pool – Kemp knew the lay-out well; it was similar to his own company's ships, both lines having had their vessels laid down by Vickers-Armstrong's yard in Barrow-in-Furness. He'd dined aboard the *Orduna* alongside the berth at Woolloomooloo in Sydney, with the then Staff Commander Pope. All the pomp and glitter of a great liner, the white-jacketed stewards, the ship's orchestra, the gilded mess jackets of the officers, the superb menus, all in the past, all now burning to extinction.

'They're still jumping over,' he said to Champney. 'So goddamn many of them!' With the best will in the world, the *Wolf Rock* couldn't take them all. Kemp had sent his signals to the other ships but they hadn't been necessary: the camaraderie of the sea was holding, and the nearer ships were moving in to stand by and assist the rescue operation. Two of the destroyers, alerted by Kemp as to his intentions, were acting as close guardships, pumping away with their multiple pom-poms at the Nazi attack. The air was thick with puffs of smoke and with shrapnel as the heavier ack-ack blazed away with the smaller weapons, but still the Stukas were coming in.

Kemp, his binoculars trained from time to time on what was left of the *Orduna*'s bridge, caught a glimpse of two men still there: obviously, Pope and the OC Troops. They wouldn't leave until the ship was clear of all personnel. And they wouldn't have a hope by that time . . .

There was another near miss, this time very close to the hull. Below in the engine-room, Chief Engineer Turnberry felt the full impact. The whole compartment juddered and rang with noise, the light flickered, dimmed and came back again. Turnberry was flung bodily from the starting platform, ending up on the greasy deck plating with his right arm twisted beneath his body. He felt agonizing pain, tried to get up, fell back with a gasp. As he tried again to get to his feet he saw a river of water run down the bulkhead on the starboard side: sprung rivets, and the seam was weeping. He made a big effort; the pain in his arm and another in his side made him cry out, and then he passed into unconsciousness as his second engineer reached him and bent over him.

Fifteen seconds later Champney took the report by voice-pipe on the bridge. 'Second engineer, sir. Chief's hurt and there's a sprung seam to starboard. We're making water fairly fast.'

'Will the pumps cope?'

'Don't know yet, sir – '

'Keep reporting,' Champney said. He slammed back the voice-pipe cover and went out of the wheelhouse to join the Commodore in the bridge wing. By this time the *Wolf Rock* was in among the survivors and already men were grasping the jumping nets and clambering up, all along the sides. As the first of them reached the deck and were helped aboard by the *Wolf Rock*'s seamen, an aircraft came screaming out of the sky, its machine-guns blazing away into the water, raising a myriad pockmarks, finding easy targets in the crowded gap between the two ships.

FIFTEEN

'Those awful screams,' Susan Pawle said suddenly, her eyes wide and her fists clenched. She hadn't spoken for some while, had just lain in her bunk staring blankly. Sub-Lieutenant Finnegan had left her now, taking his part in the hauling of survivors over the guardrails, a case of all hands. Rose Hardisty was sitting beside her, with her knitting, and was trying to shut her ears to the terrible sounds from outside. The Stuka had passed and re-passed, disregarding the stream of fire from the close-range weapons, firing blindly down into the water and then raking the port side of the *Wolf Rock* as the survivors climbed the jumping nets. Their screams as the bullets ripped into them were close enough to be heard in Susan's cabin. 'What's going on, PO?'

'It's those Germans,' Rose Hardisty said uncertainly.

'Oh, I *know* that!'

'Yes, ma'am – '

'Tell me. I'm not a child.'

'Oh no, ma'am.' Rose Hardisty hesitated, wondering how far to go. Then she plunged; after all, war was war and they were all in it very positively now. 'The aeroplane's shooting at those poor soldiers, ma'am. The survivors. In the water and up the side of the ship . . . '

'Oh, God!' Susan lifted her still-clenched fists. 'What's everything coming to? Those *bastards*!'

Rose Hardisty felt a slight sense of shock at the word, coming from the young lady. 'Yes, ma'am, that they are. But don't take on, now. Nothing we can do is there, dearie?' She caught herself up sharply. 'Oh! Beg pardon, ma'am.'

163

'What?'

PO Hardisty, flustered, explained.

'Oh, don't be silly, PO.'

'No, ma'am.' Rose Hardisty knitted stolidly on, easing a cramp in her legs by stretching them out farther. She wished that Mr. Finnegan was with them still; he was such a nice young man and so polite, and good-looking too. If anything should happen, he would be a tower of strength, but, though it was obvious he liked Mrs Pawle, he'd been very restive about being below with her while things were going on up top and he'd taken the first opportunity of leaving. Rose Hardisty could understand, of course; men were like that. She remembered her young male charges in her nanny years, so much more combative than the girls. And often very rude with it . . . and the things they used to pick up! Miss Hardisty remembered little Master Donald, who at the age of not quite three had picked up very common language from a village boy and, when rebuked for some really trifling matter long forgotten now, had told nanny she was 'a fuckum bloosance.' Rose Hardisty had interpreted bloosance easily enough but had been stumped by fuckum, and she recalled, with a middle-aged blush, the embarrassment when she had asked cook for enlightenment. Little Master Donald, now a major in The Blues − Rose Hardisty always kept up with 'her' families − had unfortunately had the makings of a Petty Officer Ramm. She was, however, sure that Mr Finnegan, American though he might be, never used such language.

Even in the midst of war, even in the midst of attack, there was a placidity in the occupation of knitting and the regular click of needles that somehow settled the mind back into happier and safer days before the world had gone mad. Rose Hardisty found little sense in war; the last one hadn't really settled anything in spite of the sacrifices and her old dad's best efforts in the stoke-hold of Admiral Beatty's flagship. And now just look at what this one had done to the poor young lady in the bunk, her life in ruins and her only in her early twenties − and lost a husband too.

Rose Hardisty knitted faster, her head shaking a little from side to side as the needles flashed in her hands and her lips moved as she counted stitches.

She was about to cast off when the *Wolf Rock*'s luck ran out and the bomb hit. The whole cabin seemed to lift into the air and sway curiously, a very funny feeling and an alarming one, then it dropped suddenly and left Rose Hardisty's stomach behind as it did so. She dropped her knitting. She gave a cry of dismay as she saw that Susan Pawle had fallen from the bunk – the retaining board had come adrift and her young lady was lying on the floor and was in obvious pain. As she bent to see to her, Mr Finnegan appeared, blood running down the side of his face, which had a nasty gash.

'Oh my, sir,' Rose Hardisty said. 'Just look at you!'

'Bomb splinter,' Finnegan said briefly. 'Don't worry about me, I'll be okay.' He bent down by Susan, his face showing his concern. He looked up. 'I'm no medic. Do we lift her, or do we wait for the doc? Don't want to add to the damage.'

Miss Hardisty knew that the wait for Dr O'Dwyer would be a long one. She said they would lift; the young lady would be more comfortable in the bunk. As they lifted her, Susan Pawle screamed. She was still screaming as they laid her as gently as possible in the bunk.

ii

The bomb had taken the *Wolf Rock* slap in the eyes of the ship, right for'ard beyond the hawse pipes and the anchors. The fo'c'sle-head was shattered, the links of the cables parted and the anchors smashed away from the bottle-screws and Blake slips. The force of the explosion had driven down into the fo'c'sle mess, the seamens' living space now filled with troops wounded in the vicious machine-gun fire from the Stukas. It was now a charnel house, filled with mangled flesh and bloodied strips of khaki drill. In the midst of the carnage Dr O'Dwyer moved like a zombie, overwhelmed by death and suffering, not knowing what to do, where to start. It was all too much for one doctor to cope with and after one appalled look he stumbled back into the fresh air, emerging on to the fore well-deck shaking in every limb.

From the bridge Kemp looked down on the destruction, at Harrison examining the cargo hatches with the ship's carpenter. Tod Ridgway, bosun, lay dead by the windlass below the break of the fo'c'sle, his head and shoulders a crumpled, shapeless mess. The fire hoses were in action, their jets pouring water over the

165

hatches. Harrison disappeared below with the carpenter. The jumping nets were still heavy with soldiers; the *Orduna* herself was burning now to the waterline; in addition to the fire, she had taken another bomb that had fractured her fuel tanks and her bunker oil was escaping, pouring a thick blanket of choking black that spread out fast among the men in the water.

The liner's purser was among those who had clambered aboard the *Wolf Rock*. He came to the bridge to report.

Kemp asked, 'Captain Pope?'

'Last seen on the bridge, sir. That's all I know. He'd given the order to abandon . . . I think he intended staying.'

Kemp nodded. Pope was the sort to do exactly what ship-masters' were popularly suppposed to do: go down with their commands. In the RN the idea was that the ship and captain were a single entity, one and indivisible; Pope would see it in the same light. He'd been that sort of man.

The *Orduna*'s purser asked, 'You knew him, didn't you, Commodore?'

Again Kemp nodded. 'I was Mediterranean-Australia Lines before this lot.'

'I know. Captain Pope spoke of you. He said he was glad to be sailing under your command, sir.'

For the third time Kemp nodded but didn't trust himself to speak. Pope wouldn't be all that glad by now, assuming he was still alive which he almost certainly would not be. A spirit, pass-ing overhead, looking down on tragedy, of the loss of all those lives, the loss of a great ship? Kemp felt a great weight settle on his shoulders: he had let poor Pope down, hadn't been able to do anything to help when the crunch had come. Looking down into the fore well-deck, he caught sight of Dr O'Dwyer making his way aft, stumbling and bumping into everything in his path. The *Orduna* had carried two doctors, two nursing sisters; and there would be an RAMC detachment with the troops. Kemp asked, 'What about your medical people? Survived – or not?'

'The nursing sisters were in a boat, sir. I don't know how they've made out.'

Kemp put a hand on his shoulders. 'Do something for me, Purser. Find any medics you can and ask them to contact our own doctor. They're all going to be needed now. Down below, there's a young girl who's recently had a leg amputated. . . . '

It had seemed like hours, weeks, a lifetime even; but in fact it had been going on for little more than twenty minutes before the Stukas withdrew, pursued by the Seafires flown off by the aircraft-carriers. Ten of the Stukas had been destroyed by the combined efforts of the ack-ack and the attentions of the British fighters; the loss to the Seafires had been four, shot down by the Nazi fighter escort. Kemp counted the score: those four aircraft gone, one of the destroyers standing by the scattered convoy sunk, the *Orduna* burned out and one of the armaments carriers blown up while the survivors from the transport were being embarked. He didn't yet know about the main fleet but it was, Kemp thought, not exactly a British victory.

He looked around the convoy. The ships were by now widely separated, and were mostly heading west still. The situation, as Kemp remarked to Finnegan who had now joined him on the bridge, was under control for the moment, at least until another wave of dive bombers came in.

'Which might not be long. I'll not reassemble the convoy yet.'

'I guess not, sir. There's still the surface . . . the Eyeties.'

'Yes. You'd better get that face seen to, Finnegan.' Kemp could see right through into Finnegan's mouth as the sub talked, could see his teeth through his cheek. 'Where's Dr O'Dwyer, by the way?'

'Making himself scarce, sir. I reckon he's shit scared if you ask me.'

'I didn't ask you, Finnegan, and I'm not asking you now. Go and report to one of the medics from the army, or the *Orduna*'s doctor if he's survived.'

'I'm okay – '

'You don't look it. That's an order, Finnegan. Get yourself bandaged before the next attack comes in.'

Finnegan went down the bridge ladder. Soon after, the various reports reached the Commodore and Captain Champney: the cargo holds were intact and such fires as had broken out had been doused, the hoses still playing on smouldering wreckage. In addition to the bosun and the ack-ack gunner, four seamen of the *Wolf Rock* crew had been killed. The *Orduna*'s doctors, both survivors, were at work together with two RAMC doctors and a number of medical orderlies. The transport's own nursing sisters had not been accounted for as yet but the rescue operation was still proceeding, currently without interruption from the Nazis. Jock Campbell was tearing his hair and was on the verge, like Dr O'Dwyer, of giving up. Troops were everywhere, below and along the decks, lying on the hatch covers, crowding the boat deck and impeding access to the bridge ladders. Peter Harrison was trying to sort them out and bring back some semblance of order.

The trouble spot was the engine-room. Chief Engineer Turnberry had a broken arm and some rib damage but had been given a temporary repair by the RAMC and was carrying on grimly. His engine-room was a foot deep in water and he believed the ingress was overcoming the pumps. The seam had widened a little and the second engineer had a gang working, trying to make a seal.

Kemp asked, 'What's your assessment, Chief?'

'Hard to say, sir. If we can't seal it, well, the engine spaces will flood.'

'And fast, by the sound of it.' Twelve inches in so short a time was very bad news. Kemp did some sums in his head. They wouldn't have long if the pumps failed to cope. Like Horncape in the *Langstone Harbour* somewhere behind the convoy, they would be in need of a tow. And a tow at this stage would seriously affect the manoeuvrability of the reduced escort.

There was, however, some good news and it came via Yeoman of Signals Lambert as he read off a lamp flashing from the *Nelson*. 'From the Flag, sir . . . Italian fleet has suffered severe damage and is running for home. Am pursuing.'

Kemp looked out towards the distant battleships and cruisers. The sound of heavy gunfire was still there, still loud and continuous as the for'ard batteries of the big ships flung their projectiles across some twelve miles of the Mediterranean. The gun flashes could be seen, and the billowing clouds of black smoke that followed them. Kemp leaned over the bridge rail and called down to the troops massed in the well-deck, then turned aft to repeat his words to those aft, the message that the enemy was on the run. A storm of cheering rose from the decks, went on and on. Petty Officer Ramm, in the port wing of the bridge with Able Seaman Cardew, was sardonic.

'Just done what they always bloody do, that's all.'

'Run away?' Cardew wiped a hand across his sweat-streaked

168

cheeks: his anti-flash gear was wet and clammy, and no longer a nice virgin white. 'They say the buggers carry their heaviest guns aft, to fire while buggering off – right, GI?'

Ramm nodded. 'Admiral's wasting 'is bloody time, chasing. Them Eyeties have got the legs of those old battle-wagons . . . twenty-two knots flat out, my arse!'

'Well, I'm glad enough to see 'em go,' Cardew said with feeling. 'When an Eyetie projy hits, it bloody blows up just as much as a Jerry one.' He paused. 'Kemp going to – '

'Commodore Kemp to you, Able Seaman Cardew. The enemy may 'ave fucked off but I'm still 'ere to keep you sods up to the mark, all right?'

Cardew grinned. '*Commodore* Kemp, then. I was going to ask, is he going to – '

'I'm not party to what takes place in the mind of the Convoy Commodore, Able Seaman Cardew, but if you're going to ask, is he going to fall out the guns' crews so they can do a loaf, I'd say we're still a long, long way from home and there's plenty of Nazis stationed in Sardinia and bloody Sicily.'

'I wasn't going to ask that, GI,' Cardew said. 'I was going to ask, d'you think we'll head in for Malta now?' The word had spread that the engine-room was flooding and they might find themselves without power, wallowing in the water like a lop-sided duck.

'Don't know, do I? I reckon it'll be on the cards.' Ramm chuckled. 'Wouldn't mind a night ashore, down the Gut! All them tarts.' Strada Stretta, known to generations of British seamen as the Gut, was a kind of paradise to be descended upon as soon as libertymen were piped after a ship arrived in the Grand Harbour. Wine, women and song, and dirt cheap too, all of it. It had to be admitted, there were compensations in the sea life. Even in wartime . . . Petty Officer Ramm had started to elaborate on the pleasures he'd enjoyed down the Gut when he was interrupted by urgent signals from Cardew, who was indicating someone behind his back.

Ramm turned to find PO Wren Hardisty. There was a funny look on her face, sort of faraway and worried, and Ramm believed she hadn't heard what he'd been saying, which had been fairly lurid, anyway would have been in female ears. Ramm lifted an eyebrow, enquiringly.

169

Rose Hardisty said, 'I'm looking for First Officer Forrest.'

'Won't find her up here, PO Hardisty. Commodore'd do his nut if – '

'Where's the Commodore?' she asked in a flat tone.

Ramm gestured. 'Starboard wing.' He looked at her closely. 'Anything I can do, is there, eh?'

'No,' she said. 'No, there isn't, thank you, PO Ramm. The Commodore . . . it's that poor young lady. Third Officer Pawle.'

'Bad, is she?'

Rose Hardisty answered as though she couldn't bring herself to believe her own words. 'She's been seen to by an army doctor. A major. He says her back's broken. She may never walk again.' Tears rolled down Rose Hardisty's cheeks. 'He didn't say, but I think it's my own fault. I told Mr Finnegan, I said, Dr O'Dwyer wouldn't be any use and we'd better lift her back into her bunk.' She turned away, rather stumblingly, making over to the starboard side of the bridge. Ramm watched the movement of an ungainly backside, like a couple of fullsize Stilton cheeses rubbing together. Poor old cow, he thought, she's really upset. And no wonder: he found he wasn't unmoved himself.

SIXTEEN

'Vessel ahead, sir. Fine on the starboard bow.'

The report came from the masthead lookout and on the bridge of the *Langstone Harbour* all the binoculars swung onto the bearing which was being indicated visually by the outstretched arm of the seaman in the crow's-nest. Something, some ship, had already been picked up on the escorting destroyers' radar, and one of them was making ahead, investigating at full speed. It was a day of sunshine now, sunshine and deep blue water, the Mediterranean at its best after the foul weather that had accompanied the convoy all the way from the Irish coast; the streaming, tumbling wake of the destroyer reached back towards the *Langstone Harbour* like a brilliant white sash across a blue dress as the freighter came on behind the rescue tug. All seemed to be peaceful: Captain Horncape had heard the distant sounds of the heavy gunfire some hours back but these had faded.

He went into the chart room and looked at the chart, worked out his position by dead reckoning from the last fix, and noted it with a cross in a neat circle. At their current speed, Malta lay some thirty-two hours' steaming – or towing – ahead.

He had a word with his Officer of the Watch. 'We should raise Zembra within the next two hours, Phillips. Distant to starboard.'

'Yes, sir. By which time we'll be in the Narrows.'

'That's right. That's when the buggers'll attack. On the last lap . . . just our luck!' Horncape lifted his glasses once again. Now the ship ahead was coming into view: he thought she had little movement and there was no smoke. He studied her for a while, frowning. 'She looks like – ' He broke off as the distant ship started flashing towards the destroyers. 'Signalling,' he said.

171

They waited. Within the next three minutes the answering destroyer began calling up the *Langstone Harbour*, sending slowly. Horncape gestured to his second officer, who read the signal and noted it down on a signal pad. When the message was complete, he read it off to Horncape.

'Destroyer reports *Wolf Rock* ahead, sir – '

'The Commodore!'

'Yes, sir. Commodore reports engine-room flooded, ship without power, convoy scattered but re-forming. Commodore intends entering Malta under tow.'

'Well, I'll be buggered,' Horncape said softly. 'Me and John Mason Kemp . . . what a way to meet again, both of us lame ducks under tow. We're going to make it, though.' To enter the Grand Harbour with his vital cargo intact would make his imminent silver wedding day into something never to be forgotten. He wondered if Nesta was going to spare a thought for him. He would like to feel that she did, as he took his ship on towards the Sicilian Channel and that last lap.

ii

Kemp had made the decision after a good deal of thought during which he cleared his mind by a frank discussion with Captain Champney and Finnegan. There was, Champney agreed, no alternative but to enter Malta. The split seam had widened, the packing was proving ineffective, and the pumps were not coping. Turnberry had reported that in his view the engine-room would flood within a couple of hours.

'You'll request a tow, sir?' Finnegan asked.

Kemp snorted. 'What else?'

'Sorry, sir.' Finnegan paused. 'What about the convoy?'

'I have that in mind, of course. You have a penchant for stressing the obvious sometimes, young Finnegan. The convoy's going to pass close enough to Malta – the farthest from Sicily and the toe of Italy the better. I shall see the *Wolf Rock* into the Grand Harbour . . . then I shall transfer to another ship in the convoy. Whoever's detailed to tow us in will hand over to the harbour tugs on arrival and can then take us off to catch up the convoy and embark at sea.' Kemp paused. 'Draft a signal to the Flag, Finnegan, outlining what I've just said.'

172

'Aye, aye, sir. Then we wait for the reaction from the Admiral, I guess.'

'You guess well, Finnegan. But anticipating the Admiral's concurrence, you'll tell Petty Officer Ramm and all staff to prepare to transfer with me.'

'Yes, sir. And the Wrens?'

Kemp said, 'The WRNS detachment is under orders for Trincomalee, which means they'll have to keep with me. You can tell First Officer Forrest that I'd like a word with her – if she can fight her way through the soldiery! I have to consider Third Officer Pawle, you see – and Wren Smith.'

'Yes, sir.' Finnegan left the bridge, passing Petty Officer Ramm waiting to climb the starboard ladder. He passed the Commodore's order. Ramm said, 'Malta, eh. Thought as much, I did, sir.'

'Sure. But not to remain.' Finnegan passed the rest of the orders: the transfer of the Commodore's staff to another ship. As he moved away he was aware of a sour mutter under the PO's breath, something about sod that for a lark. Pushing through the throngs of khaki-clad figures lying, sitting and standing about the decks, Finnegan found Jean Forrest in Susan's cabin. PO Wren Hardisty was with them, her face a mess. Susan was lying very still and Finnegan realized that under the sheet she was encased in plaster. Her face looked haunted but although she had obviously been crying, her cheeks were dry now.

Finnegan was overcome with embarrassment. Avoiding the girl's eyes he spoke to Jean Forrest. 'Commodore's compliments, ma'am. He'd like a word . . . on the bridge.'

'On the bridge?' Jean Forrest gave a rather shrill laugh. 'The last time I went up there, I was threatened with death. Almost.'

'This time it's different, ma'am. If you'll come with me, I'll push through the troops for you. Act as an escort.'

She said, 'Oh, I'll manage. I'd sooner you stayed with Susan if you can be spared.' She lowered her voice. 'She's been asking for you, as a matter of fact. You did some good before. See if you can do it again.'

'Sure,' Finnegan said, still much embarrassed. 'I'll do my best, anyway.'

'Good,' she said, and gave his arm a squeeze before she left the cabin. He stood by the bunk, looking down in concern but trying to keep it out of his face: he had to be cheerful, keep her spirits

173

up, but he hadn't an idea in the world of what to say that wouldn't sound forced and trite.

Rose Hardisty came across and stood beside him. She said in a flat tone, 'It's that Dr O'Dwyer, that's what it is. If he'd been any use I'd *never* have lifted her, but I knew he wouldn't come that quick. Not in time. And she was lying there.' She went on impulsively, 'It's the drink, sir. I'll say that whoever tells me I shouldn't do. It's not right, specially in wartime, is it, sir?'

Finnegan said, 'Well, I guess it's not for me to comment, ma'am, PO I mean. But I don't reckon you should blame yourself any. You did what you thought best and me, I reckoned you were right.' He turned and found Susan staring at him and he gave her a smile.

There was no answering smile on the girl's face. Their voices had carried. In a hard tone she said, 'For God's sake, don't argue about it now. It's done. Like me.'

Finnegan shook his head. 'Not you, ma'am, Susan. Far from it. You'll be okay.'

She laughed, another hard sound. 'Where did you study medicine?'

He flushed. 'Sorry. It's ... it's just that I'm dead sure you're going to be okay.'

'Oh,' she said, 'I'll live. That army doctor assured me of that. In a bloody wheelchair. The rest of my life.'

'He didn't say that?' Finnegan was shocked.

'Oh, no, he didn't say it. They don't, do they? Always reassuring, look on the bright side. So I'll live, yes. As I said, in a wheelchair for the rest of my life. Do you know what that means, do you really think that's what I want?'

'Well, now – '

'I'd rather die. There's nothing to live for anyway. There hasn't been, ever since – ' She broke off; tears ran down her face.

Rose Hardisty came across, eyes troubled, close to tears herself. 'Now, ma'am, don't take on. Things'll come brighter one of these days, they always do if you don't give in.' She bent and straightened the blanket over Susan's body. 'There now,' she said, back again in the nursery. '*That*'s better.'

Finnegan felt himself superfluous: he was doing no good and he knew he looked as awkward as he felt. And he would be needed on the bridge, maybe. Also there would be much to see to

174

in getting the Commodore's staff and equipment ready for the transfer after they reached the Grand Harbour. If they did. As he left the cabin he realized that Susan Pawle had asked no questions about what was going to happen; maybe she just didn't know about the engine-room and the Commodore's dilemma about to be resolved in a change of destination and the transfer. Very likely she didn't; but Finnegan believed that she genuinely didn't care any more. She might even welcome the quick end that could come from a bomb in the next attack by the Stukas. Finnegan was very thoughtful as he climbed to the bridge. This war was turning out somewhat differently from what he'd expected in the heady days, seeming far off now, when he'd left home to join in the fight for freedom via Canada and the Royal Canadian Naval Volunteer Reserve. Guns and shells were on the menu, and sinkings, and death – he'd known all that, of course. It hadn't worried him; he would come through whatever happened, and he would see Adolf Hitler topple from his grisly pinnacle of power. He would be there, along with the Canadians and the Yanks and the French and the British Empire when the grand victory parade was held, as held it would surely be, in London, plus a ticker-tape welcome through the New York streets to the returning veterans. All that was part of war, part of his own plan as he saw it. What he had never reckoned on was what was happening in the cabin he had just left, a young and vital girl wishing only that she could die because of the double tragedy inflicted by the Nazi war machine.

Once again he encountered Petty Officer Ramm. Ramm asked, 'How's the young lady, sir?'

Bitterly, Finnegan told him, releasing some of his own frustration at being able to do damn-all to help. He saw the hard look in Ramm's face and the way the P O's fists clenched. In a wooden voice Ramm said, 'Them buggers!' and turned away, trying to march along the crowded deck, shouting for a gangway through the troops and cursing luridly about brown jobs when he stumbled over out-thrust, weary feet.

iii

'It'll depend on the Admiral, of course, Miss Forrest,' Kemp had said. 'But you'd better prepare your draft for transfer with my staff.' He paused, lifting his binoculars to rake the skies to the

175

north, expectant of attack at any moment. The convoy was reassembling under his orders since it had to maintain some kind of cohesion and make its easting through the Mediterranean for Alexandria and Port Said; but Kemp was not intending to bring the ships into any close formation and had signalled a warning that the scatter order might come again. He turned back to Jean Forrest when he found the skies clear.

'The only question mark is around your Mrs Pawle. And that Wren Smith. Not that there's much of a query about Mrs Pawle, of course. She'll be landed to the Bighi naval hospital.'

Jean Forrest nodded. 'I'll see that everything's ready, Commodore.'

'Let the army doctors have charge of her meanwhile, Miss Forrest. Not Dr O'Dwyer. If he doesn't like it . . . he knows what he can do.'

She grinned. 'Take a running jump?'

'That's putting it politely. Has he been seen around?'

'No.'

'That's blunt!'

'Well . . . he's been seen I admit. Wringing his hands. I think he knows when he's not wanted.' She added after a moment, 'I don't think it's quite his own fault, Commodore.'

Kemp snorted.

'No, I mean it. He has a history – I've talked to him. He opened up – '

'When drunk?'

'Yes,' she said. 'Very drunk! Anyway, he talked about himself. In the last war . . . I gather it was what we'd call shell shock. They deal with it differently now. But back in fifteen or whenever, they – '

'Yes, I know. I was in that war too, Miss Forrest. In destroyers and minelayers – lieutenant RNR. So you're saying it was that that led to the bottle. Whatever the reason, the man's no damn use as a doctor.' Kemp's tone was dismissive of any further discussion about Dr O'Dwyer. 'Now, what about that blasted pregnant girl? What do we do with her, for God's sake?'

'She's part of the draft, Commodore.'

Kemp gave a short laugh. 'Even pregnant?'

'Which she still insists she isn't.'

'Quite a change of story – but we've been into that before. My recommendation is that she's put ashore in Malta and left as a problem to the authorities there. However, I doubt if the decision lies with me. It's your pigeon, I fancy!'

Jean Forrest said, 'Yes, I suppose it is. Have you specific reasons for recommending she's landed, Commodore?'

'Yes, very. Disruptive influence. I may be the old so-and-so whose world is bounded by the bridge and is scarcely human, but I do have eyes and ears. I understand there's been hanky-panky between your Wren Smith and the Chief Officer. I also understand that Petty Officer Ramm has been, shall we say, trailing his coat at her door – ' Kemp broke off, having been interrupted by an involuntary giggle. 'Now what have I said, Miss Forrest?'

'Just something rather old-fashioned, Commodore.' Jean Forrest had had a vision of the Blenheim brigadier, trailing his coat outside her door in Oxford.

'I'm an old-fashioned man,' Kemp said, 'but that won't prevent my putting it into basic English if you wish.'

'It's quite all right,' she said with a touch of rather wicked primness. 'I did get your drift. And I agree with you. I've certainly no wish to carry that girl on.'

'Give her the order, then,' Kemp said briskly. 'Bag-and-hammock, immediately on arrival.' He was about to go into further details, ask Miss Forrest if there were any WRNS detachment in Malta, and if not, to whom Wren Smith should report, when there was a shout from the yeoman of signals.

'Flag calling, sir, via *Glamorgan* as repeating ship.' The *Nelson* with the main battle line was now well out of visual signalling distance and was using the cruiser as an intermediary. Lambert read off the signal. 'To Commodore, sir. Your 0830 concur. You will be taken in tow by *Probity* and will hoist your broad pennant in *Orlando* on rejoining. Message ends, sir.'

'Thank you, Lambert. Acknowledge.' Kemp turned to Miss Forrest. '*Orlando* – another Orient liner. We certainly don't want Wren Smith running riot about a liner, do we? And we'll take that decision upon ourselves ... making the assumption the Flag's too busy to be bothered!'

Jean Forrest left the bridge for an unwelcome interview with Wren Smith; and as she went down the ladder a report reached Kemp from the masthead lookout, the report that a destroyer was coming in fast from the east. Shortly after this the signalling

177

started up again: the *Langstone Harbour* was reported only a short distance to the westward. Later, while the *Wolf Rock*, her engine-room evacuated, was taking up a tow from the destroyer *Probity*, the laden freighter with her vital food cargo was seen hull down, emerging gradually over the horizon behind her own tow, the ocean-going rescue tug cleaving the blue water with its bluff bows, bringing Jake Horncape to rejoin the convoy.

Kemp sent him a welcoming signal. Two lame ducks now, he said. Two lame ducks that were going to make the Grand Harbour come what may. That signal had scarcely been sent when the Flag broke wireless silence to report the next attack coming in but not, this time, the Stukas. The destroyers screening the battleships, way out ahead, had picked up a nest of submarines on their Asdics.

iv

'All hell's being let loose,' Steward Botley reported to Jock Campbell.

'Where, eh?'

'Miss Forrest's cabin.' Botley clicked his tongue. 'Such language! I dunno . . . talk about Billingsgate.'

'Not Miss Forrest?'

Botley jeered. 'Not likely. She sent for that Wren Smith, the one with the – '

'Yes, I know all about that.' Jock Campbell's eye wandered to his keyboard: the key of the linen store hadn't been absent since the pongoes had embarked. Mr Harrison would be missing his oats right enough. 'So what's going to happen? Don't tell me you didn't hover, Botley.'

'Didn't need to, not really. That little tart was shouting the odds and getting nowhere fast. She's to be shoved off the boat in Malta. I reckon she was hysterical . . . flinging all sorts of charges around.' Botley paused, eyeing the chief steward somewhat circumspectly. 'Said if she was landed in bloody Malta she'd bring out a load of dirty washing.'

'Oh, yes?' Jock Campbell suddenly felt uneasy. 'Such as?'

'She's going to say that Ramm had tried to rape her.'

'That all?'

'No, it wasn't,' Botley said. 'She's going to implicate Mr Harrison. Forced her to have it off.'

'Go on, Botley.'

'In your linen store, Mr Campbell. That's what she said.'

'I see. And Miss Forrest? How did she react?'

Botley shrugged. 'I dunno. She was keeping her voice down, all ladylike. But it's going to set the cat among the bloody pigeons, I reckon, if that girl does what she threatened.'

'You can say that again.' Jock Campbell pushed himself back at full arms' stretch from his desk and stared blankly at the deckhead above him. He had suddenly become a very worried man. Petty Officer Ramm may or may not have tried to rape the girl – probably hadn't, Ramm was no bleeding fool – but it was a certain fact that Mr Harrison had had it off with her. It was likewise a fact that the venue had been the linen store of which only he, Jock Campbell, had the key. There was no way anybody could get that key from its locked keyboard except himself, or with his connivance. If asked, Jock Campbell would not deny the facts. He prided himself on never having told a lie. Chief officers were chief officers, but chief stewards also had their responsibilities and were little kings in their own territories. The Company in London would not take kindly to a chief steward who'd hired out his linen room for fornication. They wouldn't sack him, not in wartime, but as soon as the war ended he would be in disfavour to say the least and would quite likely not be offered a ship. And a chief steward eased out for being in dereliction of his duties and responsibilities would face the end. No other Line would employ him, except maybe as a cabin steward like Botley, or a saloon waiter aboard a liner. And the home in Liverpool, if it remained standing against Goering's perishing *Luftwaffe*, depended on its lord and master bringing home the lolly as a chief steward. What was he going to say to Mary, when the chop came? And in fact the chop *could* come even while the war lasted. There were plenty of blokes coming up for chief stewards' berths: he wasn't the only one available to the Company. If he got pushed out in wartime, well, he knew the next step: no longer seagoing, he would be called up for military or naval service, end up as a pongo or an ordinary steward, berthed in a hammock on the messdeck of a warship and emptying the officers' piss-pots. And the last person to help him would be that Mr bloody Harrison . . .

179

When the word came down from the bridge that the convoy was about to come under submarine attack, Jock Campbell was a very heavy-hearted man, sharing some of Susan Pawle's outlook: he might just as well be blown to Kingdom Come, honourably, and be done with it. At least Mary would get a decent pension from the Company.

SEVENTEEN

Chief Engineer Turnberry plus all the rest of the engine-room and boiler-room complement was now mostly on deck. With the engine-room flooded and the tow buttoned-on the *Wolf Rock* was proceeding slowly with no power of her own, lower in the water than was usual. Turnberry and his second engineer were taking watches turn and turn about on the watertight bulkheads. If those reinforced bulkheads, running right across the ship immediately for'ard and aft of the engine spaces, should fail to take the load of the water and started to spring their seams then the *Wolf Rock* would be in real trouble and would probably go down like a stone as the sea rushed through to bring its weight to bear on her stability.

It was in fact unlikely; but it could happen. And now the Eyeties were coming in with their submarines, and just one torpedo hit on the *Wolf Rock* would be the end.

Pressing through the massed troops while his second engineer took the watch, Turnberry climbed to the bridge. He approached Champney.

'How's it going, Captain?'

'Convoy and escort are altering course to come closer to Malta, Chief. We'll break off on the signal from the Flag.'

'With the *Langstone Harbour*?'

Champney nodded. 'Yes. And our own escort which'll take off the Commodore's staff after we've entered.'

'I heard a buzz . . . Kemp's going across to the *Orlando* – right?'

'Yes – '

'Lap of luxury. All right for some.'

181

'Just as likely to get a fish. Or a bomb.'

'I never said not.' Turnberry looked around, looked at the unruffled blue Mediterranean. 'Where are these submarines, Captain?'

Champney gestured ahead and to port. 'Two groups. One dead ahead, the other off the port beam.'

'No sign of them being attacked.'

'They're still distant, Chief. The escort's after them. We'll hear the depth charges before long.'

'And we're getting nearer to Malta.'

'Slowly, yes. Too damn slowly!'

Turnberry looked down at the crowded decks. 'Those poor buggers,' he said. 'Not much chance, if we go down. Too far off Malta for swimming, I reckon! Have you any plans for them, Captain?'

Champney's answer was brief. 'No. What can I do? Boats enough for the ship's company only. Two Carley floats. My job's to dodge the torpedoes in the first place and I can't even do that under tow. I'm hamstrung, Chief . . . dependent on the destroyer to swing us as necessary – and in time. It's a tall order.'

Turnberry nodded. 'I feel somewhat superfluous too. No bloody engines! We just sit and take it. No help anywhere.'

'There's the escorts, Chief. And God. Don't forget it's Malta we're making for now.'

'So what?' Turnberry looked blank.

'Dobbie. Sir William Dobbie's the Governor of Malta. Late the Royal Engineers . . . who're all said to be mad, married and Methodist. I don't know the truth of that somewhat wide statement. But I do know Dobbie's a very religious man.' Champney grinned. 'A lot of prayer could be wafting out towards us, Chief. Guardian angels being invoked . . . that kind of thing. Heaven keeping a good watch.'

Turnberry stared. 'You believe in all that, Captain?'

Champney said, 'Yes. As a matter of fact, I do. I've known prayers to be answered before now. And I'm doing my share of praying, I can tell you!'

'Well,' Turnberry said. 'I suppose it can't do any harm.' He wondered if the Old Man had been doing any praying for his engine-room. If he had, it hadn't worked, that was for sure. He left the bridge, went below again and descended the steel ladder

182

into the after tank space, now emptied, the narrow compartment immediately adjacent to the watertight bulkhead, making heavy weather of it with his arm in a sling. He had words with his second engineer: there was some water on the deck, not much, but enough to show that the seams were tending to weep a little and that was not good news. But it was a very slow ingress; it would be a question of time and Turnberry believed they could make it. Malta was now within around a day's distance. Aboard the ship, they were doing all they could. Now they were in Mussolini's hands. And God's.

ii

By this time the destroyers of the escort had picked up their targets and were homing in, following the urgent *ping-ping* of the Asdics. The submarine packs were not far off the convoy, and the concussions of the depth charges could be felt throughout the *Wolf Rock* as they exploded below the water to bring great spouts hurtling into the sky. Lambert reported the bow of a submarine emerging from the sea on the port beam, a bow that fell back, sliding to the bottom probably, as Kemp picked it up with his binoculars. Below at the watertight bulkhead, Turnberry watched the seams in growing alarm: the depth charges had been too close for comfort. The reverberations had increased the seepage of water. The attack continued, more and more heavy explosions sending their shock waves through the *Wolf Rock*'s plates.

Reports of the watertight bulkheads reached Champney and Kemp.

'Nothing we can do,' Kemp said. 'What's your assessment, Captain?'

Champney shrugged. 'Fifty-fifty. The Chief'll be doing what he can. Which won't be all that much. There's little enough room down there for rigging more shoring beams and such. He's already put chocks across to the bulkhead aft, and – ' He broke off as a voice-pipe whined in the wheelhouse. He went inside, listened, came back with another report.

'Chief's hurt,' he said.

'Badly?'

183

'Very badly. A shoring beam came down, a long drop. He's pinned to the deck and unconscious.' Champney added, 'O'Dwyer's been informed and is on his way down.'

Kemp met his eye. 'Your ship, Captain. But if I were you, I'd ask for an army doctor.'

'I was going to say the same thing,' Champney said. As he turned to call down to the deck, a signal came from Captain (D) in the destroyer flotilla leader: his radar had picked up the approach of a strong body of aircraft from the northwest. This signal had just been received when the aircraft-carriers were seen to turn into the wind and start flying off their fighters. And in the same instant specks were seen in the sky, keeping high until they were over their targets, and then coming down at full throttle like angry wasps, tearing off from their squadrons and dropping to the attack. Within the next half minute the machine-guns were raking the crowded decks of the *Wolf Rock* and men were scrambling for cover and bodies were falling over into the sea as the bullets bit. Screams came up to the bridge and Kemp, looking down, saw the decks red with blood. At his side a naval gunnery rate fell slack in the straps of the Oerlikon. Kemp pulled the body clear and laid it on the deck, and took the man's place, getting his sights on as the next Stuka came down in its dive.

iii

It was Chief Officer Harrison who found Dr O'Dwyer. O'Dwyer had emerged from his cabin just as the first of the Stukas had come in. He had stood for a moment listening to the racket and had then turned back. Harrison, descending from the bridge to go down to the tank space aft of the engine-room, saw him and went into his cabin behind him.

'You're wanted, doc. The Chief's bad. Don't say you didn't know. The bridge had the report you were on your way.'

'The army doctors . . . they're more up-to-date – '

'They have other things to do now, that's if they're still alive. Get down there, or else.' Harrison loomed over him, big and threatening. 'Now's the time to justify your existence.' He reached out and seized hold of O'Dwyer, turned him, and propelled him out of the cabin, along the alleyway and down

184

towards the engine spaces. From outside came the roar and shriek of the attacking Stukas, the concussions as the bombs exploded, once again close along the *Wolf Rock*'s sides. There was more machine-gun fire, the rattle of bullets on metal, the chatter of the ship's ack-ack armament and the stench of cordite. O'Dwyer was shaking uncontrollably. He had his bag with him, the ready-prepared bag with hypodermics and pain-killing drugs: it fell from his hand as the ladder, the vertical steel-runged descent into the tank space, was reached. Harrison caught it in time.

He said, 'Over you go.'

'I – I can't. It's a death trap down there. You don't seem to understand.'

Harrison, his face grim, his shirt clinging wet with sweat, said, 'Get down where you're needed. Or do you want me to truss you up like a bloody chicken and lower you on the end of a rope?'

O'Dwyer stared at him, his face working, eyes wide and red. He was seeing again his experiences in the last war, hearing not the present sounds of attack and defence but the roar and thunder of the German artillery on the Western Front, the terrible chatter of the machine-guns that on the Somme had mown down twenty thousand British and French troops in the first ten minutes of the battle, hearing the desperate cries of wounded men as they were brought back to the field dressing station, hearing the crump of the shells that had landed well to the rear of the front line. Suddenly he screamed and as Harrison moved towards him threateningly he took a step backwards, caught a leg against the hatch coaming, and toppled over. His body bounced once off the steel bulkhead and then he went down like a stone, another scream echoing back behind his fall.

Harrison was going down the ladder like a monkey when the torpedo hit.

iv

On the bridge, they had had no chance of avoiding the enemy's strike. Kemp had spotted the torpedo trail, coming in on the starboard beam. He called to the yeoman of signals.

'Lambert, make to *Probity*, haul round to starboard!'

185

'Aye, aye, sir.' Lambert, feeling in his guts that this was the end, clacked out the urgent message on his Aldis. Almost immediately the towing destroyer altered to starboard and the towing pendant took a sharp angle to the *Wolf Rock*'s bow in a last-ditch attempt to narrow the target, to head both ships towards the torpedo and manoeuvre so that it passed harmlessly along one side. In a ship under its own control this might have been successful even at so late a stage; but under tow the process was too unwieldy and slow. While the *Wolf Rock* was starting to turn, the torpedo hit. There was a vast explosion just below the waterline on the starboard beam; the ship lurched sickeningly, the deck trembling beneath Kemp's feet as he braced his body against the guardrail in the after part of the bridge and looked down.

'Slap in the engine-room,' he said to Champney. 'Lucky in a way . . . seeing it's already full of water! But we'll be main deck awash any moment now. That's if the transverse bulkheads don't hold. I'm going down to see for myself, Captain.' He looked around. 'Where's Finnegan?'

'Here, sir.' Finnegan's head appeared at the top of the starboard ladder. He was streaked with sweat and oil. Kemp gestured him back down the ladder and started towards it himself. Finnegan clattered down ahead of him. Kemp said, 'We'll take a look at the damage, Finnegan.'

'I've already been down as far as possible, sir. I reckon it's been contained by the water, largely anyhow. The bulkheads. – '

'Our last hope,' Kemp said. 'How's the girl, Mrs Pawle?'

'Dead scared, sir.'

'Let's hope that's a good sign.'

For a moment Finnegan looked puzzled; then he ticked over. If Susan was showing fear, fear that she might die, then maybe she preferred to live after all. But that was a long shot: no-one would want to die in pain and terror, in rising water or in the red hell of a burning metal box. He followed the Commodore down the internal ladders towards the water-logged engine-room, now presumably a shatter of twisted ladders and broken machinery. The ship felt desperately sluggish, becoming more so as the waters extended as far as the remaining bulkheads fore and aft, the last bulkheads that would have to hold if the ship was to survive. He knew what would be in the Commodore's mind: abandon, or

186

not? The troops who had survived the machine-guns might be safer off the ship or they might not. Finnegan remembered the last time, knew that Kemp also would have that in mind – the gunning down of the swimming men. As they came towards the remains of the after tank space Kemp set his mind at rest on that point.

'We'll stay aboard as long as possible, Finnegan. It's the only hope. Not that it's much.' Kemp had the troops foremost in his mind: they were targets, so long as the attack lasted, wherever they were. But at least the ship offered a little more protection than the water, and they were to some extent defended by Petty Officer Ramm's close-range weapons.

Kemp and Finnegan reached the tank top abaft the engine-room. As expected, it was flooded, the water coming up to well over the deck above and sloshing to starboard as the *Wolf Rock* settled with a nasty list. Kemp had difficulty in keeping his feet, found himself impacting heavily against submerged projections as he moved.

A moment later he saw a body coming to the surface of the scummy water: Turnberry, dead as mutton, maybe from that blow on the head from the shoring beam, maybe from drowning. Kemp pulled the body clear of the water. Finnegan said, 'The doc went down there, sir. So did the chief officer.'

'You're sure of that?'

'I saw them, sir.' Finnegan didn't add anything to that statement. It was a hundred to one that O'Dwyer and Harrison were both dead; there was no point, as he saw it, of saying anything now to the discredit of a dead man. Up to a point, O'Dwyer, like Harrison had died in the execution of his duty. That was good enough. And Finnegan said nothing further when Kemp commented that Dr O'Dwyer had turned up trumps in the end.

Kemp turned away, back towards the ladder leading to the midship superstructure. He said, 'The ship's wallowing . . . like a slug in a plate of porridge. But I've a feeling she's going to stay afloat for long enough.'

'I'll get the flags out, sir. For the Malta arrival.'

Kemp gave him a sharp look. 'Is that meant to be funny, Finnegan?'

'Why, no – '

'There'll be no damn bullshit when we enter, Finnegan. The only flag we fly will be at half mast.'

Finnegan wished he could recall thoughtless words. Old Kemp didn't like losing men and never mind death's inevitability in time of war. When the convoys were out, so was the enemy. And so it would go on, convoy after convoy, time and time again, until the whole goddam thing was over and done with. Finnegan's hope was that so long as it all lasted, he would sail the seas with John Mason Kemp.

v

No attack ever lasted as long as it felt it had; when the Stukas came under the darting Seafires, they withdrew: there was always another day, another convoy. Likewise the Italian subs: the destroyer escort accounted for another two beside the one that had surfaced so briefly earlier. Two depth-charge-damaged boats that also surfaced stayed there until they were blasted out of the water by the 6-inch batteries of the *Glamorgan*, the nearest of the heavy cruisers. The attack had left its mark: two more armaments carriers sunk, two more shattering explosions, sheets of orange and white flame, flung debris to rattle down into the Mediterranean or over the remaining ships of the convoy. All that, and much blood to stain the decks of the *Wolf Rock*, many bodies to be given a sea burial.

As the attack was called off and a kind of silence came, Kemp reorganized the remains of the convoy into its ordered lines for the onward passage through to Alexandria, Port Said and Trincomalee. Next day, in the late afternoon, the gallant, bomb-torn island of Malta was raised on the starboard bow. Kemp made his signals to the ships in company: the *Langstone Harbour* behind her tug would break off from the convoy with the Commodore's ship and would enter Malta. The remainder would steam on at convoy speed and would be overtaken by Kemp aboard *Probity*, when the Commodore with his staff and the WRNS contingent would be transferred at sea aboard the *Orlando*. Just for now, it would be goodbye. It was also hail and farewell by exchange of signals to Jake Horncape aboard the *Langstone Harbour*: there would be no opportunities for a meeting of one-time shipmates; Kemp's job was to leave Malta the soonest possible and rejoin his convoy.

Later, as the evening shadows lengthened and the day drew with Mediterranean suddenness towards dark, the *Wolf Rock* and the *Langstone Harbour* approached the breakwater across the entry to the Grand Harbour. Signals were exchanged between the Commodore and the Naval signal station at Lascaris: among other things Kemp reported that he intended landing a WRNS rating believed to be pregnant. He asked for instructions as to her disposal. Aboard the *Langstone Harbour* Captain Horncape was also receiving signals, congratulatory ones containing his berthing instructions and advising him that discharge of his cargo would begin immediately, the precious foodstuffs being lightered off while his ship was still in the stream off Fort St Angelo. A part of Jake Horncape's mind was on his silver wedding anniversary, this very day . . . he hoped Nesta had remembered.

As the *Wolf Rock* came slowly through the breakwater behind *Probity*, now assisted, as was the *Langstone Harbour*, by the dockyard tugs, Kemp became aware for the first time of the crowds of Maltese citizens and British servicemen lining the shores of the Grand Harbour. From the parade ground of Fort St Angelo, famed in history, from Customs House Steps and the battlements of Lascaris, from Sliema Creek and French Creek and Dockyard Creek, from overburdened *dghaisas* being propelled by their single oars across the fairway of the Grand Harbour, a storm of cheering rose. There was not much response from the troops aboard the Commodore's ship; they were all too weary, too deadened by their experiences of the Stukas' raking fire, too conscious of so many of their mates who'd been colandered in that terrible fire. The decks, washed down now by the hoses, showed no mark of all that beyond the structural damage and the scored paintwork and woodwork where the bullets had hit or richocheted, but the memories were fresh enough. Before the light went, those aboard the entering vessels could see the waving and the flags, could sense what their arrival meant to a beleaguered garrison and a starving population battered near to insensibility by the long German and Italian bombardment.

Finnegan, on the bridge with Kemp, was impressed by the poignancy of the occasion and said so. 'They're mighty glad to see us, sir.'

'Yes,' Kemp said sombrely. 'And I'll tell you something, young Finnegan: I wouldn't like to be in their shoes later tonight.' He

189

said no more; Yeoman of Signals Lambert, overhearing, understood: probably before the Commodore had left the ship to rejoin the convoy, before the discharge of the *Langstone Harbour*'s cargo was even begun, the Eyeties and the Jerries would be over the island once again, bombing, strafing . . . Malta wasn't the place it had been in peacetime, though no doubt the bars and brothels would be as busy as ever. Lambert thought of his wife back in Pompey and wished there was a chance of mail coming off, but knew there wouldn't be. They would all have to wait for news of their families until a good while after arrival in distant Trinco.

On the shattered fo'c'sle Petty Officer Ramm looked across at Malta, glad – the only one who was – that there would be no mail. Bad news could always wait so far as he was concerned and he was still apprehensive about that Pompey barmaid. He would have appreciated a run ashore in Malta, fill himself up with booze so as to forget for a spell, and maybe spend a quid or so on a woman. Turning, he looked aft. He saw Wren Smith, waiting mutinously with her metaphorical bag and hammock and being cat-called by some of the troops.

'Missed opportunity,' Ramm said to Able Seaman Cardew.

'Eh?'

'Never mind, lad. Probably wouldn't have looked at me any road. Not enough bloody gold on me sleeve.' He was thinking of Chief Officer Harrison, now confirmed as dead along with Dr O'Dwyer. Jock Campbell, below with his work sheets and his stores lists and his once-again sacrosanct linen room, was also thinking of Harrison. Not that he wished anyone dead, of course; but death did wipe out a worry or two. Wren Smith could fulminate all she wanted once ashore, and no doubt would, but with Harrison gone so was her sting. Nobody was ever going to believe her. Jock Campbell felt he could look forward to a secure future once again.

In Susan Pawle's cabin Rose Hardisty stood by for the arrival of the naval doctor and sick-berth attendants from the Bighi hospital: it had been confirmed by signal that Third Officer Pawle would be lifted off in a Neil Robertson stretcher and taken to Bighi. She would go alone. Rose Hardisty had pleaded with First Officer Forrest to be allowed to leave the draft and stay with her. Jean Forrest, whilst understanding, had been adamant.

'I can't interfere with drafting orders,' she'd said.

190

'But ma'am, perhaps Vice-Admiral Malta – '

'No, Rose.' Jean Forrest had dropped formality and put her arm around Rose Hardisty's ample shoulders. 'I'm sorry, but there it is. We're wanted in Trincomalee, all of us. It's a question of duty. I'm sure you of all people understand that.'

'Well, yes, ma'am. . . . ' She did, too; into Rose Hardisty's mind came a vision of little Master Donald to whom she had once been a fuckum bloosance and who was now sweating it out – which was not her normal way of thinking – in the Western Desert, a major in command of men, all doing their duty. She could do no less. Whatever would little Master Donald think of nanny!

Kemp's thoughts as the *Wolf Rock* came past Custom House Steps amid the continual cheering, and as he prepared to disembark into *Probity*'s motor boat, were chiefly of the losses of ships and men. The dead also had their part to play in this tumultuous welcome and they would not be forgotten. Not yet, anyhow: Kemp had too many memories of the last war to imagine that heroes would live for ever.

He laid a hand on Captain Champney's shoulder. 'Time to say God-speed, Champney. And the best of luck go with you.'

'You too, Commodore. It's been a pleasure to have you aboard.'

The two men shook hands warmly. Kemp caught the eye of his assistant. 'All ready, Finnegan?'

'Just about, sir. Staff and WRNS mustering in five minutes.'

Kemp nodded. Looking ahead he saw that *Probity* was already unshackled from the tow and was turning short round in the Grand Harbour's restricted water to point once again for the breakwater, her motor boat ready at the falls for lowering. Below on the *Wolf Rock*'s embarkation deck, First Officer Forrest was lining up her girls with the assistance of the PO Wren. Kemp was starting down the ladder to take a last look around his cabin when Yeoman Lambert reported the final signal before leaving.

'From Vice-Admiral Malta, sir, addressed Commodore. Am to be informed urgently whether or not pregnant Wren is married.'

Kemp stared, caught Finnegan's eye, and gave a short laugh. He said, 'Well, I suppose admirals will be admirals. The information is probably much more important than any delay to the convoy as a result of detaining its Commodore. Lambert?'

'Yessir?'

191

'Make, Vice-Admiral Malta from Commodore, subject of your enquiry is unmarried but a bush in Victoria Park Portsmouth would have a tale to tell.' Kemp started down the ladder. 'Come on, Finnegan, we have a convoy to catch up.'